Dream Rider

Dream Weavers, Book 3

Kimberly Dean

Published by Tiger Eye Productions, LLC

Dream Rider
Copyright © 2023 Kimberly Dean
All rights reserved.

Cover design by oliviaprodesign
Vector design by Marisha

ISBN-13: 979-8-9855505-4-2

CHAPTER ONE

Dust was flying when Emily arrived at the park. It hung in the air like a curtain of grit that stung her eyes and made her cough. Engines revved, sounding like a nest of large, angry hornets, and colors whizzed by. The chaos overwhelmed her senses, and she had to stop to get her bearings.

Where was he?

Tires skidded as a racer hit the brakes to navigate a turn, and a plume of dust rose. She'd stopped in the wrong place. Seeing the breeze push the dust cloud in her direction, she scrambled out of the way.

Great. Dirt, noise, and adrenaline. All her favorite things.

Pushing her hair out of her eyes, she spotted the bleachers that had been set up outside the motocross track. They were positioned behind a four-foot-high wooden fence with ten-foot-high netting on top of that, so it gave the appearance of safety. Best of all, it wasn't downwind. Coughing up the dust she'd swallowed, she made her way over to the bleachers and climbed halfway up so she could get a better view.

Which one was he?

She watched a lone rider race past, and she let out a squeak when he went airborne. He landed just as quickly, making it more of a skip than a jump, but her gasp still dropped into a scowl.

It wasn't Zane, but HR was going to have fits over this.

Shaking her head, she settled in and began methodically searching for him. He'd be in a pair, since he'd brought a guest—which was the crux of the problem—but how was she ever going to pick them out? The riders were all dressed the same, albeit in different colors, and they all wore helmets. Fortunately, the course wasn't overly busy. School was back in session, so that took away most of the teenagers who probably congregated here. It was also the middle of the day, when sensible people were meeting with potential clients in conference rooms or restaurants.

Not at a motocross track.

Yet the Solstice Adventure Park was busier than she'd expected it to be on this beautiful autumn day. The sun was shining, the temperature had cooled from the summer's extremes, and the breeze that had nearly given her dust inhalation actually felt nice. No doubt, it had tempted more than one rider away from work and responsibility.

Unfortunately, work was the precise reason she was here. Why Zane Oneiros had become her responsibility was beyond her, but someone had to keep the golden goose out of trouble.

Yeah, like that was doable.

She let out a snort that was drowned out by the rev of another engine and the scrunch of tires against dirt.

"Is everything okay?" a voice called.

Emily glanced around, not sure if the question was for her. When she met the gaze of another woman seated higher on the bleachers, she pointed to her chest and lifted her eyebrows.

"You seem nervous."

Nervous. Freaked out. Irritated. Pick any of the lot. "I'm looking for someone who's not supposed to be here."

The woman sat up from where she'd been lounging back against the bleachers. She had long, dark hair gathered into a ponytail and was wearing a bikini top and skimpy shorts that showed off both her tan and her legs. How Emily could have missed somebody else sitting here, much less this woman, spoke to her urgency.

"A kid?"

"God, no." Although, in a way, it fit.

"Boyfriend?" the woman guessed.

Emily's belly gave a funny squeeze. "Well, he's a boy, and he's a friend."

The beach goddess laughed and gave her a knowing wink. "Mine is in the green."

She pointed and let out an appreciative whoop when her boy/friend made the skip jump in front of them and headed down the straightaway.

So that eliminated the green jersey. One down. Emily scanned other riders as they went by. They were all geared up to the teeth. Make that the top of their heads. From the helmets with the dark visors to the padded gloves and shin-high boots, they looked like futuristic warriors.

"How long is the race?" she asked. "Where's the finish line?"

She needed to know so she could pluck Zane off his bike by the scruff of his neck and move this so-called meeting to someplace more civilized.

"They're not racing. Today, at least," the woman said. "They're just having fun."

"So, this could go on for a while?"

"Yup." The woman took a sip of her drink. She looked totally relaxed, not bothered at all by the dirt or the noise. "Boys will be boys. Sometimes they need to blow off some steam."

That was what worried her. Emily began clicking her thumbnail against her ring finger, a habit she'd had since childhood. Oh, this was so not good. Even if she did find them, how was she going to get them off the track? Standing and waving didn't seem like a good idea. If she distracted them, they might hit the jump wrong or skid into the wall. She was here to prevent a calamity, not cause one.

"Looks like you need a pressure valve, too," the woman said after a moment.

"Huh?" The question made Emily do a double take, and she missed a group of riders who zoomed by.

"Honey, you're way too high-strung."

"No kidding."

"Maybe you should go out there with them."

"What?" The suggestion caused another head spin that nearly wrenched her neck. "No, this is the source of my stress. What if he—*they*—get hurt?"

"They have protective gear, and none of these riders are newbies. You can tell by watching them." The woman's forehead scrunched when she saw that wasn't the right answer. "Okay. Maybe this isn't your outlet, but they're having fun. Don't they look free and energized? Don't you find that appealing?"

Emily didn't know about that. All she saw was chaos. Controlled chaos, she had to admit. The riders were on a track with turns, bumps, and jumps throughout—including one over a puddle of water. *Ew.* Add mud to the mix? This was so not her thing. It looked impulsive and dangerous.

And, maybe *secretly*, like fun… if someone could guarantee that no wipeouts or accidents would occur. Which, of course, they couldn't. That was part of the draw.

She looked over the course, trying to follow the action. It wasn't an oval, but a snakelike route that twisted back onto itself. There were uphill portions and downhill slopes, and the track was so rutted, she wanted to take a rake and smooth it out like a Zen gardener. She spotted a few ponytails hanging out from under the helmets, but overall, testosterone hung over the park in a cloud nearly as thick as the dust.

And there, almost as if she'd summoned him with the thought, was Zane.

Her gaze was drawn like a magnet to a rider dressed in blue. His helmet concealed his face and blond hair. Nothing distinctive stood out, yet she knew it was him. She might not have seen that athletic, aggressive style as he'd been riding a desk in the office, but the enthusiastic "Yee-haw" he let out as he flew over the jump confirmed it.

She curled her fingers around the wooden seat beneath her when he showboated, twisting the handlebars of his bike to cockeye the front wheel before straightening it out for the landing. The show-off move caused him to lose ground to the rider in red next to him, who gunned his engine to rush ahead.

Oh, God. She tilted her head back to stare at the crystal-blue, cloudless sky. Pete Larimer, their potential client.

And billionaire.

Her mouth had gone dry. "Excuse me, but where did you get that drink?"

The sunbather gestured to her right. "Over there, at the concession stand, but I don't think they have the strong stuff."

"I'm just looking for something wet." Unlike some people, Emily knew when *she* was on company time.

She bought herself a lemonade and returned to her spot in the stands to wait it out. Yelling at them wouldn't get them off the track. In fact, it might make them lose their concentration. She was here to stop anyone from getting hurt, not to cause an injury.

Too soon, the riders completed a loop and were back within sight. Zane wouldn't notice it, but she gave him the stink-eye as he and his new friend went zooming along. She had to admit there was grace in the way they both moved. They balanced on two wheels, leaning into curves and coming off their seats to lessen the impact of the bumps. And they did it all without thought while controlling the loud, powerful engines between their legs.

Her face heated as her thoughts veered off on a totally different track, and she scooted down the bench to find a bit of shade.

The woman next to her wasn't fooled. "So, you see what I mean."

Emily took another drink of her lemonade. "Maybe it does look appealing," she agreed. Especially the rider in blue. "But they're supposed to be discussing a business deal, not risking their necks."

That little detail hadn't stopped either of them.

She watched the two as they raced. Larimer was smoother in his riding somehow, which surprised her. Zane was all aggression and zest. He charged into corners, waiting until the last moment to brake and veer around them. He attacked the jumps, just like the other riders did, but he seemed more focused on getting air than going fast.

"Oh!" she gasped when she saw the berm collapse as Larimer went into a turn. She jumped to her feet, but there was nothing she could do as dirt slid down the incline. She was sure he was going down, but he jammed his foot into the ground and gunned the engine until his back wheel found traction. He shot forward as if out of a cannon, completely oblivious to her near aneurysm.

"He's good," the beach goddess said. "That your guy?"

"No." Before Emily could think better, she said, "The other one."

"Ah, the daredevil, then."

"Yeah. The daredevil." That summed him up pretty well.

The woman stilled and then sat up straighter. Her hand went to her throat, and despite the warm sun pouring down, she seemed to shiver. "Is that an Oneiros?"

Emily was so stunned, she turned in her seat and gave the woman her full attention. "Yes, that's Zane. Do you know him?"

"I'm acquainted with the family." The woman looked around and began collecting her things. "Would you look at the time? I need to be going."

She hooked her purse over her shoulder, stood, and hitched up her low-riding shorts. As an afterthought, she grabbed her drink and began carefully stepping down the wooden planks. A skateboarder heading to the skate park saw her, accidentally braked, and flew headlong into a stuttering run before he caught himself.

Yeah, the woman was that eye-catching.

"You don't need to wait for your boyfriend?" Emily asked.

The woman blinked, but then waved her hand. "Oh, he's not my boyfriend. He's a client."

Client? And she dressed like that? It was all Emily could do to stop her head from tilting, but she straightened up fast when the woman stopped to dig into her purse. She held out a business card.

"I'm Hunter. Call me if you're interested in breaking those chains and learning how to go with the flow. Stress isn't good for anybody."

Emily looked at the card in her hand. *Hunter Mahina – Life Coach.*

Ah. Shame on her and her wayward brain. She smiled ruefully. "I'm Emily, but I'm afraid my stress might be too built-in."

"You never know." Hunter glanced over her shoulder to watch the riders bouncing along the track. She settled her sunglasses over the bridge of her nose and gave a quick grin. "It could be fun."

Zane suddenly looked in their direction—or maybe he was looking for Larimer. Either way, Hunter turned on her heel, gave a wave, and left.

Emily settled in to wait, sipping on her lemonade and trying to ratchet down her nerves. She thought about texting the office, but what was she supposed to say? She'd found them, but she hadn't arrived in time to stop the craziness. Saying that everything was fine would be tempting fate. All she could do was sit here and watch.

Yes, she should watch... in case someone needed to call for help...

Rationalizing her way into it, she gave in to the secret pleasure.

She never got to watch Zane and just appreciate him. They were friends, and she was hesitant about crossing that line. They talked all the time, but sometimes she sneaked peeks out of the corner of her eye. Here, away from the office, though, she could indulge. She could watch the way he moved full-on, feel the cocky energy he radiated, and daydream a little.

Yes, she found it all appealing. The energy, the exuberance, the man…

She took another sip from her drink and heard the annoying sputter as she reached the bottom of the paper cup. She glared at the biodegradable straw. She didn't need the judgment on her flight of fantasy.

But it was time to rein it in anyway. She saw the riders in blue and red exit the track and put down their kickstands. Pulling on her cloak of responsibility, she climbed down from the bleachers and walked over to them. Her jagged nerves got some relief when they turned off their engines. Larimer swung his leg over the bike to dismount, while Zane remained seated to undo the strap under his chin and pull off his helmet. His hair stood up every which way, and a streak of dirt ran across his cheekbone. It was the smile on his face, though, that made her stomach go all fluttery.

"Man, that was awesome," he said.

Larimer walked over, and they gave each other an enthusiastic high five.

Zane hung his helmet on a handlebar and pulled off a glove. He swiped a hand through his sweaty hair, shoving it back into some order before his gaze swung up.

"Em!" he said with that same bright smile.

Even prepared, she wasn't ready for it, but she had long experience with his charm offensive. Her lips quirked, but she managed to lift an eyebrow. "Zane."

"Pete. this is Emily Hutchins. She works with me at High Score."

The billionaire took off his helmet, and Emily immediately saw why so many magazines like to put his handsome face on their covers. The green eyes and black hair were a potent combo. His grin was as wide as Zane's as he held out his hand. "Nice to meet you."

She shook his gloved hand and felt the sweat and grime that clung to the nylon and neoprene.

"Oh, shoot. Sorry about that." He pulled his hand back,

removed the glove, and wiped his hand on his equally sweaty and grungy racing pants. "Well, that's not going to be much better."

She laughed. For a tech icon, he seemed down to earth. Yet she saw his guard come up as his gaze swung to Zane. He was questioning why she was here. It was obvious he thought they were teaming up on him.

Zane rolled his eyes. "I'm in trouble again, aren't I?"

Emily wasn't sure how to answer. Pete Larimer was standing right there. "Um, maybe we could talk over there?"

She should have stayed hiding in the stands and caught him afterward.

"That would be a yes." Letting out a laugh, Zane caught her empty glass of lemonade. Popping off the top, he tilted it back and gobbled up the melting ice cubes. "Mmm, lemonade. Where'd you get that?"

She pointed to the concession stand that stood centrally located between the motocross track, the skateboarding park, and the half-pipe that eagerly awaited winter snowboarders.

"You had lunch yet?" he asked.

She was surprised to find him looking at her. "No."

"What do you say, Pete? Want to join us?"

"Are you kidding me?" Larimer was already moving in that direction. "I haven't had a chili dog in years."

Zane winked at her as he dismounted and took off his other glove. Emily narrowed her evil eye on him, glad to have a target, but his grin only widened. Together, the three of them headed for the haute cuisine of the adventure park sports concession stand.

Emily felt a bit disconcerted being accompanied by two such handsome men. She was used to catching looks as she walked through the hallways with Zane at work, but this was on a different level entirely. Larimer was taller, but both were lean, athletic, and definitely male. She felt like the cheerleading captain being accompanied by the quarterback and star receiver. The wallflower deep inside her got a thrill out of it, even though she knew she was the odd one out.

She placed their orders as the guys went to wash up and then found a picnic table where they could wait for their food. Rather than brave a public restroom, she cleaned her hands with the hand sanitizer she kept in her purse. Her pulse rate sped up again when she saw Zane striding across the grass toward her. The dirt was gone from his face, but he still looked like a road warrior in his boots and gear. He dropped onto the bench at her side while Larimer took the seat across from her.

Oh, was he still here?

"So why is Zane in trouble?" the tech giant asked.

Emily felt pinned. It wasn't a discussion she wanted to have out in the open. She didn't usually meet with clients. That was Zane's job.

"HR probably doesn't like that we're here. You know, the 'liability.'" Zane curled his fingers to emphasize the word.

Exactly, the liability. Emily rounded her eyes at him. "Why the air quotes? It *is* a liability. Someone could get hurt doing what you two just did."

His blue eyes twinkled, and, across the table, she heard Larimer snort.

"You didn't get permission." This time, she swept her best shaming look over both of them.

"Because I knew I wouldn't get it."

Emily puffed up with air, so stunned by the attitude, she forgot she was supposed to be all nicey-nice.

Zane slapped her on the back to get her breathing again. "Relax. I ride with my brothers every chance I get, and this guy was a motocross champion when he was a teenager."

"And your top salesman here is the only one who did enough research to find that out." Larimer pointed at Zane, who promptly nodded and gave his new friend a fist bump across the table.

"That doesn't guarantee that one of you won't crack your ribs. Or your heads." Emily knew she should shut up, but she was wondering if that was what had happened before she'd gotten here. Why weren't they taking this seriously?

"That's why we're wearing all the gear," Larimer said. He pulled at the neck of his shirt to show a chest protector underneath.

Was Zane wearing a chest protector?

She wanted to look, but that would cross a very different line with HR. And it was probably best not to think about his chest.

"That's not the point," she said.

"I have insurance," Zane said patiently, "and I know this guy must be covered up the wazoo."

"And past," Larimer muttered.

Emily's head was beginning to pound. Fine. Let the tough guy break an arm. He could deal with the pain and inconvenience. Insurance would pay for it—but then the press would come to report it all and tie their company to the incident. That would cost them more than the medical bills.

Zane frowned when he saw the way she was rubbing her temples. "Okay, okay. We promise we'll go during off-hours and on our personal time from now on."

Larimer perked up. "Trail dirt biking?"

"Hell yeah."

Emily squeezed her eyes shut and rubbed her temples harder.

The concession stand lady arrived not much later with their food. She had puffed-up gray hair and wore a hot-pink T-shirt that showed a frog riding a skateboard and saying "Ribbit." She put a plate of loaded nachos in the middle of the table and then began passing out the chili dogs.

"Whoa," Zane said, holding up his hand before Emily even saw her plate. "No onions on hers."

"Oh, sorry about that. I'll bring you another one, dear." The woman looked over the table. "Anything else? More water? Lemonade?"

"I'll take a large water, extra ice." Larimer was eyeing his chili dog like an after-schooler eyeing a Little Debbie snack. He launched into it before the server returned, and his eyes rolled back into his head. "Oh, man. I've missed this."

Emily quietly considered him. This was why Zane was so good at what he did. He was loud, incorrigible, and unmanageable, but he outsold all the other salespeople in the company because he established relationships.

She couldn't do that, not like he did. She was friendly enough, but her circle was small and tight.

Larimer wiped his mouth with a napkin. "So, what do you do at High Score, Emily? HR? Lawyer?"

"Project manager," she said as she reached for a nacho chip.

"What type of projects?"

"Usually me." Zane reached for the fresh chili dog, sans onions, that the concession stand lady brought to the table. "Thanks, beautiful."

The woman turned nearly the color of her T-shirt. "Oh, you," she said, with an embarrassed wave.

"You're Zane's manager?" Larimer asked, watching as Zane set the plate in front of her.

"No, but I get called in to talk to him quite often."

"Because they figured out that she's the only one I listen to," Zane said as he passed her the mustard.

She rolled her eyes. "Right. You listen. *That's* what happens."

Larimer's lips twitched as he looked at her, but then they were all diving into their food. Dirt apparently didn't supply the calories a motocross rider needed. As much of it as they'd eaten during their ride, the men still both managed to finish their hot dogs and were tucking into the nachos before Emily made it halfway through hers. She tried to eat healthy, but she had to admit that the concession stand food was delicious. She'd sat outside under the bright sun and in the fresh air. That always seemed to rev up a hunger meter, didn't it?

"So, Emily," Larimer said before he took a swig of water. He'd already downed two glasses since getting off his bike. "What do you think of High Score's software? Do you use it?"

She blinked and looked at him like a deer in the headlights.

She didn't have a pitch to give him. This wasn't what she did.

Zane elbowed her. "Go ahead. Tell him your honest opinion."

"Um, all right." She wiped her hands and thought about it. "I like it. Performance reviews are always hard for me. I'm not comfortable tooting my own horn, but the way we gamify it makes it easier. I score points for doing things on my action list, and the software automatically notifies my manager. It makes the task more tolerable."

Zane made a sound around his gulp of lemonade. "She says tolerable. I say fun."

"I told you I wasn't a salesman," Emily muttered.

"And thank God for that."

Larimer laughed. Hooking his knee up onto the seat, he turned and looked around the park. The sunlight left dappled shadows across the complex. The leaves on the trees hadn't started to turn colors yet, and the air still smelled fresh and sweet. The temperature today was perfect, but right on the edge of having a bite in it to signal colder weather coming. He took a deep breath and lifted his face to the sun's rays. "Thanks for this, man. I spend so much time in meetings in manilla-colored conference rooms that I sometimes forget this part of me. Sales ploy or not, this was fun."

"I hate conference rooms," Zane said.

"True story." Emily chose her last nacho chip.

Larimer gave Zane a steady look. "Seriously, let's do the trail bike thing. If you don't have a bike, I have one you can borrow."

Emily's head jerked up, and she nearly spilled her lemonade. "But…"

"During off-hours," Zane said.

"That's really not the point," she insisted.

"We could go up to Comet Tail Park," Larimer said.

"At least don't make plans in front of me," she said a little louder.

"You got it."

For the love of Pete. Well, not this Pete. Emily rolled her

eyes as the two men shared another fist bump.

"Nice to meet you, Emily." Larimer held out his hand to her.

She accepted the handshake. His hand felt warm and big as it closed over hers. This time, there was no glove, and the contact was skin to skin.

"I'll be in touch," he said as he stood from the table.

His fingertips swiped ever so gently over hers as he pulled his hand away, causing an unexpected pitter-patter in her pulse.

Wait. Had that last comment been meant for her or Zane? Or High Score?

She glanced at Zane, but he was staring at her outstretched hand.

Larimer cleaned up his side of the table and took the paper plates to the trash bin.

"Bye, Mr. Larimer...er, Pete," Emily called as he headed out, back to his busy office and schedule.

She looked at Zane. He'd gone uncharacteristically quiet. "Did I ruin it?" she asked.

"What?"

"Did I botch the sale?" She bit her lip. "I didn't mean to get in the way. Human resources sent me out to catch you. I was supposed to stop you before you went out on the track."

"How did they figure out we were here?" He held up his hand when the answer came to him. "Wait. Let me guess. Wes."

She nodded. His brother worked in the company's customer success area. They'd been talking about what a nice day it was, and Wes had mentioned how he wanted to join the guys out on the track. It was the first she'd heard of the outing. Same for the HR executive who'd been walking by. Naturally, she'd been sent on the mission to take care of the problem.

Emily sighed. She sometimes hated being such a fuddy-duddy rule-follower. Larimer was young, but his company was huge. If it adopted High Score's software, it could launch their mid-sized company into the stratosphere. "I blew it, didn't I?"

Zane looked at the way she was flicking her thumbnail against her ring finger and reached out to stop her. "Hardly. I think he's in."

All in.

* * *

Zane cleaned up their empty plates before Emily could read the look on his face. He liked Pete Larimer. Under all the hype and brilliance, the guy was all right. That didn't mean he wanted to sit here and watch the dude's attention home in on his... his... *coworker.*

Zane jammed the paper plates into the trash bin. "Shit."

He made the mistake of inhaling the stench rising from the garbage that had been sitting in the sun too long. Yeah, this was a rotten turn of events, all right.

Planting his hands on his hips, he looked at Emily. He knew what had just gone down. He had eyes, just like Pete Larimer did.

She sat at the picnic table looking girl-next-door pretty in her sneakers, jeans, and High Score T-shirt. So pretty, it made him ache. She had her chestnut-colored hair half up in a clip, with the rest tumbling down her back. It wasn't long, and it wasn't short. It was just the right length to swing around her shoulders as she moved.

And when it came to the way she moved—

Her brown gaze landed on him, catching him mid-fantasy, and he rubbed the back of his neck. Sighing, he headed back to the table.

She started to climb off the bench, but he wasn't ready to go yet. He so rarely got her out of the office. Yeah, he took her to lunch all the time, but she was always on such a set schedule. A salesman and a project manager? The two didn't mix well.

But damn, how he wanted to mix.

Climbing up on the picnic table, he sat atop it and watched a kid obviously new to motocross attempt the baby jump in front of the bleachers. The afterschool crowd was starting to show up. The kid made it, even though he had to put his foot out on the landing to balance himself. That was how you learned—by falling down and getting back up, not by stopping yourself from trying in the first place.

But he'd already tried so many times with her.

"You think Larimer's still interested?" she asked. "Even after all the liability stuff?"

The guy was interested, all right. Zane did his best not to snarl.

"He owns a company. He knows about lawyers and HR, and all that comes with it." Zane rolled his head on his neck. "I know I went around the system, and I shouldn't have. I just ran across this biking thing in his bio. It was something we have in common, and yeah, it was a way in. But more so, it sounded like a good time."

"I know." Climbing up onto the table, Emily took a seat next to him. "Sitting in the office at a desk isn't your thing, and it shouldn't be. Kevin doesn't like it when his salespeople spend too much time in the office."

Kevin was their CEO and, fortunately, his biggest supporter. The guy knew that deals were made where the clients were.

Zane shook his head. "I'm sorry they sent you out here to rein me in. It's not your job."

"*I'm* sorry I have the crossing-guard personality that lets them use me like that." She watched a chipmunk as it discovered a tortilla chip that had fallen off their table. "I wish I could be more fun."

"You're fun."

She let out a laugh that disagreed.

He nudged her with his shoulder. "Stick with me, kid."

She gave him a weak smile. "I'm serious."

"So am I."

The newbie appeared again as he finished his first lap around the track, only the kid wasn't being aggressive enough on his half-sized bike. He went up for the jump at about half the speed he needed to, and... *splat.*

"Oh, no." Emily flinched. "Not the mud."

"It will cool him down." Before the stuff dried out and got all itchy. Zane knew from experience.

They both sat there, primed to go help, but the kid waved off a park employee. He pulled his bike off the course, scraped the mud off his goggles, and climbed right back on.

"Are you really going to go riding with Larimer again?" she asked as the kid zipped up the incline with more determination.

"Sure." Zane loved to ride, and he wasn't going to let his employer, of all things, stop him. So maybe he couldn't do it as a replacement for a sales meeting. They couldn't dictate what he did in his free time.

"He acted like Comet Tail was something different."

"It is." Zane nodded to the track. "This is motocross. It's a race on a closed route with planned obstacles. Trail riding is just like it sounds, riding on trails out in the countryside where it's allowed, like Comet Tail Park. The bikes are different, too, but you probably don't care about that."

"Out in the country? What if you have an accident? There's nobody around like here." She pointed at the park attendant who was now handing a towel to another racer who'd come off the track.

She sighed. "Sorry. There I go again." She eyed him up and down. "At least you're wearing more protective gear than I expected."

Zane liked having her gaze on him, but he was surprised when it got stuck on his riding boots. His boots? Really? Excitement lit in his gut. "Do you want to try it out?"

"What?" she squeaked.

Oh yeah. She'd slipped with that look, and he'd caught her. "Take a ride around the track? I could teach you."

"Me? Out there?" She laughed nervously. "In my dreams."

And, just like that, his excitement centered in his crotch. "I can make that happen."

Her eyebrows lifted. "Well, that's bold, but you can't get

inside my head as easily as you do with other people, Zane Oneiros."

She had no idea what he could do once night fell, and people drifted off to sleep. "How much do you want to bet? Lunch?"

"On what?"

"That I'll get you on a dirt bike tonight in your dreams."

The look she gave him was flabbergasted. "Why would you make that bet? You won't know if it happened or not. All I'd have to do is tell you I didn't dream. You'd never know."

"I'd know."

Time slowed in that moment, and her breath hitched.

"Come on, Em. That's what dreams are for, trying new things and working through your fears."

"I'm not scared. I'm… I'm thinking through all the angles. Why are we even talking about this?"

His gaze dropped to her lips. Because they never talked about this… and sometimes you had to stop thinking and jump.

He was about to take the leap when his phone beeped with an incoming text message.

"Fuck," he muttered.

"Oh," Emily said, pulling back sharply. "That might be work."

And it might be the worst timing in history. Zane pulled his phone out of his pocket, and his jaw clenched. "It's Pete."

"Uh oh. Is it bad? Is he pulling out?"

"He wants a fifty-seat subscription." Zane's gaze flicked up to meet hers. "He wants to give it a test run in his *project management* organization first."

Her face lit up in delight. "Really?"

"Yeah." Zane began jabbing a reply with his thumbs. He liked seeing her happy, but he wanted to be the one to make it happen.

"But that's good news."

"Right."

"So why are you frowning?"

Because the playboy had also asked what her relationship status was. The question flashed at Zane from the screen, making his brain squeeze dangerously.

Dude, he typed back before he could stop himself. *She's my work wife.*

He jammed the phone back into his pocket when she tried to look over his shoulder to see. Climbing off the table, he held out a hand to her.

"I don't understand," she said. "Fifty seats is great."

"Yeah?" Zane growled. "Well, I want more."

CHAPTER TWO

The bastard hadn't gotten the message.

Zane stared at his phone later that evening, going through the conversation one more time. Was Larimer not paying attention to what he'd said, or was he just flat-out ignoring it? Because there was no misinterpreting the message he'd laid down. *Dude, she's my work wife* clearly meant *back off.* And the appropriate response to that was *Sorry, man. I didn't mean to make things uncomfortable.* Not *Awesome, then you know her well.*

Know her well? Yeah, he knew Emily well. He knew her at work. He knew her dreams.

But everything in between?

Well, that was a little cloudier. Zane shifted his weight. People's work personas didn't necessarily match what they were like at home, and dreams were often a magnified version of everything.

It was the next question that really got him, though. *Is she seeing anyone?*

No, she wasn't. She hadn't dated anyone since that Ivan or Evan or whatever his name was. The city engineer had bored her, and they hadn't even slept together. At least, the guy hadn't slept over…

Zane started a walk around his garage and then expanded it out to the end of the driveway. Maybe she was seeing someone, but she hadn't shared that tidbit with him. He did tend to get testy whenever the subject came up.

And she flat-out never asked him about his love life.

Huh. She'd never offered to set him up, either. What was that about?

Think you can put in a good word for me? Larimer had typed.

"Abso-fuckin'-lutely not," Zane said out loud.

The stream of water hitting his neighbor's mums took a jump. Apparently, Mrs. Washington wasn't as hard of hearing as he'd thought.

Irked beyond belief, Zane stomped back to his bike. He'd been tuning it up, but at this point, he'd better pack away his tools before he started taking his frustration out on the thing. He wiped down the tools and stowed them, but his phone felt heavy in his pocket. There were a lot of answers he could send to that question, but he held back and typed nothing at all.

Because he didn't want to be unfair to Emily.

He'd known her for three years. They'd started at High Score on the same day and bonded through the sharp curve of onboarding. They were work buddies, but it hadn't grown to anything more than that. Would it ever?

He didn't want to step in her way. Pete Larimer, nosey interloper that he was, seemed to be a good guy, all smart and successful. Em deserved a good guy.

He was a good guy, too.

"Hell." Zane slammed the drawer shut on his tool cart and tossed the rag in the bin. Man, he was twisting himself up over this. He did not do well with mind games.

At least, not this kind.

Planting his hands on his hips, he looked at the evening sky. He knew one way to possibly get some answers, but the sun was still well above the horizon. It wasn't close to bedtime yet.

Bedtime, when people slowed down, stopped all the craziness, and settled in to recharge. To sleep and to dream.

"Screw it." He could get a head start on his night job.

Slapping the button to close the garage door, he headed

into the house. He locked up, snacked on a Pop-Tart, and headed upstairs to his bedroom. He liked his house, with its sharp edges and modern style. Larimer might be swimming in money, but Zane's own pockets weren't so shallow. Despite most of his brothers thinking he was a layabout, he made a good living. As a software salesman, he made more than the geeks who wrote the code, for sure.

He tugged off his T-shirt and threw it into the hamper in the closet. He'd taken a shower when he got home from riding, but he did another quick wipe-down to get rid of the oil and grime he'd managed to collect while working on his bike. He brushed his teeth, stripped down to his briefs, and lowered the temp on the air conditioning. By the time he crawled under the sheets, it was dusk.

It was early, but some of his younger charges were probably already in bed. He could lead them into their dreams about unicorns and puppies and spend more time with Emily. He already knew he was going to spend her whole dream with her, because that was one thing he had that fancy CEO Pete Larimer didn't—a Greek god family lineage.

He was a freakin' Dream Weaver, and Emily Hutchins was one of his charges.

"Relationship status that, Larimer, you putz."

Zane punched his pillow, stretched out on the bed, and worked to clear his mind. Once he went under, his spirit form would travel into the dream realm, and, as his body rested, he'd guide the sleepers assigned to his care into dreams.

Sleepers like Marilee.

He felt her brain waves calling for him the moment he crossed into the dream realm. She wasn't one of his younger charges, but rather one of his oldest. He was glad she'd managed to fall asleep early tonight. Her sleeping hours had shrunk over time, and bestowing dreams upon her was sometimes a challenge. They were what she needed, though, to rest and restore her mental state.

He manifested at her bedside, which tonight was the recliner in front of her television. It was still on, but he didn't need the noise to cover his presence. She couldn't detect him in the parallel realm. Sleepers were unaware of the work that he and his brothers did every night, but he kept his guard up anyway. His older charges were particularly susceptible to sleep raiders as sleep became more capricious with the passage of time.

Tonight, nothing malicious was around. No Apneacs, no Night Terrors, no Spasmodics. He settled his palm on Marilee's forehead and caught one of her passing brain waves. He led her into REM, the state of dreams, and waited to see what would appear.

"Ah, a classic." John Wayne was dealing cards on her back porch. It wasn't a surprise, given the movie that still played on the television.

Zane removed his hand from her forehead and let his senses scan outward. Another sleeper called out for him, and he dematerialized. He was off to his next stop. He had no time to linger tonight.

Except with one sleeper in particular. For that, he'd made a date.

* * *

By the time Zane showed up at Emily's apartment, he'd bestowed three dreams of puppies, a spy noir, a forgotten test dream, two dreams of falling, and one nightmare involving a monster.

The bad dreams were as important as the good ones when it came to a dreamer's mental health, but he was really hoping for a good one for Emily. He could change the direction of a dream at will, but he wanted to see where she'd take it first.

He materialized at her bedside, alert for anything unusual. With a new moon on the horizon, there was little light. The shadows were deep, and outside, not even crickets chirped. On guard, he searched the room. There was nothing, but the pinch in his shoulders didn't ease. He always felt uncomfortable here, like he was intruding. Overstepping.

He wasn't. Dream weaving was his birthright and his duty. He had countless sleepers that depended on him to visit, but it was different with her.

He wanted an invitation to enter her bedroom.

"Ah, Em," he said with a sigh.

She was lying on her side with one knee pulled up and her hands tucked under the pillow. She always burrowed into the thing, tucking her temple into the softness. Her breaths were steady, and her lips looked soft. The weather was that in-between kind where the weight of the comforter was never right. At some point, she'd gotten too warm and kicked it off. Her Solstice Satellites nightshirt had pulled high, and it rode over her hip, allowing pink panties and long, smooth legs to show.

Zane groaned. There was a lot of empty, beckoning space on the other side of that bed. But he wasn't in the physical realm, and he was here for something else.

He had a bet to win.

Laying his hand over her forehead, he tracked her brain wave patterns. She'd moved past light sleep and into deeper delta waves. Both provided benefits, but it was time to lift her into the dream realm.

Catching a wave, he guided her up... up... until her brain activity increased, her muscles locked down, and her heart rate sped up. He let her take the lead from there, choosing the storyline and participants.

"And here we go."

He smiled when the sports park appeared, complete with him, his bike, and all his gear. What do you know? He hadn't even had to work for it; she'd chosen the dream all by herself. One little suggestion over lunch was all it had taken.

The temptation was too strong. He couldn't watch this from afar.

He wanted to participate.

His brothers warned him all the time not to hitchhike, but he hopped into the slipstream and took a dream ride. She was already dreaming about him. It was nothing for him to slide into the role she'd made for him in her mind.

Suddenly, he found himself back at the park, with the

smell of exhaust and the grit of dirt in the air. Engines buzzed like bees, and the sun's rays heated the back of his neck. Emily was standing between him and his bike, looking it over with an equal mixture of curiosity and dread. He looked her over just as closely.

"It's not going to bite," he said when she didn't notice him.

Her hair lifted from her shoulders as she spun around to face him. It swished right back into place when she stopped. "This is crazy. It's much too dangerous."

"Yet you're here. You must be tempted."

Her cheeks flushed. "That's because I… You…"

He walked closer. So, she *was* tempted. "Emily, if you want to go for a ride, just say so."

She glanced wistfully over her shoulder at the bike. "I don't know how."

"I can teach you."

She laughed. "I've seen you ride. You're way too aggressive."

"We'll take it slow. I'll make sure you don't get hurt." Her job was to look for risks and mitigate them so project goals could be reached, but she held on to the "what-ifs" too tightly. She needed to let go a little and enjoy life.

He was happy to teach her how to do that, too.

He looked her over from head to toe. She was still wearing the T-shirt and jeans she'd had on earlier in the day. "Street clothes won't do. Why don't you change in the locker room?"

The dream skipped, and there she suddenly was, dressed in biker gear from head to toe.

Just as suddenly, Zane had a hard-on. "Da-yum, Em."

The look shouldn't suit her, but it did.

The protective long-sleeved jersey was hot pink, with a logo that matched his own, and the pink theme ran right down to her toes. The look was a combination of cute and tough at the same time, and he had to move the helmet he was carrying to hide his reaction. "Come on, biker chick. Let's walk through the controls."

He was impressed at how accurately she'd re-created his bike. He only had to adjust a few details to make it operable. If she retained any of this when she awoke, he wanted to make sure it was right. She paid close attention as he demonstrated the clutch, the throttle, the brakes, and how to shift. "Remember, your left hand is the clutch, and your right hand is the throttle."

"Where's the brake again?"

"There are two, but let's stick with using your right foot for the rear wheel for now. You'll shift with your left foot."

She did that thing she did with her hand whenever she got nervous, flicking her thumbnail against that of her ring finger. "It's too much. I'll never even get it going—or I won't be able to stop."

"That's what this red button over here is for. If you get into any trouble, it's the kill switch."

She blanched and took a step back. "Kill switch?"

"For the engine," he said quickly.

She was already backtracking. "What was I thinking? This is crazy. I can't do this."

"Hold on." He caught her hand before she went into full flight mode. "Just try sitting on it."

"What if it runs away with me?"

"It can't do that when it's not started."

The side-eye she gave him told him there'd be hell to pay if he was messing with her, so he stepped back and presented the bike like a game show host. He liked to push it, but he wasn't stupid. He wouldn't do anything to lose her trust. He knew how valuable it was and how rarely she gave it.

"I promise not to trick you into anything."

Her brown gaze was steady and serious. Finally, she turned it on the bike. She wanted to do this, he realized. Badly.

When she lifted her leg and straddled the dirt bike, sweat popped up on his brow. She looked cute sitting there. Cute and *hot*. Just once, he wanted to see what would happen if she slipped the leash and did something wild and crazy without overthinking it first.

"How's that feel?" he asked.

"Dangerous, but... *badass.*" She wrapped her hands around the handles, reveling in her newfound power. She gave them an experimental stroke and shot him a quick grin.

Whoa, talk about a kick-start.

"And that's how you rev an engine," he said, his voice suddenly gravelly.

She nodded, but then she caught what he'd said... and what she'd done... Her head spun around, and he used the opportunity to plop on her helmet. It was hot pink with lightning bolts down the side. Dangerous, and badass. Definitely.

"Okay, let's go through everything again."

He walked through the controls, letting her touch and figure out how to operate each one. When he quizzed her, she had the answers down pat. Finally, there was nothing to do but give it a go.

"Ready to take her on a test spin?" he asked.

"What?" She let go of the handlebars as if they'd become too hot to touch. "No."

"Come on. Give it a try. See if you can get it moving without killing the engine."

"Uh uh." She wiggled back on the seat, trying to find a way off it, because he was standing too close by her side.

He caught the handlebars when they twisted, and the bike began to tip. "You'll love it once you get started."

"Nuh uh."

"I thought you said you wanted to have more fun."

That, finally, got through to her. She sat for a long moment, looking at the bike she was astride. *His* bike. He could practically see her assessing the trade-off between the risks and rewards, and his hopes sank. He rarely won when it came to that calculation.

"Ride with me?"

She might as well have hit him upside the head with a two-by-four.

Zane thought fast. It wasn't an option he'd considered

because it wasn't feasible. *In the real world.* A dirt bike wasn't meant for two, but they were in the dream realm where anything was possible. And the thought of her riding behind him, holding on tight?

He jerked his thumb at her. "Let me in front."

She clambered off, and he mounted the bike. Just like that, he wove changes into the dream that lengthened the dirt bike and added footrests.

"Here," he said, leaning in to help her get her goggles into place. "You don't want a face full of dirt."

He put on his own helmet, latched it under his chin, and, finally, crooked a finger at her.

Time to put up or shut up.

She took a tentative step toward him, but then her hands were on his shoulders, and she was swinging her leg over the bike. She sat down behind him, but she tried to leave space between them. That wasn't going to work. They had to act as one, balancing the bike on the straightaways and leaning into the curves. Reaching back, he caught her behind the knees and tugged her forward until she was snug against him. "Hang on to me and do what I do."

If he could remember what that was...

Heat poured through him when she cautiously wrapped her arms around him. There was nowhere else for her to put her hands but against his waist, and her body was pressed all along his back and outer thighs.

"Ready?" he asked, his voice doing that gravelly thing again.

"No, but let's do it."

He grinned. That was his girl.

He stomped on the kick-start, and the engine roared to life. Settling down, he revved it and felt her arms tighten around him.

Oh yeah. He officially loved this dream. He might even store it for recurring play.

He put the bike into gear, and they took off.

* * *

Emily clung to Zane. Her heart was in her throat, but excitement exploded outward from her belly.

"*Eeeee*," she squealed. They were racing down a straightaway so fast, her hair should be on fire. "Zane!"

He turned his head to yell over his shoulder, "We're only in third gear."

That was fast enough. The wind was whipping by, and they were balancing precariously on two wheels. Worse, there wasn't the metal of a car surrounding and protecting them.

"Here comes a turn. Lean when I lean."

Lean? Seriously?

She clung tighter and tried to follow his lead. She didn't want to lean too far or not enough, but going anywhere from straight upright was terrifying. The dirt track had tight turns, and the dirt was sandy. It spurted upward when their back tire drifted. Instinct had her putting her foot down as they struggled to gain traction, and Zane did the same thing. The tire tread dug in, and then they were darting forward again.

Up a huge, terrifying mound of dirt.

She tried to bury her head into Zane's back, but the stupid—no, make that "wonderful, life-saving, protective"—visor of the helmet got in the way. Instead, she tucked her chin against his shoulder and squeezed her eyes shut. She didn't want to see. She didn't want to know.

Ahhh, she *had* to know what was coming.

She opened her eyes in time to watch as they ascended the bump and went hurtling into the bright blue sky. Exhilaration burst inside her, even as her stomach dropped. She couldn't help but let out an alarmed *whoop*.

They landed before she could process the sensation, and they were off to the next thrill and terror.

"You okay?"

Emily flinched when Zane spoke right into her ear. It took her a moment to realize the helmet suddenly had built-in speakers and a microphone. When had that happened? "Holding on," she said.

He laughed. "I can feel that."

They were climbing a hill, and gravity pulled at her. She realized how tightly she was squeezing him. She was plastered against his back, and her thighs pressed into the outsides of his. She could feel the power of the machine beneath her—and the strength of the man in front of her. "Sorry."

When she started to loosen her grip, he let go of the handlebar to catch her wrist. "Don't. I'm not complaining."

She quickly latched back on. She needed both his hands firmly on the controls. "I'd prefer that oxygen get to your brain."

He let out a bark of laughter. "That isn't where the blood's going right now, darlin'."

The tires spun, digging in and kicking up more dirt. The trail was rutted and bumpy enough to rattle her teeth. She saw the mud jump approaching and screeched, but then they were flying. Air rushed past them before the dry ground rose to meet them again.

They landed like an airplane greasing the runway, and, this time, her shout was one of triumph.

She couldn't count how many times they circled the track. Her balance got better, and she learned how to use the muscles in her legs to cushion the landings. The ride was a thrill, and so was the man taking her on it. She spread her fingers wider against Zane's flat stomach. He felt warm and hard against her. Muscled and in control.

She was exhilarated when he finally veered off the track and stopped.

He looked over his shoulder, and their helmets bumped. "Like it?"

"Loved it."

She could see his wicked grin in her mind, even if she couldn't see past his goggles to his face.

"Want to try it yourself?"

"Never in a million years." Although the idea wasn't as completely terrifying as it had been before. "Maybe if we found a nice, flat place with no trees."

What she really wanted to do was continue riding with

him, but all good things had to come to an end. Holding on to his shoulders for balance, she climbed off the gutsy little dirt bike and pulled off her helmet and goggles.

The breeze that lifted her hair felt blissful.

"Whew." She felt like she was floating. "Is it always like that?"

"Not even close." He took off his helmet. His face was flushed, and his eyes were bright. "That was special."

Yes. Yes, it was.

Emily started to step back to give him room to dismount, but he looped his arm around her and pulled her back toward the bike. And him.

"*You're* special," he whispered.

He looked at her, making sure she understood what he was saying. When she didn't protest, he pulled her into a kiss that shocked her right down to her tough biker-babe boots.

The feel of his mouth on hers was hot, intimate, and cataclysmic.

Emily let out a sound of surprise as pleasure burst like fireworks inside her chest. This was the ride she'd always wanted to take… the risk that she'd never worked up the nerve to try… He kissed like he rode, all in and right on the edge. Lifting her hand to cup the nape of his neck, she kissed him back.

He felt sweaty and male. Their mouths ate at each other's, and her adrenaline surged all over again.

This was Zane—and he was kissing her. Like a woman, not his buddy.

One of his women… The countless women who fawned over him every day…

A big, red, flashing warning sign lit up her brain, and she pulled back, breaking the contact of their mouths. Never date a coworker. That was a hard and fast rule.

His arm tightened around her. "Em?"

Embarrassment flooded her, and she lurched back, away from the bike…

And straight out of the dream.

With a jerk, Emily awoke to darkness. The buzz of the motorbike faded until it was only the hum of her refrigerator in the kitchen. Zane's arm around her morphed into the twisted sheet of her bed. The sounds and pictures of the dream faded, but emotion still clogged her chest.

Kicking off the covers, she rolled onto her back. Her heart was racing, and her breaths were jagged.

She could still feel his lips against hers... his arm around her... and her body pressing flush against his. It was what she wanted, but she'd crossed the line. The line of what was "appropriate"... the line of professional colleague to intimacy...

"Damn it," she cursed, scrubbing her hands over her face. What was wrong with her?

She couldn't go after what she wanted most, even in her dreams where the possibilities were endless.

CHAPTER THREE

Zane was so not in the mood for this. He slouched in the conference room chair and watched the legal team and HR take turns chewing on him. Right now, they were pointing at words in some document they'd pulled up on the video screen. Their jaws were flapping, and their mouths were moving, but he'd tuned them out long ago. Now, they were just trying to outdo one another.

Tilting his head back, he stared at the ceiling. It was an interior room with no windows or, at this point, air. That didn't mean the meeting was private. The walls and door were made of glass, and anybody walking by could plainly see the shitshow that was happening. They didn't call it "the fishbowl" for nothing.

He snapped his head back down. "Enough!"

Since it was the first thing he'd said since the castigation had started, the outburst surprised the suits enough to briefly shut them up.

He took the opportunity to get a word in edgewise. "I made a sale with the biggest, most important client we've ever had. Yeah, it's only fifty seats right now, but if we prove our value—which is someone else's job, not mine—the potential reaches to the sky."

He held up a finger when one of the suits leaned forward, clearly with the intent to argue. "Not just with Larimer's company, mind you," he continued, "but with all the other companies it would influence. What more do you want from me?"

The leaner piped up anyway. "So, the end justifies the means? What if Larimer had been injured? What if he'd wiped out into a fence? What if he'd broken a leg or dislocated his shoulder?"

"Hell, it was motocross. We weren't trying to jump the Grand Canyon."

"This company wouldn't survive that kind of a lawsuit."

"Or the media coverage," somebody from HR piped up.

"We both signed waivers at the adventure park," Zane said.

"With the park," the lawyer sputtered. "That wouldn't prevent his legal team from coming after High Score."

"You can't take clients, even potential clients, to that sort of an environment," another lawyer said. Her tone was soothing, and her eyes were gentle, as if she were trying to help him understand.

"Or any of our employees," the overly irate leaner added.

Zane narrowed his eyes on the guy. He looked constipated.

"It's not like Larimer's a newbie," Zane said. "He's *won* motocross races before."

It had been years ago, when the guy was a teenager, but they didn't need to know that.

"It's not on the approved activities list."

Apparently, it didn't matter. What the hell was an approved activities list, anyway?

"If you don't like meeting in the office, couldn't you go to a nice restaurant?" the female attorney offered. "Talk over a hot meal?"

Zane cocked his head as if that thought had never occurred to him. "With a glass of wine or a beer?"

"Of course."

"Or two or three?"

The woman blinked. "Well, all things in moderation."

"But it's a valid reimbursement. I know because I've done it." Sitting up in his chair, he propped his elbows on the table. "What if I do that—all legal-like and list-approved—but the client gets in an accident on the way home? He's under the legal limit, but we paid for the drinks."

"You should get him a cab or an Uber. High Score would cover that."

"Okay, different situation. How about I take someone golfing and we're talking business, but some old geezer on the next hole shanks one and clobbers our client in the head?"

Muttering started, but Zane was just working up a head of steam. "Or we do something safer like go for a pleasant walk outdoors. Yeah, let's say we're walking by that little lake downtown. What's it called?"

"Serenity Lake?" the female lawyer asked.

"That's the one. What if we're walking by it, and we run into an urban alligator—you know the type, the ones that are dumped by people who can't take care of them anymore and grow to monstrous sizes in the sewers. What if one of those monster alligators rushes us as we're having this nice, safe, walking business meeting, and it bites Larimer's leg? What then? Think of the media. What's our liability there? I'm the one who suggested the walk. I led him by the lake. Maybe I even stepped aside and let the gator bite him, because I'm faster. What then? Huh? Would I get dragged into this conference room then, too, so you could bite off my ass that the big, bad gator missed?"

He was on such a roll, he didn't hear the door open, or the company CEO walk in.

"What the hell is going on here?" Kevin Frye asked. He looked around the room filled with high-salaried employees, and his expression grew stormy as dollar signs rattled around in his head. He might be dressed in jeans and a High Score hoodie, but he was the man in charge.

"Gatorgate," Zane said.

The leaner across the table sputtered. "That scenario isn't

even feasible."

"Mr. Oneiros was reckless with a potential client," a HR crony said, tattling to their boss. "He took Pete Larimer *dirt biking.*"

"And?" the CEO asked.

Zane crossed his arms and sat back in his chair again.

The leaner had the audacity to smirk. "We're addressing the infraction now, sir."

"Infraction? I heard he got the sale, and nothing happened," the CEO roared. "Give the man a bonus!"

The leaner stopped leaning. In fact, he sat up so sharply his finely coiffed hair seemed to stand on end. "But... but sir—"

"But nothing. This might be the break we've needed to get higher-tier customers." The CEO spun around, and his sneakered heel knocked against the glass door in a resounding thump. "Get out of here and do some real work—like writing up the damn contract."

The room fell into silence as their boss stomped off in the direction of engineering. The bubble of tension in the room had been burst, and everyone in the room was dripping with the fallout.

Zane lifted an eyebrow at the one-time leaner. The guy's face was flushed, and his constipation was obviously worsening. One by one, he and the other muckety-mucks began picking up their laptops and legal pads.

Zane was more than ready to leave, too, but he bent down to pick up a pen from the floor and returned it to the one woman who'd tried to help him. "Sorry for snapping, Monique. I didn't have a good night."

"Uh," she said, her eyes softening with compassion. "I hope you weren't worried about this meeting."

Yeah, this was what had him knotted up. Right.

But it was good to have allies in enemy corners. "I know you're looking out for the company."

"I don't want you to get in trouble, Zane. I'm trying to keep you out of it." She smiled and dropped her voice to a whisper. "It was a rather genius way to get an appointment with Larimer, though, and you did your homework to know he was an experienced rider."

Ally made. Zane knew when to take the win. He gave her a wink and turned the other way as she and the land sharks headed back to their desks.

Unfortunately, that put him on a direct course for Emily.

"Shit," he muttered. This was not his day. He should have stayed in bed. He could have taken a double shift and covered for Mac, who did Dream Weaver day duty.

But a dream ride was what had put him in a funk in the first place, wasn't it? That was what had twisted him up all night, not that stupid interrogation of a meeting.

That dream. That awesome, thrill-inducing gut punch of a dream.

He shoved his hands into his pockets and headed Emily's way. She'd already seen him. Hell, everyone in the bay had a front-row seat to the show that had just happened. It would look strange if he didn't go talk to her.

Because they were work friends.

And, apparently, nothing more than that.

He kicked a scrunched-up ball of paper that was lying on the floor. He'd thought he'd discovered her true feelings for him as they rode around that imaginary motocross course. She'd been laughing and screaming and holding him so tightly, he could still feel her curves plastered against him. When she'd climbed off the bike, all happy and excited, she was the most beautiful woman he'd ever seen. It had felt right to pull her into his arms.

It had felt right to kiss her.

The moment their lips touched, his brain had short-circuited. His adrenaline had kicked in, along with his hormones, because he thought she was kissing him back—but then she'd jerked away, and he was suddenly holding thin air.

She hadn't been able to get out of the dream fast enough.

Talk about a gator bite in the butt.

Fuck.

* * *

Emily saw Zane walking toward her, and she flashed hot and cold. She'd been watching what was happening in the conference room. It had been like a train wreck, impossible not to watch, and she was concerned for him.

But then there was that dream... That dream that she could only remember bits and pieces of, except for one part—the part where he'd kissed her.

He was going to ask if she'd dreamt about him—she knew he was. He'd teased her that he'd get her on a dirt bike, and she'd obviously let him get inside her head. It wasn't tough when he was already in her blood.

She flushed hot again.

"Are you all right, Zane?" Priya asked as she passed Emily's desk.

Startled, Emily glared at her coworker, before she realized how out of line she was. Right. The meeting. Where was her head?

"It's all good," he said.

Why would Zane ask her about her dreams when he had more important things on his mind? Like his livelihood. Emily's stomach gave a sickly twist. She was a terrible friend.

Daphne turned in her squeaky chair and slid her candy bowl in Zane's direction. All the project managers were based in a pod together, although it probably made more sense for them to be co-located with the teams they supported. "I can't believe the way they ambushed you," the redhead said.

Zane took a butterscotch.

Of course he took a butterscotch, Emily thought grumpily.

She watched the way the women in the project management pod fawned over him. Zane Oneiros was a woman magnet. He was dressed like everyone else in jeans and a black High Score T-shirt, but none of the software geeks looked like he did in the standard uniform of the tech industry. Women were drawn to him like flies, and he was too nice to shoo them away. Too nice and too flirty.

He wasn't flirty with her until he was in her dreams, though, so who really was the one with sex on the brain?

Her cheeks heated. What was wrong with her today?

"That sure boomeranged on them, though, didn't it?" Not bothering to stand, Priya walked her roller chair closer to the candy dish by shuffling her feet.

"Urban gators?" Astrid said with a snort. Astrid, who was ill-tempered and focused on retirement from the company where "kids" ruled...

Zane swung his gaze up, his eyes that piercing blue. "You can hear what's going on in there?"

"You can when the company CEO holds the door open. What are we supposed to do? Plug our ears? 'What if he gets bit, because I'm faster?'" the woman said, imitating his lower voice. "Where do you come up with this stuff?"

He shrugged and spun his butterscotch out of its wrapper. "I guess I got on a roll."

"They'll think twice about jumping you again," Daphne said as she smiled and tilted her head at him. Emily squeezed her hands into fists when her coworker twisted a lock of her red hair around her finger.

"You did break the rules," Astrid noted.

Zane knocked on her desk as he walked past. "Yeah, I did. and I should know better." At last, he looked in her direction. "Emily tried to tell me."

She had.

He was finally at her desk, and she had no idea what to say to him. With talk of gators and CEOs yelling, more than the project managers in her pod were watching. She swiped up her water bottle and started walking, knowing that he'd follow her.

"Are you in trouble?" she asked quietly so the others couldn't hear. Her heart dipped. "You didn't get fired, did you?"

He sucked on his candy as he walked by her side. "I got a bonus."

A bonus?

He'd gotten a stinking bonus?

She shook her head in disbelief. "Only you."

"Yeah, that's me. The lucky one."

He rolled his shoulders as if he hadn't shaken off the meeting. They made it to the snack area, and she pushed her water bottle under the fountain dispenser. He settled his hips back against the counter and folded his arms over his chest.

Finally, he met her eye to eye. "So, did we go riding last night?"

Emily died a little inside.

He didn't know. He *couldn't* know how she'd embarrassed herself last night. "You can't be asking me this right now."

"You're turning red. I assume that means yes?"

"Yes," she hissed. She'd been remembering more of the dream than just the kiss. She'd seen blips of them racing around the track as if the hounds of hell were on their tail. She remembered holding on to him tightly and leaning into a curve. "I suppose I owe you lunch. Where do you want to go?"

"Not today." That piece of candy in his mouth had to be nearly gone with the way he was working on it. "Rain check?"

"Sure." He didn't want to talk about what had just happened in that conference room? A ribbon of panic curled deep inside her chest. Their rhythm was off. Talking to each other was usually easier than this. "Are you sure everything's okay?"

Unguarded for a split second, he looked hurt.

On impulse, she touched his arm. "Zane, you're good at what you do. Don't let the tight-asses in legal get you down."

Tight-asses like her?

"I shouldn't have gotten involved. I'm sorry."

He stared hard at where she touched him. "I know that I don't do my best thinking when I get going with a full head of steam. I go with my gut, and I don't have the best filter in the world. But just let me know when I cross the line... about anything. Okay?"

"Okay." She wasn't following.

He lifted his head. "No, promise me. Promise me you won't go along with any of my crazy ideas if it's not what you want."

"I promise."

He nodded and bit down so hard on the candy that she heard a crunch. "There's one thing I need to know."

"What?" At this point, she was ready to tell him almost anything.

"Where's the throttle on a dirt bike?"

"The right handlebar grip."

Emily's chin jerked up in surprise. Where had that come from?

His lips curled into a sad smile. "Catch you later, Em."

She watched him go with her mouth hanging open. He couldn't know. He'd taken a wild guess and triggered something she vaguely remembered... or had read somewhere... He couldn't know the rest of it. There was no way that he knew about the kiss or the way she'd chickened out.

Yet as he walked away, it felt like their problems were deeper than dream level.

It felt like their work friendship was in jeopardy.

CHAPTER FOUR

Zane trudged into IHOP on Sunday morning with his sunglasses and bad attitude firmly in place. The smell of syrup made his stomach turn, but the overriding promise of carbohydrates kept him moving forward. Toast with butter, he could handle. Maybe a breakfast sandwich.

He winced when a busboy dropped a tray of silverware onto a cart, and the clatter drilled into his eardrums.

"Hi, Zane," two pretty girls called as he passed their booth.

Their singsong voices made his shoulders clench. He lifted a hand to say hello, but it barely reached hip level. Sisters, if he remembered right. Or was it cousins?

It was hard to think.

If Sunday morning breakfast wasn't a somewhat mandatory family meeting, he wouldn't be here. He'd still be in bed with his head under a pillow. But it was, he was here, and he wasn't going to complain about it. He and his brothers needed to keep in touch about what was happening in the dream realm. They'd learned the hard way that Dream Weavers had to have each other's backs.

He entered the back dining room and saw his brothers seated at two tables they'd pushed together. It looked like five of them had made it so far. He pulled out a chair, collapsed into it, and grunted at them. He was here. That was about as much as they were going to get from him today.

"You walked by the sorority sisters without so much as a smile. What's up with that?" Bobby asked.

Sorority sisters. That was what they were.

Tony looked him over. "You either had the best night of your life or the worst. I can't tell."

Zane didn't like the way Mr. Muscles was looking at his hair. He took a swipe at it and found tufts sticking out. He combed his fingers through them, trying to get them to at least lie flat. Hell, he'd never claimed to be a fashion model.

"Did you go?" AJ asked. Zane lifted an eyebrow, which must have made it over the level of his sunglasses, because his brother pointed at his chest. "Harbingers of Mayhem. Did you go to their concert last night?"

Zane looked down. He was wearing the T-shirt he'd bought. It had been hanging off the corner of his dresser when he rolled out of bed, and it hadn't smelled all that bad, so he pulled it over his head before coming here.

"Yeah." His voice sounded like a frog on Ambien.

"Oh, hon." Sally stopped in her tracks when she caught a look at him. "Coffee?"

Zane nodded, but then thought better of it. He didn't need his brain rocking around inside his skull. "Please."

"Were they any good?" Wes asked. "I haven't listened to their new release yet."

Zane gave a thumbs-up. The band was about the only good thing from last night.

"You go with anyone?" Tony asked.

Zane let out another grunt. And that would be the not-so-good part. "A gal from work."

"Emily?"

His stomach did another gnarly turn. "Daphne."

"Who's that?"

Zeus's Thunderbolt, could they not leave him alone?

"Ooh." Wes sat up straighter in his chair. "The redhead in project management?"

"Wait," AJ said. "Isn't that Emily's area?"

Emily. Zane's head throbbed.

"Yeah, yeah. She's really pretty."

The pressure inside Zane's head spiked. "You want her, Wes? You can have her."

"Emily?" Tony's eyes popped open wide.

"Daphne," Zane said, the frog voice going deeper, more prehistoric. It would serve Wes right. Then again, his younger brother might like it.

Daphne, the redhead from project management, had no comprehension of personal space. She'd tried to drape herself all over him last night. If he'd known she was so handsy, he never would have gone. It was only when the band started playing and she felt the need to "sexy dance" that he'd gotten his personal bubble back.

Gah, but he was hungover.

He lifted the napkin that was covering the muffin basket on the table. He needed something nice and spongy. Not too sweet. He'd drunk too many beers last night, using the sloshing glass technique to keep Daphne the Draper at a distance.

"Are you dating her now?" Tony asked.

"What?" Zane said, his head snapping up. *"Ow.* No, she had an extra ticket."

He'd learned to avoid that trap the next time.

AJ cocked his head. "Were you trying to make Emily jealous?"

The muffin flew out of Zane's hand. Without even thinking about it, he let it fly. It bounced off AJ's chest and landed on the tines of his fork, causing it to jump and clank against his plate. Another ringing drilled into Zane's eardrums.

"Hey!" Tony leaned forward, ready to stop a fight. "What the hell was that for?"

He was the oldest, and therefore most senior, Dream Weaver present. He was also the biggest.

Zane rubbed a hand over his face. He was spoiling for a fight, had been ever since Larimer put a kink in his tail.

"Sorry." Emily wasn't the one who was feeling jealous. He squinted, but someone had already turned the blinds on the window to stop the laser-like rays of the morning sun. After the nearly moonless night, the brightness was too much for all of them. "I should have thrown that at this one." He jerked his thumb at Wes.

"Who? Me? What did I do?"

"All this yapping about Emily... You told her that I was taking Pete Larimer to the motocross course in front of someone from HR."

"Oh. Yeah. Right." Wes shifted uncomfortably. "I heard you guys ran into an alligator?"

Storm clouds gathered in Zane's head. "There was no alligator!"

"No? Weird. I wonder how that rumor got started." Wes saw another banana muffin in the basket, and he grabbed it.

Zane let out a growl. "That doesn't mean that I didn't get in trouble, you stool pigeon."

Wes glanced up, but he didn't stop peeling the paper liner off the muffin. "With HR? What are they going to do to you?"

Do?

"Well... nothing," Zane grumbled.

Except pay him more. That would not make his case here.

He leaned back in his chair when Sally returned with a pot of coffee. She filled his cup, and he sighed in appreciation. "You're an angel, Sally. Truly."

"Think you might want to try something to eat?"

"Maybe a breakfast sandwich and some hash browns?"

If he asked, she might get him a pillow and clear a booth for a nap.

"I'll get you to the head of the line."

Bobby lifted a hand. "Hey, Sally. Could I get some more... water?"

Too late. She was already making a beeline for the cook.

"Pete Larimer?" Tony frowned. "Isn't that the tech gazillionaire? You took him dirt biking?"

"He's a better rider than I am," Zane said defensively.

"All I said was that I wanted to go, too." Wes took a bite of his muffin. "I don't know why you're so hacked off at me."

"Because now Larimer wants Emily's number," Zane snapped.

Heads came up at that.

"*Ahhh*, and there we have our answer." Tony pointed at the muffin sitting in front of AJ. "Are you going to eat that?"

AJ snatched it up quickly. "Yes."

The guy might be quiet, but if food came within reach at this breakfast table, you grabbed it unless your belly was already full.

"How'd he meet Emily?" he asked. He didn't bother stripping the muffin before breaking off the crunchier muffin top. "I didn't think she was involved in sales."

"She isn't, but after Wes talked to her, she hurried out to the adventure park to try to stop us from riding."

Wes slowly leaned out of reach. "She did?"

"Of course she did. Do you not know who she is?" Em was his protector. She tried her best to keep him out of trouble.

"What does she think of this Larimer dude?" Tony asked. "Is she interested?"

Okay, that question just hurt.

"They seemed to get along well enough." Zane looked into his coffee. Wasn't it supposed to predict his future? No. That was tea leaves.

"Did he ask her out?"

"He texted me after he left to see if she's single."

"Ouch."

"Yeah," Zane replied. Putting him right in the middle…

AJ looked at his muffin as the magnitude of the situation sank in. With a shrug, he offered half of it back. The bottom half. Zane wasn't about to be picky. He tore off the paper skirt and nearly consumed it all in one bite.

He'd go with that being his main problem. He wasn't

going to tell them about taking a ride on one of Emily's dreams... Or being shot down in spectacular fashion when he'd made his move and kissed her... Some things were too personal to share, even with brothers.

"I'm debating if I should set them up."

"What?" Wes said. "No."

"You can't do that," AJ agreed.

"Why not? They're both good people," Zane said.

"But you like her," Wes said.

Zane stared at his muffin, and then dropped what was left of it onto his plate. Yeah, but it only went one way, now, didn't it? At least romantically.

"I don't get it," Bobby said. "Women fall all over each other to get to you. If you want her, why not go get her?"

Tony shook his head. "Because she's his kryptonite."

AJ nodded. "With her, it's real."

Zane dragged a hand through his wayward hair. Normally he didn't mind the spotlight, but all this attention was making him uncomfortable. Not to mention, his head was pounding worse than ever. "Are Derek and Cael going to show today? I've got places to go and things to do."

Like back to bed to sleep.

"They're out of town," Tony said. "This was the weekend they're camping up at Saturn Lake with Devon and Shea."

Their girlfriends.

Zane shifted in his seat. At least some of them were having luck in the relationship department. "All right. Then let's get this meeting started—and before any of you jump down my throat, I had a late night, but I did get to all my charges."

It was time to get down to business. Dream Weaver business. This was the time they set aside for talking about their common night job of bestowing dreams on the sleeping public.

"That's good," Tony said. Missing sleepers had been a problem in their past. "My charges are all taking dreams well, except for the ones who are getting too much screen time."

The blue light from computer screens and cell phones played havoc with people's natural sleep rhythms.

"Same here." Bobby reached for the pitcher of water that Sally had brought to their table and refilled his glass. "I have a couple of charges, though, who fall asleep fine, but wake up in the middle of the night and can't get back to sleep. It's like the Sandmen aren't giving them large enough doses, or something else is going on. I can't lead people into dreams if they're awake."

The deepest sleep tended to happen early in the night, and people dreamt more as the night wore on. The dream state was closest to waking, though, and sometimes sleepers overshot.

"It doesn't sound like screen time is the problem there," Tony said. "Keep an eye on them. Maybe try to get to them earlier in your rounds."

"Good idea. Will do."

Not every Dream Weaver kept a regular schedule. Zane sure didn't. He went wherever the calls came from, and then doubled back to check on sleepers he hadn't heard from. Emily was one who slept like a clock. Regular and on time.

Shit. Did every thought he had have to lead back to her?

"I have a question about teenagers," Wes said. He was still on the learning curve. "They sleep later than anyone else, including me. I can't sleep the day away on weekends to keep up with their dreaming. What am I supposed to do?"

"Coordinate with Mac. He can pick up where you leave off."

"Okay."

"AJ, how have things been for you?" Tony asked.

"Fine."

"Zane? Anything else you want to bring up?"

Zane took another drink of his coffee. He'd been eyeing the Tabasco sauce next to the salt shaker, wondering if he could hack together a hangover cure, but that was a risk even he wouldn't take.

"I do," he said. "My bedwetter. You all told me he'd grow

out of it. Well, he hasn't, and I'm tired of sitting back and not helping the kid out."

"What stage of sleep is he in when it happens?" Tony asked.

"It doesn't seem to matter. He doesn't wake up—or the poor kid is too anxious to sleep at all. He doesn't want to wake up and find out it's happened again."

Bobby's attention was drawn away from the sorority sisters who hadn't given up, just changed the object of their attention. "I have sleepers who would pay dearly to sleep that hard."

"Yeah, well, my kid would give up his piggy bank not to have to wear diapers to bed at age ten."

Wes groaned. "Poor guy."

Tony crossed his muscled arms and leaned his elbows on the table. "Sounds like the Sandman is dishing out too much of the stuff in his case."

They rarely crossed paths with Sandmen. Their particular skill sets were needed at different portions of the sleep cycle, but just because they doled out sleep, it didn't make Sandmen any better than the sleep raiders that were out there trying to steal it. This kid was a case in point.

"You might need to hunt down his Sandman," Tony said.

"What's he dreaming about?" Wes asked.

"Normal things," Zane replied. "School, tests, football, riding his bike…"

"What's his home life like?"

"Single mom—a good mom—and a little brother. They spend every other weekend with their dad, who seems to have his act together."

"That can still be stressful," AJ said.

"Maybe he's clinging to sleep as an escape?" Wes offered.

Zane thought about it. It wasn't an avenue he'd considered, but it was a different take on the problem. "Maybe I need to think outside the box on this one."

"Not too far outside the box," Tony said, pointing his finger in warning.

"Yeah, yeah." You take one dream ride—or ten—and suddenly you had a reputation to deal with.

AJ straightened. "There's Sally with our breakfast."

Dropping their discussion, they sat back in their seats.

"Thanks, Sal," Zane said when she served him first.

"I hope it makes you feel better."

Zane caught Bobby's eye roll across the table. "Me too," he responded, sugar-sweet.

Working together, his brothers helped pass the rest of the plates of food to the right people.

Zane tested out a bite of the hot breakfast sandwich, and his eyelids fluttered closed when the biscuit melted on his tongue. Oh yeah. This was going to help soak up the leftover alcohol in his system.

He nudged Wes's shoulder. "Do you want the Larimer account?"

"Seriously?"

"They'll need someone to onboard them to the software and support them. I can make it happen, if you want the pressure of that kind of customer."

"I want it."

"Good, then you can come dirt biking with us when Larimer and I go up to Comet Tail."

"Wait." Wes stopped the syrup carousel from spinning round and round. "Isn't that what got you into trouble in the first place?"

"Yeah, but it's also what helped me land the account. You in?"

"Won't HR be watching you?"

"Most definitely." Zane winced at how much maple syrup Wes poured on his waffle. "I promised I'd go outside work hours."

He'd promised Emily, at least, and he wasn't going to break his word to her.

"Was that good enough for them?"

"Our CEO didn't have a problem with it."

"All right, then. I'm in."

Good. Zane liked Pete Larimer, but it would be wise to have a buffer with him. A non-Emily buffer… someone who could stop him from knocking the guy off his bike if he brought her name up again.

Zane took a bite of his hash browns and felt almost normal. "One other thing… Can you give me a lift when we leave here? I took an Uber."

"Sure." Wes stirred his bite of waffle in the lake of syrup on his plate. "Still feeling too hungover to drive?"

"Nah, I'm good now, but I need to pick up my Camaro at the auditorium where I left it last night."

"Daphne drove you home?"

"We took separate ride-shares after the show."

Wes looked at him sharply. "You didn't spend the night together?"

Zane had to give a hard swallow to get his bite of breakfast sandwich down. "No."

When she plastered herself against his side as he tried to navigate his way down the stairs from their seats, he'd had enough. Even drunk.

"I'm serious," Zane said. "If you like her, don't let me stand in your way. Ask her out. But trust me, you can do better."

Going out with the woman hadn't been worth it for him, for sure. It hadn't gotten his mind off anything, which had been the idea. Partly, at least… If Emily was so repelled by the thought of kissing him, he had to move on. That was what the concert had been about. It hadn't been a date. He hadn't done it to get back at her or to make her jealous.

He stared at his breakfast sandwich, which had suddenly lost its taste.

Had he?

* * *

Emily awoke on Monday morning to her phone chirping out a happy little melody. She swatted to stop it before it distracted her. She wanted to catch any dreams before they faded from her memory, but figments of thoughts pulled apart and feelings floated away. It was already too late.

With a sigh, she rolled onto her back. She'd slept well, but she was frustrated. She'd tried all weekend to recapture the dream she'd had about Zane. She wanted to see if she could will a different outcome or, at least, keep the dream playing.

But she'd had no such luck.

The only dream she could remember had to do with work.

She groaned when the snooze alarm went off. This time the music seemed more annoying than pleasant. Swinging her legs off the side of the bed, she sat up and rubbed her eyes.

Monday morning, and she didn't feel like she'd had a weekend.

She needed to start planning better for her time off.

Pushing herself off the bed, she made her way to the bathroom. Fall had arrived, but there was still a lot happening. She could have gone to the farmers' market or the arts festival the news anchors on TV had hyped. There'd been a sign advertising a skateboarding competition at the adventure park, too, but she'd spent the weekend washing and detailing her car. It needed the attention, and she'd felt happy when she finished. She liked checking boxes off her to-do list, but really?

She couldn't wait to tell that story when someone at work inevitably asked what she'd done this weekend.

"What a barrel of monkeys I am."

At least she'd taken time to bake banana bread to bring into the office. It was Zane's favorite, and she still felt bad about her involvement in the whole dirt bike fiasco. Things had felt so strained between them that she felt compelled to make a peace offering.

The work pod was empty when she made it to the office. She put the banana bread on the table and hurried to fire up her laptop. The work dream had been anticlimactic, but it might have given her an idea how to reorganize her team's work so they could get to the navigation bug that users were reporting.

She was deep into exploring the idea when Astrid showed

up, and then Priya. Neither were morning people, so they didn't disturb her with more than a hello.

The same couldn't be said of Daphne.

A muscle in Emily's cheek twitched when her talkative coworker arrived.

"Morning, everyone," the redhead said, waving a green smoothie. "Did you all have good weekends?"

Emily wore headphones for a good portion of the day to block out the woman's incessant chatter. She really didn't care about the latest thing some influencer had done or the hottest trend on social media. She reached for her desk drawer out of habit, but her fingers froze around the handle.

"Zane and I went to see Harbingers of Mayhem Saturday night," Daphne was saying loud enough to make sure everyone heard. "We had the best time."

"Our Zane?" Priya asked.

"Is there another?" Daphne giggled. "I was supposed to go with my neighbor, but when I saw how down Zane was after that meeting with the legal team, I figured he needed a pick-me-up."

"What about the neighbor?" Astrid asked.

"Oh, it's all right. He doesn't really like that kind of music."

"But you'd planned to go with him."

"It's not a big deal. I'll bring him some takeout after work or something."

Astrid shook her head when Daphne pulled up a video of the concert that had already been posted online and began looking for herself.

"That's the way to make friends and influence people."

She shot a look her way, but Emily couldn't breathe. Daphne and Zane had gone out?

"Oh, pooh. This was shot from the wrong angle." The redhead leaned her hips back against the table in the center of the pod. When she bumped into the plastic-wrapped loaf of banana bread, she reached back and pushed it out of the way. "You can't see the cute leather skirt I wore."

"So just tell us." Priya spun around in her chair. She wasn't a morning person unless there was gossip to be had. "How was the show? What's Zane like outside of work?"

"*Hot*, but I guess he's that way inside of work, too." Daphne laughed as if she'd made the funniest joke ever. "The band was good but too loud. I had to get close to talk to him, although that wasn't necessarily a bad thing."

Emily's heart squeezed. She vented to Zane about Daphne all the time. The woman drove her nuts. She hadn't known that he liked her. He'd never said anything.

Maybe there were other perks.

Tears pricked at her eyes. Sniffing hard, she made herself dig out her headphones and put them on, but like a glutton for punishment, she couldn't stop listening to the conversation behind her.

"We had so much fun together. He bought us both T-shirts and way too many beers." This time the laughter spread outside their pod area, and a quality analyst looked up in annoyance.

Daphne went back to her phone. "I have pictures." She began sweeping her finger across the screen until she found what she wanted. "Here we are during the opening act."

She waved the phone around so everyone could see, and Emily flinched when it was shoved under her nose. She had to admit, the two of them made an attractive pair. Daphne had snuggled up close to her date with her arm around his neck and her head against his shoulder. Emily's gaze lit on Zane with his mussed blond hair and bright blue eyes. The smile on his face was wicked.

Or was it strained?

She couldn't tell, because the phone was yanked away before she could make up her mind. It was probably wishful thinking anyway.

"He's a big fan of HoM," Daphne said.

Emily knew he was. She was, too, enough to know that nobody called them HoM. People were always surprised by her taste in music.

"They're a little heavy for me," Daphne added.

"Then why did you buy the tickets?" Astrid sniped.

"Because guys like them. Are you not listening?" Daphne let out a breathy sigh. "I spent most of the show concentrating on him anyway. Isn't he dreamy?"

She waved another picture at them, this one a solo shot of Zane in his new black Harbingers of Mayhem T-shirt. The cover of their new album sat against his muscled chest, and the sleeves fit snug against his biceps.

Emily's throat felt thick.

The headphones weren't going to be enough. Folding up her laptop, she tucked it under her arm and headed out of the pod.

"He's definitely the best-looking guy who works here," Priya agreed, "although his brother is super cute, too."

Emily began to walk away faster, but not before she heard Priya ask, "When are you going to see him again?"

Oh, God. Again?

She couldn't take it if Daphne and Zane started seeing each other for real. One date was enough to make her feel queasy.

How had the night ended?

The prickle in her tear ducts became sharper. Turning into the commons area, she wove her way back to a soft chair with a boxy footrest in the corner by the windows.

It was her favorite quiet place. Her hideaway.

She quickly sorted herself out, opening her laptop and tucking her chin into her chest. If she appeared deep in her work, it might dissuade people from talking to her, because talking was something she absolutely couldn't do right now.

That or see her screen.

Tears blurred her vision, but she steeled herself to keep them from falling. She was so angry with herself.

What did she expect? For Zane to be a monk?

She knew he wasn't. He had the looks of a Greek god and a personality that drew people. Guys wanted to go dirt biking with him, and women wanted to take him to bed. Daphne was bold, and she'd asked him out to a rock concert. *Her* way of reaching out was baking banana bread.

Emily rubbed her temple to hide the flare she felt on her face, and she jumped when her phone rang. She hurried to pull it out of her back pocket, and a piece of paper fluttered down to her lap as she looked at the screen. There was no name on the caller ID, and she didn't recognize the number.

"Damn marketers."

She rejected the call and turned her attention to the small piece of paper in her lap. It was made of sturdy stock, but it was worse for the wear. It had clearly gone through the laundry.

She flipped it over. It was the business card from the woman at the adventure park.

The life coach!

What was her name again?

Emily lifted the card into better light and squinted. Hunter something. The last name was gone forever, but she could just make out the phone number.

A shot of adrenaline went through her.

They said that the definition of insanity was continuing to do things the same way and expecting different results. She wanted to learn how to take more chances and live life more fully… even if it was only in her dreams. For once, she didn't open a spreadsheet and chart all the pluses and minuses of the idea. She simply held the card up to the light and dialed the number.

It was time to do things differently.

CHAPTER FIVE

Emily was waiting at the coffee shop when Hunter arrived. The life coach was dressed casually in black shorts and a lavender tank top, with a billowy white men's shirt open over the top of it all. She'd rolled the sleeves up to her elbows and carried a large woven bag. She looked like she was ready for the beach rather than a counseling session.

"Hey," she called, spotting Emily right away.

Emily stood from the table she'd nabbed for them. The coffee shop was busier midmorning than she'd thought it would be. Out of habit, she glanced at her wrist.

"Am I late?" Hunter asked as she walked over.

Two minutes.

"No," Emily said. She searched for an excuse as to why she'd looked at her watch, but she couldn't come up with one.

Hunter winked.

Had she arrived late on purpose? To see how Emily would react? To see if that caused her stress? To show her that time was just a construct?

"I had trouble finding a parking spot," Hunter said.

Emily laughed self-consciously.

"Don't try to outthink me," the life coach said with a smile. She dumped her oversized bag onto the bench on the other side of the table and searched through it for her wallet.

"This isn't a test. I'm only here to help."

"I appreciate you getting me onto your schedule so quickly," Emily said. She'd only called yesterday—but she might have been awake half the night wondering what a meeting with a life coach would entail.

"I had a client reschedule because he's taking scuba-diving lessons." Hunter looked at the blackboard with the coffee house's offerings listed in chalk. "Shall we order?"

"Sure," Emily said. Her mind was stuck on the scuba-diving lessons.

"Don't worry. I'm not going to push you into the deep end."

"Am I that transparent?"

"No, I'm that good." Hunter stepped up to the counter. "I'd like a double-shot quad espresso macchiato with whipped cream."

"Wow," Emily said, the word slipping out.

Hunter shrugged. "You'll have to get your nutritional coaching elsewhere. I need the caffeine. I don't have much energy this time of the month."

"Ah," Emily replied. She was lucky; she only had to deal with an occasional cramp now and then. Still, what would it hurt to spice up her order? "Can I get a pumpkin spice cold brew?"

"Mm, that sounds good. It's getting to be the season, isn't it?"

They took their orders back to the table and got situated. Hunter took out a notebook and a pen. She pushed her hair back over her shoulders, sipped deeply from her double-octane coffee, and finally met Emily's look. "I have to admit, I'm surprised you called."

"I'm surprised, too. I've never done anything like this."

"Ask for help?"

Help? "No. Well…" Is that what she was doing? "Maybe."

"It's funny, isn't it? We've all gotten so busy with our schedules and accomplishing things, we've forgotten how to do what comes naturally."

Schedules and to-do lists *were* natural for Emily. "Like what?" she asked.

"You know… Smell the roses, jump into rain puddles, dance naked under the moon…"

Dance naked? She lifted an eyebrow. Why didn't she start with dancing? And they might as well come to an understanding right now that the "under the moon" thing wasn't going to happen. "I don't know if I want to go that far."

"Good point. What *do* you want?"

Zane.

The split-second answer surprised Emily, but she couldn't say it out loud. That was something she needed to think long and hard about on her own. She took a sip of her pumpkin drink and tried to reframe her answer. "To be looser."

"*Oh!* Okay."

Emily gasped. "Not like that! I meant… adventurous, spontaneous. More open to opportunities."

Although her dream *had* been about opportunities in the direction the life coach was implying.

Hunter gave a closed-lip smile as she sucked more energy-providing caffeine from her coffee cup. "I can help you with either."

"Let's start with being more of a go-getter."

"Still applies," Hunter teased, but she let her off the hook. "You're saying that metaphorically, you want your own dirt bike."

Emily shifted in her seat. The guess was a little too spot-on for her comfort. She didn't want to ride on her own, but she wanted to ride with Zane. Although… saying that out loud wouldn't sound right, either.

Oh, this was not going well.

Hunter sat back. Her dark eyes were all-knowing, as if she could see past a person's shields to their vulnerabilities. "Tell me about your background. What were you like growing up?"

Emily relaxed. That was easier for her. No urban alligators waiting to pop up there. "The definition of normal. I grew up in a small town with my mom, dad, and sister. I moved to Solstice after I graduated from college."

"What do your parents do for a living?'

"My dad's an actuary."

"An act-u-what?"

"Actuary… He's in insurance."

"Got it. And your mom?"

"She's a librarian."

"Okay." The life coach wrote something in her notebook, but with her drink in the way, Emily couldn't see it without being obvious. "Is your sister older or younger?"

"Younger." The picture was becoming clearer in Emily's own head, and she crossed her legs. She'd never stepped back and taken a long-distance view of her life before. "She's the wild one. She kind of went the other direction from me."

"So, you're the firstborn, overachiever, all-around good kid."

"That's me." On the dot.

Hunter cocked her head. "Try this on for size. You were always held up as an example, never got in trouble, got good grades…"

Emily poked a bubble in the foam of her coffee with her straw. "Captain of the tennis team."

"You're athletic? Excellent."

"I used to be. Well, I guess if you count Zumba, I still am." And Zumba was a form of dancing, although she followed the instructors' moves. She was very good at picking up choreography, but not so good at going freestyle.

She was beginning to see a pattern here.

Hunter made another note in her book. "How about work? I know you were on the clock the other day, but I don't quite understand what you do."

"Project manager. I keep everyone on time and budget." Emily jabbed her straw into the frothy drink until it hit the bottom of the glass. More and more, it seemed like she nagged people.

Hunter scrunched her nose in understanding. "Do you like

what you do?"

"I'm good at it."

"That's not the same thing. If you could do anything, what would you choose?"

Emily looked at her blankly.

"All right, let's narrow it down. Is there any other job at your company that interests you?"

She thought back to her early days at High Score. She'd been happy to get in the door as the company was taking off. "Maybe a product owner? They're the ones who investigate the market, talk to users, and determine what features the software needs."

"So, forward thinking."

Emily nodded.

"With more risks and uncertainty," Hunter said. "Interesting."

It was, but the life coach flipped her notebook over to the next page and didn't give Emily time to think about it.

"Tell me about the Dream We—the dreamy coworker from the other day. The one on the bike."

Emily stiffened. "Dreamy" had been Daphne's word for him, too. "What do you want to know?"

"Were you sent to get him because of your job? Or are you friends?"

"Friends."

"Are the two of you close?"

"Very. Or, at least, I thought we were." Emily pushed her pumpkin spice drink away and folded her hands together. "We're good friends."

"But you want to be closer."

She pressed her lips together reflexively.

"Okay," Hunter said. She flicked her pen. "You don't have to tell me everything."

Emily looked across the coffee shop and out the front window at the busy street. "Daphne gave him butterscotch candies."

Hunter waited for a long moment. "Is that a euphemism?"

"No…" At least, Emily hoped it wasn't. "I'm ready to try something new. Work or play, it doesn't matter. I need to break out of the box I seem to find myself in."

"Okay, let's explore the area of play. What do you do in your spare time?"

Emily sighed. There was another one of those questions. *What are your plans for the weekend? What do you do for fun?* She did things she enjoyed, once she got her chores and errands out of the way. They just never seemed to be exciting enough when she shared them with other people.

"Hey, I'm not here to judge. To each their own. My goal is to help people find their joy."

Emily shrugged. "I enjoy baking and gardening. Flowers." She flipped through the pictures on her phone and shared them.

"Those are beautiful."

"Thanks." The small bit of reinforcement made her feel better.

"What's this patch over here?"

She leaned forward to look. She saw straight lines of impeccably weeded flowers, but of course, Hunter was pointing at the bare patch of dirt that was the bane of Emily's existence. "The area is shaded, and I'm having trouble finding anything that will grow there."

"Have you thought about wildflowers?"

"Wildflowers?"

"The woodland kind can be pretty hardy."

But they grew haphazardly, and you never knew what you were going to get… what colors might pop up… and vegetation filled in around them.

"Tell me what you're thinking," Hunter said.

Emily played with the wrapper from her straw, folding it up into tiny squares. "That they're ragged and unpredictable… and beautiful."

"Small steps."

She tilted her head. That was it? Her assignment was to plant new types of flowers? She could do that.

"You know, they have some over at the park on Sagittarius Street." The life coach began packing up her notebooks and drained the rest of her coffee concoction. She pointed out the window. "I have an idea. Let's rent a couple of those scooters and zip on over to the park to check them out."

"Scooters?"

"I'm too tired to walk all the way over there." She swung her legs out from under the table. "Are you coming?"

Emily looked around. Wait. How had they jumped from planting wildflowers to riding scooters? She slid out of the booth and hurried after the woman. "I can drive."

"And give up your parking space?" Hunter shook her head and put on sunglasses. "We'll be there and back before you'd find a spot near the park."

"But the kids are back in school," Emily protested. The park shouldn't be busy, although that didn't mean the parking situation would be better.

The bell over the door to the coffee shop jingled as Hunter exited. She had more energy after her shots of espresso, although the prospect of trying something new seemed to invigorate her more.

Emily, on the other hand, could feel herself withdrawing.

She looked in dread at the scooters in the checkout rack on the curb as she followed Hunter outside. They all looked to be motorized.

"I think we just put our credit cards in the slot and check one out." Hunter ran her fingers over a sign as she skimmed the words. "Yeah, and then we check it back in wherever we want around town, and it will bill us by the hour."

"But... But..." It wasn't the cost. "These things are dangerous."

Emily had seen reports on the news about people getting into accidents when they took the scooters onto the street. And then there was the problem of them cluttering the sidewalks... and people not replacing them properly... The story had been quite negative, although the reporter also talked about the convenience and the speed of getting around.

"I've heard they're pretty instinctive," Hunter countered. "Even easier than the old-fashioned ones you have to push."

Emily flicked the tip of her ring finger against her thumbnail. She'd said she wanted to be more impulsive, but when it came right down to it, making the switch was hard. "We don't have helmets."

That had been the final point of the news segment. The scooters may be relatively easy to ride, but protective gear wasn't offered due to hygienic reasons. Riders needed to supply their own. When they didn't and they fell—rare as that might be—they got hurt.

Hunter sighed, but then bounced up onto her toes and pointed across the street. "There's a bike shop right there. You want a helmet? We'll go buy helmets."

Emily whipped her head around. There couldn't be.

But there it was, Big Dipper Bikes… taking advantage of their location across the street from a scooter rental and eliminating another of her excuses. "That's way too much to spend for a four-block trip to look at wildflowers."

Hunter planted her hands on her hips. "But that's the point."

Not waiting for another excuse, she headed across the street. Jaywalking, while she was at it. Emily frowned. Maybe the woman wasn't such a good influence after all.

But if she wanted to mix things up, she needed to push her comfort level a little.

She clicked her fingernails together more quickly. What was she supposed to do?

As she was deliberating, a young kid came up the street to return a scooter, followed by what looked like his grandpa. Both were smiling and laughing—and not wearing helmets. They didn't help her decision one bit.

Looking both ways, she zipped across the street to catch up with her new friend.

"Shouldn't that kid be in school?"

"Hm?" Hunter looked around, trying to follow, but her attention returned to the window of the bike shop. "Ooh, look. A lavender one. That will match my outfit."

Her cute outfit, with fun lavender slip-ons to match her tank top.

Emily glanced down at herself and felt like a stick in the mud. Surely she could do better than the grays and blues she was wearing. Maybe she needed to mix things up in the wardrobe department, too, and wear more than High Score T-shirts to work. With a sigh, she pulled open the door to the bike shop and went inside.

Too soon, they were back at the scooter rack, with their new helmets in place. Without hesitation, Hunter swiped her credit card, unlocked a scooter, and pulled it off its charger. She looked over the controls and found the power button. "Look, here's the throttle where you control the speed."

"Where's the throttle on a dirt bike?"

"The right handlebar grip."

Emily stared at the scooter that stood in front of her. She felt almost called upon to ride the thing now. She fiddled with the chin strap of her hot-pink helmet. More and more, that dream she'd had was feeling prophetic.

"And here's the brake." That seemed to be enough information for Hunter. She pushed off and hit the gas.

Or, in this case, the power.

She was off and flying down the sidewalk way too fast. When she hit the brakes, the tires squealed, and the back end swung out. Her big bag smacked her in the back, but she just let out a whoop and hopped off. Laughing, she looked back at Emily. "Come on, it's fun."

Fun or insane? There was such a fine line between the two.

Hunter returned at a more sedate speed. "The accelerator doesn't take as much as I thought. Come on, I just started too fast. You can do it."

Taking a deep breath of courage, Emily checked out the scooter that was taunting her now. There were only two wheels, one in front and one in the rear, making it worse than a skateboard. The handlebars rising from the front of the board should provide more stability, though. How did she even get on the thing? She placed one foot onboard, and then switched to the other. Her fingers turned white around the handlebars as she tried to work up the nerve.

Hunter reached out to steady her. "Just get it moving and step on. You'll get the hang of it."

Emily turned the throttle wheel a notch. When the scooter began moving, she had to step onboard or be left behind. She was ready to jump off if she needed to, but the scooter remained amazingly steady. The only reason she wobbled was because she was going too slow. She cranked it up another two notches and felt the breeze lift her hair. It made her smile. She ventured a left turn, and it went better than Hunter's attempt had.

"You ready to head over to the park?" the life coach called.

Emily looked at the path they had to take. They needed to stick to the sidewalks and off the streets, but foot traffic looked light. All the other children were apparently in school where they were supposed to be.

"Okay."

They pushed forward, and the whir of the electric motors increased in pitch. They rode down the sidewalks side by side, and it *was* fun. Like, super fun. Emily tried weaving a bit from left to right. It made her feel like she was surfing.

They stopped at the intersection, and she eased onto the brake to make sure she didn't go flying over the handlebars. Hunter grinned, and Emily laughed.

"How do you think your friends will react to the changes you plan to make?"

Emily thought about it for a second and started the scooter again when the crosswalk light turned green. "It doesn't really matter, does it? I'm doing this for myself."

"Good answer. I think we can work together well."

"I'd like that," Emily said. Because look at her. She was

already riding an electric scooter and wearing a hot-pink helmet. It didn't have lightning bolts like the one in her dream, but she could fix that.

"Woohoo!" Hunter took off on her scooter, switching it up to a higher gear. "Then follow me!"

* * *

Zane found Emily sitting on the curved sectional in the commons area at High Score later that afternoon. Her feet were propped up on the massive hassock in the middle of the gathering area, and her computer was in her lap. Her hair had swung forward to hide her face, and he took advantage for a long look.

She was sleek; he liked that about her. Slim and an easy kind of sexy. There wasn't the hint of tomboy in her, but she didn't go overboard with makeup or faddish clothes. She was just girl-next-door appealing, and he wanted to gobble her up.

But he couldn't let that show, especially now that he knew what he knew.

Stupid Greek god dream insight.

Settling for some chocolate-covered pretzels in the snack area, he headed over to talk to her. He was glad to find her out of her pod area. There were way too many ears over there.

And Daphne.

He winced. What a mistake that had been.

"Hey," he said, plopping down beside her. He passed her the bowl of pretzels. They were her favorite of the snack selection, although the chocolate-dusted almonds had truly been her top choice until they mysteriously stopped appearing two months ago.

The uproar over that still hadn't died away.

"Thank you." She put the bowl down on the sofa cushion between them, within reach.

"I was looking for you earlier," he said. "Where've you been?"

Her attention returned to her computer screen. "I had an appointment. Did you need something?"

"I was going to collect on my rain check."

She looked his way. "Lunch?"

"Too late for that now." He searched through the pretzel bowl, looking for the best one—and, for once, evaluating his next move.

Oh, screw it. "How do you feel about supper?"

Her lips parted. "Tonight?"

"You free?"

He couldn't help it; the muscles at the back of his neck tensed. He wasn't asking her out, per se. It was just a couple of work pals getting together. Off hours.

With no rush to get back to the office.

"I… could do that."

He swung his gaze up and locked it with hers. The relief he felt was oversized for the request, but ever since Larimer and that dream, something between them had changed. There was a friction that hadn't been there before, and it made him uneasy. He wanted to get things back on an even keel. She might not be attracted to him the way he was to her, but she was still his friend.

One of his best friends.

He didn't want to lose her because he couldn't keep his hormones under control. She was the one person who could get through all the scattershot thoughts in his head and make things slow down and line up.

"Pick you up at six?"

"I'm the one paying up. I should drive."

He grinned. He could appreciate being chauffeured. "Works for me."

"Where do you want to go?"

He wanted to take her someplace nice and have a fancy meal, but he'd settle for nachos at the adventure park if it meant spending time with her.

"You're paying. You should decide where."

Her lips twisted into a smirk. "It wasn't that big of a bet."

"I got into your dreams, Em."

The corners of her lips fell, and he was immediately sorry

for the slip. He never should have brought that up.

"Yeah, you did." Her gaze dropped, and she fiddled with the pretzel she'd yet to bite into. The debate inside her head seemed to be strong. "I suppose that rates a burger at Hooligan's."

"Hooligan's?"

She looked up shyly. "Not good?"

"No, that's fine. That's great." Inside his head, the scattershot thoughts began flying around. Hooligan's? They went there for lunch on occasion, but she wasn't the kind of gal who went to bars at night. Too rowdy. Too loud. *Too many guys ready to hit on her,* Zane thought. But she'd be there with him.

He stood. Time to get out of here before he screwed things up. "Pick me up at my place, then?"

"At six. Not six fifteen, Zane. Don't get wrapped up in a video game or the sports report."

He grinned. There was no way he was going to be late for this. "Six," he agreed. "See you then."

CHAPTER SIX

Zane held the door to Hooligan's Bar open so that Emily could enter first. He was so hyped up his skin felt tight, and he could hear his heart thumping in his ears. The crack of the balls on the pool table and the music coming from the overhead speakers should drown that out soon.

He hoped.

Damn, but she looked good tonight. She'd dressed up. Well, not all the way. She wasn't wearing a dress or anything, but she'd put on a purple top that clung in all the right places. She'd paired it with black boots—sensible ones—that still showed off her cute butt in those jeans.

He broke out in a cold sweat when they sat down in a booth.

"You sure you're good here?" he asked. She was wide-eyed as she looked around the place. "We can go somewhere else if you'd be more comfortable."

Hell, he'd be perfectly happy with her at McDonald's.

"No, I know you like it here."

Because it was a place to hang, not to bring a date. "You don't have to do things because I like them."

"But I wouldn't get a chance to come here if you weren't with me."

All right, that sealed the deal. He certainly didn't want her venturing into Hooligan's on her own. It wasn't a rough place, by any means, but she stood out from the crowd, and she knew it. He couldn't help but grin. He wasn't about to tell her it was just a friendly neighborhood bar. If she wanted to explore her dangerous side, he was more than happy to accompany her.

"Zane," the waiter said as he brought them menus. His gaze zeroed in on Emily, and he waited for an introduction.

"Hector," Zane said, letting a sub-growl enter his tone. One that clearly said, *Stay away*. "This is Emily."

"Nice to meet you," she said.

"Nicer to meet you." The waiter smiled, showing a row of straight, blindingly white teeth. "Can I get you two something to drink?"

"Hooligan's Ale for me," Zane said, his brow furrowing.

"I'll stick with a root beer," Emily decided. "I'm driving."

If possible, the waiter's smile got bigger. "Then it's on the house. We make our own here, by the way. I think you'll like it."

"Really?" She sat taller in her seat, happy to find a perk for being responsible. "I'm excited to try it."

"Let me go get it," Hector said. "I'll take your food order when I come back."

"He's nice," she commented when he hurried off.

Too nice. And too Jason Momoa-y handsome. Zane cut off a grumble. What was wrong with the way he was delivering the message? This made two guys in a row that were ready to climb right over him to meet her. Did he need to spell it out in big, bold letters? He was surprised when the waiter remembered to bring his beer.

Emily gave the root beer a taste. "Mmm, this is good."

She licked the sweet foam from her upper lip, and both Zane and Hector froze. Realizing the dude was staring at her lips, Zane snapped the corner of his menu into the waiter's gut. "Bacon burger and fries."

Emily was more thoughtful. "Chipotle chicken sandwich for me, with coleslaw."

"Excellent choice."

Hector finally had no more reasons to stick around, and Zane was happy when the guy left the table. He took a drink of his beer, hoping it would settle him down. The golden-colored ale was smooth, but the taste reminded him of how it had kicked his butt a few days ago.

"Maybe I'll switch over to root beer, too." He rubbed the back of his neck. "I tied one on pretty good the other night."

"At the concert?"

And *damn*. He'd stepped right into that one. *Smooth move, Oneiros.*

He glanced at Emily. Her soft lips had tightened. "Yeah," he replied.

What more could he say?

She straightened the napkin dispenser at the head of the table. "Daphne said the two of you had a good time."

"No, we didn't."

Emily's head whipped around so fast her hair did that flippy thing… the one that made him want to run his fingers through it over and over again.

"You didn't?" she squeaked.

Her reaction was enough to make him pause. Was AJ right? Had he made her jealous? As soon as his hopes jumped, Zane yanked them back down to earth. He knew the answer to that. He'd taken that ill-fated dream ride. Emily didn't like the Draper… er, Daphne. Did she think he'd betrayed their friendship by going out with the woman?

Of course she did. He was so oblivious.

"No." He wanted to nip this right in the bud. He might play games with other women, but not her. "She might have enjoyed the evening, but I didn't."

The salt and pepper shakers were out of line with the ketchup and mustard dispensers, but for once, Emily didn't notice.

"Why not?" she asked.

"You know why."

Her eyes went all deer-in-the-headlights. "I do?"

He wasn't going anywhere near the problem of Daphne's

overfamiliarity, but there had been another issue. "The woman is a nonstop talking machine."

Emily blinked, and then her dimples appeared. "I told you. It's like *The View* twenty-four seven."

"There's no off button."

"Why do you think I spend so much time in the commons area?"

He'd wondered about that. "You should talk with engineering to see if you can be embedded with your team."

"You think they'd go for that?"

"Doesn't hurt to ask."

She glanced up when Hector arrived at their table with a bowl of nuts. "Complimentary," he said.

"Nuts?" Zane said. "Seriously?"

The waiter walked away laughing.

"What's going on?" Emily asked.

"Nothing," Zane grumbled as he picked out the cashews. "He's trying to impress you."

"He is?" Her gaze wandered off, following the waiter to the bar.

There were way too many men looking at her, but she didn't seem to notice.

Good. He wanted to keep it that way.

Losing interest, she took another sip of her root beer and leaned forward to talk over the music. "So other than Double-Talk Daphne, was the concert good?"

"Double-Talk?" Zane said with a snort. His cashew nearly came back up and lodged in his nose.

"Well, she talks twice as much as the rest of us."

He smiled. Double-Talk it was. "The Draper" was officially retired. Now, if he could only forget the experience. "The show was awesome. They sounded amazing."

He knew what she piped in through her headphones when she was sitting so quietly, and he loved that contrast about her.

"Did they play 'Storm Cloud'?"

"Last song before the encore." Or, at least, that was how

he remembered it. Things were getting a bit fuzzy at that point.

"I would have loved to see them."

"You should have gone."

"Yeah."

She reached out to straighten the crooked salt and pepper shakers, and Zane felt bad for bringing it up. She hadn't ventured out, probably because it wasn't the scene any of her friends would enjoy. But hell, *he* was her friend. Why hadn't he asked her to go? Forget the botched dream kiss.

He washed down the nuts with a swig of beer and set the mug down hard enough that it clunked against the table. Suddenly, he had a mission. One way or the other, he was going to get her to a Harbingers of Mayhem show.

Hector brought their food, hot from the grill, and Emily stretched a napkin out in her lap. Zane squeezed a dollop of ketchup onto his plate for his fries and watched her pick the onions off her sandwich. She'd forgotten to nix them with her order.

"Chipotle chicken?" he asked, eyeing the tasty sauce. She wasn't one for spice, although it had only earned a one-pepper rating on the menu.

"Why not?" She shrugged as she put her sandwich back together. "Time to wake up the taste buds."

His gaze fell back on her lips. There was an extra spark in her today, and he wasn't quite sure of the source. He just knew that it got him going. Her tongue darted out to capture a bit of sauce that threatened to drip from the bun onto her plate, and, under the table, he got hard.

Her eyes went wide when she tasted the sauce, but then her forehead furrowed as she considered it. He could have sworn her eyes sparkled before she went in for a full bite.

He cleared his throat. Oh yeah, full hard-on now.

She wiped her lips with a second napkin. "Speaking of my engineering team, I heard them talking about how you were chased by a garter snake at Serenity Lake."

He stopped with a French fry lifted halfway to his mouth.

"A garter snake? It was a gator."

She laughed. "It was neither."

"Yeah, but a garter snake makes me sound like a wimp. If they're going to gossip, they should get it right."

He knew there had been whispers about the two of them, and he didn't like that either. Too bad those rumors were off base, too.

"Tell me more about the show," she said.

He was happy to oblige the little metalhead inside her, and they talked about the concert. She had a major crush on the lead guitarist. Zane supposed he could deal with that.

They talked about the band and work. He started to mention the modifications he was making to his dirt bike, but he managed to avoid that disaster right at the last moment. He still hadn't made up his mind about mentioning Larimer's interest to her, and he wanted to talk about her dream even less.

"Want to play some pool?" he asked when they finished their meal.

"Yes!"

He'd seen her gaze drift over to the table more than once as they were eating. His Em was full of vim and vigor tonight.

They'd played occasionally over their lunch hour when they had time, and she always surprised him with how good she was. She knew how to shoot. There was a grace to the way she moved about the table, and it was downright unfair when she leaned over it to line up a shot.

He watched her sink a striped ball in the corner pocket. "You said you played tennis in high school, right?"

"Yes," she said, her mind already on her next shot. "Why?"

"I can see it in the way you judge the angles."

He could totally picture her placing a drop shot over the net and doing a happy dance in one of those short tennis skirts.

"Zane?"

"Huh?"

"Your shot."

The eyes in the room were upon them. She was a breath of fresh air in the place, and she seemed lighter than she had when he saw her the other day. He wanted more of this.

He wanted more of her to himself.

"What do you say we make this interesting?" He chalked up the tip of his cue as he evaluated the remaining balls on the table. "How about another bet?"

In the dim lighting of the bar, he saw her face pale. Shit. He wanted to kick himself for bringing up that dream—but he wasn't supposed to know the details, because he was just another guy, right? He hadn't been there to experience it all up-close and heartbreaking, right? He barged onward. "Whoever loses buys the next dinner."

The color came back to her cheeks. She thought about it for a moment, and then cocked her hip as she rolled her pool cue on end. "You're on."

"Like Donkey Kong." He focused on the table and got serious. This was one bet he was not going to lose. She was good—he had to give her that—but she didn't have years of practice like he did.

It would be harder for her to beg off if she was the one paying up.

Tuning out the hoots and catcalls of the onlookers who were clearly on her side and trying to distract him, he lined up his first shot.

And promptly ran the table.

"You win," she said as he walked up to her.

He stopped close and wrapped his hand around her pool cue. He dipped his head close to hers so no sneaky ears could listen in. "I'm sorry things got weird between us. Are we good?"

She looked up at him, her brown eyes deep and pure. She smiled softly, and he was a goner. "We're good."

* * *

Zane was feeling lucky tonight. He'd fixed one problem. Well, sort of… Things with Emily weren't where he wanted them, but they were nearly back to normal. It was time to go after another long-running issue.

He checked his text messages when he heard his phone ding. She'd arrived home safely.

Sweet dreams… He stopped and backspaced. *Sleep well,* he typed instead.

They'd had fun tonight, even more fun than usual. She'd been in a good mood—once they cleared up that Daphne issue—and there'd been a lightheartedness about her. One that was really appealing. Sparks had been flying.

At least for him.

You too, she texted.

He grinned. *Yes, ma'am.*

Sleep was different for him, but he appreciated the sentiment. He was going to bed to see if he could keep this lucky streak going.

He headed upstairs and went through his normal nighttime routine. He did an extra set of push-ups and then flipped over for some crunches to burn off remaining energy. Then, stretching out on the bed, he let himself relax.

He needed to talk to a Sandman about a ten-year old. It was time to do something about the bedwetting.

After the good night he'd had, transitioning over into the dream realm was easy. His spirit form went straight to Christopher's home, but he could tell from a distance that the Sandman had beaten him to the punch.

The kid was already sleeping when he got there, and deeply. The Sandman's gritty doses worked well at the beginning of the night. It was only after a round of deep sleep that sleepers started to go through the different phases, rising to light sleep and then to dreams and back down again.

That was if the sleep cycle was working properly, which was becoming more and more uncommon.

"Sandy," Zane called out.

He didn't know which one, in particular, handled Christopher's care, although that wasn't a surprise. He could count how many Sandmen he'd met on one hand. Make that a thumb. Sandmen and Dream Weavers rarely interacted, even when they shared the same charges, but Mr. Sleepy needed to cut back on his dosage with this one. Zane needed a word or two.

"Sandman," he called. He sent out a summons and was irritated when none of the kind responded. They were uppity sorts, the Sandmen, thinking they ruled the night world.

His mother, Nyx, would have a thing or two to say about that.

Zane looked around the bedroom. The shades were pulled, and the only light he saw was on a power strip that was connected to a phone charger, a computer, and a gaming station. Pretty normal. At least none of the blue-light-emitting troublemakers were on. The place was quiet and cool. Obviously, if the kid was sleeping so deeply that he couldn't feel nature's call, his bedroom was conducive to sleep.

Zane turned, and his night vision picked up a set of shoulder pads on a chair. A football helmet was on the dresser next to it, and a poster of the quarterback for the Solstice Satellites, the city's professional team, was taped on the wall.

He was detecting a theme.

He saw a calendar with Xs, once a week. Game days.

It wasn't rocket science. The kid was sleeping hard because he was tired. Zane wondered what position he played.

There was one way to find out, even if his brothers would get all up in arms about it. He could watch the kid's dream play out from the sideline like a good little Oneiros, or he could jump in and experience what Christopher was experiencing. Feel what he was feeling. The move had backfired on him the last time he'd done it, but the kid needed his help.

It was time to take another dream ride.

Zane put his hand over the boy's forehead and caught a brain wave spindle to guide Christopher into a dream. From there, he let the boy's imagination take over. Instead of watching from a distance, Zane immersed himself in the dream, entering it like an actor in a play.

He found himself in a maze.

"What the hell?"

A corn maze? No, it looked more like tall grass with different pathways mowed into it. Christopher started down one, and Zane shadowed him at a good distance back. Over the kid's head, though, he saw an X blocking the way. He backtracked quickly when Christopher changed direction. They went down another path, and there was an O.

"Twenty-two orbit, flanker pivot," a disembodied voice called.

"What?" Zane muttered.

"Hut, hut."

Suddenly, Christopher went running by, straight for the X. He skidded to a stop.

"No, *orbit*." He hurried back to where he'd begun and pivoted to go perpendicular to the path he'd run before.

"Ninety-four f-stop green."

The boy jerked to a stop so hard, his spikes kicked up a clod of dirt. He began running in a new direction, counting under his breath. On three, he turned around and waited.

A football went flying past his right shoulder, too far away for him to reach.

Zane finally caught on. The kid was trying to learn his team's playbook. He was going over it, even in his sleep.

Okay, now they were making progress.

He checked Christopher's vitals. Oops. The bladder situation needed attention.

"Okay, Chris. Take a timeout."

The dream skipped, but the boy didn't wake up. Suddenly, the grass was mowed, and it was game day. When the play was called, Christopher took off running. He knew which way to go this time, and the football was thrown right between the numbers on his jersey. He caught it, turned for the end zone, and began running as if his life depended on it.

Maybe it did.

The answer to which position he played was clear. Christopher was a receiver. He had good hands and was fast on his feet, but his adrenaline had an edge. The reason for that was right on his heels. The player chasing Christopher down was twice his size, and the lion logo on the opponent's chest looked like it had just spotted its lunch. Christopher's heart was racing, and he was sucking in air like a jet engine.

"First season of tackle football," Zane guessed. He remembered how that had upped the stakes.

He parked himself on the sidelines as an assistant coach to watch.

"Come on, Christopher," Zane shouted out amongst all the fans who were cheering. The dream was swiftly jumping from dream to nightmare—but maybe that was what the kid needed. The fear might wake him up so he could take care of business. "Jump out. Wake up, Big C. Come on, my man."

A winding brook somehow found its way on the football field, and Christopher followed its banks. The defensive back chasing him was gaining ground.

A big lake formed where the end zone should be, and there was no questioning the symbolism there. It was going to happen again. He was going to have an accident if he didn't take the hints.

But the kid was focused on the job he was trying to learn.

Poor guy. Between the pressure of the game, and the embarrassment he was dealing with every morning, he was not having a good time. He needed a win.

Zane knew how that felt.

The urgency of the situation became dire. This was not going to end well if he didn't intervene.

Zane spotted a water cooler on the sideline. He rolled it out onto the field, into Christopher's way, but the kid hurdled it and kept going.

Okay, he needed a bigger jolt, something extra to make him break away from the dream. Zane hated to do it, but the bedwetting thing had been going on too long.

"Sorry, kid."

With a flick of his finger, he changed that defensive lion into the real thing. The big cat roared. Christopher looked over his shoulder and gave a yelp. He tried to go faster, but he got caught up in the dream sludge where his legs felt like two-ton weights and his arms were heavy as anchors. Christopher cried out. The lion leapt. His fear spiked and—

Poof. The jump to wakefulness happened.

Zane swam through the flickering mists as the dream pulled apart, faded, and disappeared. He watched from the dream realm as Christopher jerked awake, and then jackknifed up in bed when he felt his pressing condition.

The kid jumped to the floor and darted down the hallway to the bathroom.

"Yes," Zane said, giving a fist pump.

Tragedy averted.

See? Dream rides weren't always a bad idea. Maybe a couple more, and the kid would learn to pay attention to the signals his body was sending him. The creek, the lake, the water cooler...

Zane was pumped. A good evening had turned into a good night.

Speaking of his good evening, where was Emily? He scanned outward, looking for her sleeping mind. Each sleeper's brain wave pattern was unique, like fingerprints, but he didn't catch it during his scan. It was getting late, and she hadn't called for him. That wasn't like her.

He dematerialized and went to find out why.

He found her bedroom empty and the comforter on the bed smooth. She hadn't gone to bed yet. That was unusual for his prompt schedule follower. He could sense her, though, awake in the house, and he heard music. Familiar music. He grinned. She was listening to Harbingers of Mayhem.

That was his girl.

Not wanting to intrude on her privacy, he faded back into the dream realm to move on to his next charge.

If he'd taken a peek, though, he would have discovered

her dancing in the moonlight.
    Wearing her Solstice Satellites jersey.

CHAPTER SEVEN

Emily and Hunter stood waiting in the hallway at the Solstice fitness center. They were early for the afterwork class they'd decided to try. Emily had wanted to get the lay of the land, but Hunter's promptness seemed due to excitement. She was bopping her head to the music coming through the glass windows of the workout room and mouthing the words. She wasn't quite dancing, but the increase in her energy was noticeable compared to the other morning when she'd been too tired to walk a few blocks to the park. Then again, some people were night owls.

Emily moved out of the way of a weightlifter who was heading to the locker room. "Are you sure this evening class isn't messing with your schedule?"

Hunter winked. "I chose it, didn't I?"

"*I* sure didn't."

The life coach laughed. "This is fine. I set my own hours. They change from day to day, because fun things like this don't always happen between nine and five."

A fluctuating schedule like that would drive Emily crazy. "You say fun. I say potentially embarrassing..."

"Come on, you're going to enjoy it, and you know it."

They were about to try another new activity outside her comfort zone. It wasn't something she would have come up with on her own, that was for certain, but she had to admit she was curious.

"Stop fidgeting," Hunter said.

Emily tucked her hand between the small of her back and the wall to make herself stop clicking her fingernails. She couldn't believe Hunter had convinced her to try a hula hoop class. She'd never been good at it, even as a kid. "How did you get me here?"

"You said you wanted to loosen up."

"Again, not like this."

"Hoop dancing is the next level up from Zumba. Or maybe you wanted to take pole-dancing classes instead? Or—*ooh!*—there's one where you choreograph your own routine and show it to everyone else at the end?"

"No, this," Emily said quickly. "This is fine."

"That one's tomorrow anyway." Hunter set her bag down on the floor and stretched her arms overhead. "So, you've tried some new things since we've met. Scootering—is that a word?—and planting new flowers."

"I played pool at a bar, too. At night."

The life coach lifted an eyebrow. "Impressive. How are you feeling about things?"

"Nervous and excited…"

"Do I hear another 'and'?"

"Maybe a little bad."

"Why?"

"I don't know. I guess because it's outside my routine."

"And that's bad?"

"No. It's… just different for me."

"What did you miss on your schedule?"

Trying not to click her nails, Emily tugged at the hem of her T-shirt instead. "Nothing that couldn't wait."

"So why aren't you letting yourself enjoy the new experiences?"

She paused. That was a good question. Why was she feeling bad about feeling good?

She stared through the window of the exercise room they were waiting to enter. People inside were finishing their strength-training class and putting their stretchy bands back on their color-coded hooks. So tidy. So orderly.

"The days just aren't long enough." She let out a puff of air. "It's ridiculous. There's not enough time in the day for people to do what's expected of them. We're supposed to sleep for eight hours, work for eight more, exercise for thirty minutes, meditate for ten, get ten thousand steps in, drink eight glasses of water, and zero out our email inbox—all while eating healthy, practicing mindfulness, and journaling our gratitude. And don't even get me started on skin care routines!"

Hunter's eyes rounded. "Whoa."

Yeah, whoa. She always felt like she had to run to keep up.

"Feel better now that you got that out?"

Emily's brow furrowed. She wasn't sure where all that had come from, but it certainly got her thinking.

"It's interesting, isn't it?" Hunter said. "Everything you listed is supposed to be healthy for you, but you're feeling trapped by it instead."

Yes, that was it exactly. She'd gotten so wrapped up in doing the right thing and following all the recommended guidelines that she wasn't enjoying anything. She wasn't living her life. She was checking off boxes and doing the tasks of living.

"You should feel proud of yourself for being here, not guilty. You've started putting yourself out there. You're enriching your life."

"Maybe… but I didn't decide to do any of those things on my own." Although she had danced in the moonlight last night to Harbingers of Mayhem… Not naked, but in her pajamas…

"Who cares? It's a start."

The door to the exercise room opened, and Hunter moved her bag out of the way with her foot. The clock had hit the hour, and people were pouring out of the exercise room to head to the locker rooms, the weight room, or their cars. They were all on the conveyor belt of life, too, ready for the next thing on their daily schedules.

When had that happened? Who had decided that everything started on the hour? Or, more rarely, on the halves? Why didn't anything start at quarter after? Or twenty minutes after or—*gasp*—seventeen minutes after the hour?

"Change can be easier if you have a co-conspirator," Hunter said over the chatter and shuffling feet. "That's why I'm here."

She gave a wave and headed into the now-empty exercise room. Emily and the other class attendees filed in after her to fill the vacuum, ready to start the next class on the magical hour. Hunter chose a spot on the far side of the room and dropped her bag against the wall. The spot was prime, right in front of the mirrored wall where they could see every misstep they were about to make.

Only with a hula hoop, it wasn't just a subtle missed step. One wrong move, and the hoop would crash to the ground, making it obvious to everyone.

Emily looked around the room at the class regulars. Most were women dressed similarly to Hunter in sports bras and leggings, but there was one guy at the back. All of them looked excited to get started. She twisted her hands in her T-shirt. If she'd known they were going to come here, she would have bought a hoop and practiced.

"Hoops are at the back of the room," a woman called as she headed to the front. "If you're new, start with a lighter weight. Loose clothing can get tangled with the hoop, so you might want to tuck it in."

The instructor wasn't anything like Emily expected. She wore glasses, and her hair was up in a smooth bun. She wore a sports bra and yoga pants, too, but hers were bell-bottom style. That made sense. They were going retro, after all.

"Ooh," Hunter said. "Let's hurry so we can get good colors."

Together, they searched through the collection. The hoops came in various sizes and weights, which was new to Emily. The sound of the swoosh was a blast from the past, though, and she liked the lightweight hot-pink one. Hunter surprised her when she went bold with orange instead of the purple one beside it.

"Who'd you play pool with?"

Emily looked up. "What?"

"Pool." Hunter swung the hoop over her head and let it settle at the small of her back. "At a bar. At night."

"Oh. It was a work thing." Emily became overly attentive to her T-shirt. Tucked into her leggings was not a look she liked. "I lost a bet."

"You lost a bet and had to go? Or you lost playing pool?"

"Both—but I think he tricked me."

"He?"

Music filled the room, a perky pop song that seemed appropriate. "All right, everyone. It's time to start," the instructor called out. "Let's warm up by stepping side to side."

Emily hurried back to her spot.

"Wait," Hunter said. "Are we talking about the motocross daredevil?"

Emily tried not to answer, focusing instead on what the instructor was doing, but that was answer enough. Hunter wasn't put off the scent.

"Oh my God, it was. Was it just the two of you, or were you with a group?"

Emily waggled her fingers to get her friend moving.

Hunter did, but she wasn't paying any attention to the instructor. "Has something changed between you and the Oneiros?"

The Oneiros? Emily knew he was from a large family, but that sounded wrong. "His name is Zane."

"Zane," Hunter said, drawing out the Z.

"Welcome, everyone." The instructor's voice came through the speakers. She was wearing a wireless microphone so she could move about the room. And move she did. Just stepping side to side, there was a graceful flow to her body. She lifted her arms to add some flare. "This is the introduction to hula hoop class—or hooping, as we like to call it. We'll teach you some basic moves and work up to some fun tricks."

Hunter scooted closer to Emily, ruining the even spacing of the class attendees and not being subtle about it at all. "What's going on between you two?"

"Pay attention."

"After you answer me."

"I don't know." Emily shut up when the instructor's gaze caught hers in the reflection of the mirror.

"Let's start with some slow hip circles to warm up those core muscles. Plant your feet and swi...vel..."

"What do you mean, 'you don't know'?" Hunter was like a dog with a bone.

"Things are *different*," Emily said.

"Why?"

The instructor turned to face them with the mirror behind her, and Emily ducked her head. She'd never gotten in trouble in class before, and she didn't want to start now.

"Try to keep your head and chest stationary," the instructor said, her voice coming through the speaker right over their heads. "Move those hips right... and back... and to your left."

Hunter glanced to see what she was supposed to be doing, and she picked up the movement quickly.

"There you go," the teacher said. "It's nice to see some new faces today. Just have fun and don't worry if the hoop falls. It happens to all of us."

The class was small, and it was hard to hide. There were only about eight students of various ages and body types. The guy at the back obviously knew what he was doing, while the others were of various skill levels. Some had wider ranges of motion. Others were precise and stiff. The common thing they all had were smiles on their faces.

Fun. They were here for the joy of it. Emily shook out her hands. They didn't care if she picked things up perfectly or not.

"What changed?" Hunter asked.

"Hip circles," Emily said, demonstrating.

"No, between you and Zane."

The instructor's eyes narrowed behind the frames of her glasses. The stage whispers were starting to annoy her.

Emily sighed. She'd already put so much out there with her rant earlier—what was one more thing? One more majorly personal thing?

"I dreamt about him the other night."

"And reverse direction," the instructor called.

"We were riding together on a motocross bike at the adventure complex... and, well, he kissed me."

"Kissed you?" Hunter stopped with her hip jutted out to the side. "The Oneiros kissed you in your dream?"

"Shh," Emily warned. "Yes, *Zane* kissed me. And I've been weird around him ever since."

"Did your mind come up with that?" Hunter asked, her voice turning serious. Emily cringed when her life coach turned to face her and gave the instructor her back. Her hips were swiveling, but her look was steady. And, honestly, not happy. "I mean... Is that something you want? Do you want to kiss him?"

"Yes," Emily said, dropping her arms. There, she'd admitted it. Out loud and to herself.

She wanted to be more than friends with Zane Oneiros.

"Get your hoops!" the instructor called loudly, trying to regain control of her class. "Stand with one foot forward and push the hoop in whatever direction feels natural, clockwise or counterclockwise. Keep it going with a forward and back motion of your hips."

And, with that, they were off and hula hooping.

At least, some of them were. Hunter was still staring.

Emily gave her hoop a whirl and started rocking her hips, only to have it clatter to the ground after no more than two rotations.

"Here, let me help," the instructor called.

Oh, God. She was heading their way. Now they were

thoroughly disrupting the class. Emily picked up her hoop and quickly gave it another push.

Hunter finally got with the program, but she didn't have much more success.

"Forward and back, not side to side." The instructor stood there, whirling her hoop as if she didn't even have to think about it. "Follow the position of your feet."

Hunter pounced on her hoop and picked it off the floor to try again. "I'm more hula than hoop."

"Ah. Unfortunately, there's no correlation between the two."

"No kidding." Hunter gave her hoop another twirl, and it started moving in the familiar *zhh-zhh-zhh*-sounding rhythm. "Like this?"

"There you go." The instructor threw a glance to check on Emily. Nodding in approval, she moved back to her place at the head of the room. "Now, try turning in a circle as you go."

A circle as they circled?

"So, how was the kiss?" Hunter asked.

Emily lost her rhythm completely.

"That good?"

Emily blushed. "I was so surprised, I woke up."

Hunter's mouth dropped open. "You hopped out of a dream where you were kissing an Oneiros?"

"Yes," Emily hissed, clenching her hoop with both hands, "and I missed all the good stuff that might have happened afterward."

Hunter laughed. And not a little. She nearly doubled over, the belly laughs were so deep.

Other students started to glare and frown, and Emily was horrified. She caught Hunter by the arm and got them both back into the hip swirls. "People are getting mad."

"Sorry," Hunter called loudly. "She kissed the guy who's supposed to 'only be a friend.'"

Emily wanted to die. Right there on the spot.

But the explanation cleared up the misunderstanding. The

growls turned into chuckles, with a "You go, girl" from the guy at the back. Glares turned into empathetic looks, because everyone understood why a situation like that warranted talking in class.

Hunter smiled broadly. The instructor began moving faster, and she was right on the beat with her.

Emily tried to hold it in. She wanted to blend in with the class or—better yet—melt through the wall, but she had to ask. "Why is that funny?"

To her, the dream had been hot, confusing, and frustrating as hell. But funny?

Hunter wiped her watering eyes and shook her head. "Oneiros means dream in Greek. You should look it up sometime."

"Oh, I didn't know that." The Oneiros. The dream. It made sense now.

"Seriously," Hunter said. "Look it up."

The music changed to a different song, one that was more upbeat and energetic. Hoops began to swish even faster.

"So, you like Dream Boy," Hunter said with a chuckle. "I think we're getting to the heart of what this is all about."

"Maybe."

"Don't change yourself for a guy," Hunter warned, switching back into life coach mode.

"I'm not." The dream and the Daphne incident might have spurred Emily to look Hunter up, but the more they spoke, the more she realized what her life had become. "This is about me figuring out what I really want, and not just following rules someone else came up with."

It was a revelation.

She didn't have to be perfect. She didn't have to make sure things went a certain way. She didn't have to carry responsibility so heavily on her shoulders. So what if the hoop clattered to the ground? It could always be picked up again.

"There you go," Hunter said.

The moment Emily stopped working so hard at it, things

got easier. Her hip motion loosened up, and her shoulders dropped from where they'd cinched up under her ears. The guy at the back of the room let out a hoot of approval, and the flush that went through her this time wasn't embarrassment. It was happiness.

"You're all doing great!" the instructor said with a smile.

Emily relaxed and paid attention as new moves were introduced. The weighted hoops were easier to control than the light ones she'd played with as a child. They moved more slowly, and the advice about the forward and back motion was the trick she'd been missing. It felt energizing to do something different. She'd memorized her Zumba instructor's routines to the point where she could have done them blindfolded.

That didn't mean hula hooping was easy.

When she tried turning in a circle, she went the wrong way, and the hoop was unforgiving. She caught it, this time, before it hit the floor. On the second attempt, it tangled in her oversized T-shirt and rucked it up to her ribcage.

"Ugh," she growled in frustration. She pulled her T-shirt over her head and tossed it on top of Hunter's bag. Focusing on the mirror, she concentrated on her stomach muscles. When she got a rhythm going this time, she could see and hear when she got it right.

"Let's move on to the vortex," the instructor called.

Hunter's eyes lit up. "Ooh, this is what I want to learn."

The instructor guided them through the ripple motion to make the hoop move up and down. It started at the hips and worked upward until the hoop was overhead, rotating around one arm.

"That looks so cool." Hunter was thoroughly engaged now. She held up her arms and tried to copy the move. It required concentration and muscle control.

"Let's slow it down and try again," the instructor said. She called out the movements one by one, gradually speeding up as they went.

And Emily got it.

Hunter gasped. "How are you doing that?"

Emily didn't know, but she kept on undulating like a snake.

"Nice," the instructor said as she walked past.

Emily's heart puffed up. She liked this side of herself. She was a girl who tried hula hooping.

"Keep going," Hunter said. She broke out of line and hurried to her bag.

Emily held up her hands when she saw the phone. "Don't you dare."

"Don't you want proof you did this? You know you're going to want to practice at home."

Well, maybe. Practice did make perfect.

"It will be something to watch when you're stuck doing those spreadsheets, or whatever it is that you do."

Emily thought about it. "Okay, but use my phone."

She pulled it out of the pocket in her leggings and passed it along. Hunter waited until she got back into the groove and then lifted the phone to record. Emily concentrated on the music and let the rhythm enter her body. She did a slow circle and then transitioned into the vortex that came more naturally to her. Hunter grinned and gave her a thumbs-up, filming all the while.

Out of breath, Emily stopped. "That's enough. Your turn."

Hunter tapped the stop button and passed back the phone. Emily glanced at the still view. Her hair was mid-swish, and her chest was mid-body roll.

For feeling so out of place, she looked good.

"Do me," Hunter said, holding out her own phone.

They switched positions, and Emily began filming her new friend. They felt like friends, more than coach and mentee, although Hunter was always the one leading her into new experiences. She somehow knew just how far to push. Emily never would have tried this class alone, but she was happy she had.

"Nice," she mouthed, holding up her thumb. She steadied

the phone, even as the beat of the music called to her.

She knew she was going to practice at home—maybe even in the moonlight.

The class was over much too soon, and there were smiles all around as people collected their things and said their goodbyes. Emily and Hunter huddled close to watch their videos.

"I still don't know how you picked up that vortex move," Hunter said.

"Either do I, but you slide from one trick to the next so smoothly, you look like you know what you're doing."

"I don't."

They laughed, but Emily flinched when her phone suddenly buzzed, signaling a text. She flipped over to the messaging app to see who it was and blushed. Speak of the devil. The message was from Zane.

"Problem?" Hunter asked.

"Nope." Emily swiped back to the video. "They're going dirt biking again."

"You don't care?"

She shrugged. "There was this whole thing at work, and he's been warned. He's not my responsibility."

"Even if he is your crush?"

Emily leveled a look on her life coach. "You can't use that against me more than once a meeting."

Hunter laughed. "Fair enough."

She went back to swishing her hoop and listening to the sound it made.

Another message came in. Emily read it, rolled her eyes, tapped her phone, and turned to put it away—but immediately froze.

"No. Oh, no." She grabbed the phone with both hands. She couldn't have done what she thought she'd just done. "Noooo!"

"What's wrong?" Hunter asked, hurrying to look over her shoulder. "Did you delete it?"

"I sent it to him," Emily said, panic making her voice

jump.

The instructor turned from the sound system with concern on her face.

"Are you sure?" Hunter asked. "What did you do?"

"I don't know. I was flipping back and forth between the apps. I must have somehow attached it to the message he sent me." Emily flung her head back and walked in a circle. There had to be a way to get it back... to stop it before he saw it... She worked in technology.

But it was right there in the sent messages folder.

"Is everything all right?" the instructor asked.

New students started coming into the room, ready for the next class. The hour hand on the wall clock was standing right on the twelve, after all.

"Nothing bad," Hunter said, circling her arm around Emily's shoulders. "She accidentally sent the video of her hoop dancing to a guy."

The instructor looked crestfallen. "But you were enjoying yourself. Why is that bad?"

"It's the friend she kissed." Hunter began directing Emily to the door. Students who were pulling yoga mats out of the large plastic bins were looking at her with concern and curiosity. The life coach swept up their things from the floor. "She doesn't realize it could be a happy mistake."

"Happy?" Emily said, whirling around. "I work with him!"

"He's not going to pass it on." Hunter stopped. "Is he?"

"No." Zane wouldn't do that—but now the thought was in Emily's head.

Oh, damn. She needed to face this head-on.

She moved away from the door into the hallway, trying to find a bit of privacy. She started texting, but her fingers fumbled, and it took her three times as long to send the message. *I didn't mean to send that to you. Don't laugh at me.*

She waited, her heart thumping and her stomach in a knot.

He texted back. *NOT laughing.*

"Oh, God."

Hunter pointed at the screen. "He said he's not laughing at

it."

"You looked good," the instructor insisted. "You picked it up well, especially since this was your first time."

"But that means that he's watched it!" Emily flopped back against the wall and let it hold her up.

She lifted the phone again. *Don't watch it,* she texted.

Too late, Zane replied.

Delete it.

No.

"Wow, that was fast," Hunter said.

Please? Emily typed.

Not in a million years.

The instructor adjusted her bag over her shoulder and smiled. "I think my work here is done." She gave a wave. "I hope to see you two back here next week."

"He's going to hold this over me as leverage," Emily said. Any time she needed him to do something to get a project moving, he was going to remind her he had this video. If he wanted his projects to jump to the top of her list, there it would be again. The video of her hoop dancing.

Hunter lifted an eyebrow. "Somehow, I don't think that's what he's going to use it for."

"What do you mean?"

Emily's phone buzzed again. *Who took the video?* Zane asked.

"Oops," Hunter said, stepping back.

Emily raked a hand through her hair. What did it matter? *A friend.*

Did you take one of her? he asked, assuming the friend was female.

He'd be surprised.

Yes. She frowned. *Why?*

Tony wants to know if he can watch it.

YOU SHOWED MY VIDEO TO YOUR BROTHER? She was dead. There was no way she could face him ever, ever again.

NO, he typed. *That's why he wants to see your friend's. I won't let him watch this one. I promise, nobody else will watch it but me.*

She read the message twice. Finally, her shoulders dropped in relief. *Thank you,* she wrote back.

Even if she was right about the leverage thing.

Thank you, he replied. *When are we going to dinner again?*

In a decade, she typed. She blew out a long breath. It would take at least that long before the heat left her face. *Maybe later.*

He returned a smiling face. *Have fun, Em.*

She backed out of the conversation and stuffed her phone into the pocket on her leg. Disaster averted, but oh how embarrassing. She wasn't embarrassed of hula hooping—it turned out that she loved it—but he was a work friend. Having him see her be that bold and free made her feel funny. She'd never made a mistake like that before, and it had to happen now. With that video? To him?

Hunter nudged her shoulder. "Maybe it will push your relationship forward. Isn't that what you want?"

"I... I don't know."

"Why?"

Because dreaming was one thing. Real life was another. "Women love Zane. They're like moths to a flame."

"He already likes you back." Hunter tapped the phone at the side of her leg. "That's clear."

But what would she do with him if she caught him? It was clichéd, but Zane Oneiros was a handsome, charming bad boy. "I don't know if I'm interesting enough for him."

"Interesting enough?" Hunter grabbed her by the arm and pulled her back into the exercise room where the yoga students were already spaced apart and ready to begin. She planted her in front of the mirror and gestured at her reflection. "This is you, Emily. You're more than enough. Trust me, that man is interested."

* * *

"Toss me that strap," Zane said as he checked that his bike was secure in its wheel chock in the back of Tony's truck. He took the right tie down from the handlebars and attached it to the front-right truck bed ring. Then, stepping around the bike, he took the left-side tie down and strung it out to the back-left one. "How's that?"

Tony tested the tightness and cinched it up a bit more. "Feels good."

"Maybe one more for the rear wheel?"

"Yeah, better to have too many than not enough."

They worked together, securing the dirt bike in the back of Tony's Ford F-150. Luckily, he had the longer bed length that had the room. Zane finally stood upright and planted his hands on his hips. It looked good to him. "Thanks for lending me your truck."

He'd done this more than once. Sooner or later, he was going to have to look into buying one of his own or renting a trailer—but that still wouldn't work well with his Camaro. Fortunately, his ride was still valuable in a trade.

He dug into his pocket and tossed Tony the keys to his car.

"Bring it back washed," Tony said.

Zane hopped out of the back end. They loaded the ramp they'd used to walk the bike up into the truck and shut the tailgate after it. He still needed to pack the rest of his gear, but they weren't going out until tomorrow.

"Wes said he's going this time, too?"

"Yeah, Larimer has an extra bike. He's having them trailered up to Comet Tail Park."

"Didn't you get in trouble doing this the last time?"

"We're all taking tomorrow off, so we won't be on company time. It's already logged into High Score's official attendance calendar."

"Does Emily know you're going?"

Zane gave him a sidelong glance. "No, but you're right. If I don't tell her, that will cause problems."

Shit. Either way, she wasn't going to be happy about it.

He tossed the towel on the rest of his gear and pulled his phone out of his pocket. They hadn't talked much since their night out to Hooligan's, but that was on him. Her dream had told him loud and clear that she preferred him in the friend zone. He'd been trying to stay there, although instincts told him to push those boundaries.

Heads-up, he typed. *Larimer and I are going dirt biking at Comet Tail tomorrow. Taking PTO.*

He took the Gatorade that Tony passed to him. It was still light out, but dusk was on the horizon. The sun was setting earlier and earlier this time of year. He loved fall, but the early sunset was another reason they were heading out tomorrow morning. It was either that or go on the weekend.

He waited for a response, but one didn't seem to be coming.

He hoped she wasn't getting her panties in a twist.

Although, on second thought…

He set down the bottle of electrolytes and pushed the thought of her panties out of his head.

We'll try to avoid the gators, he typed, hoping to make her laugh. She had to know she'd done her part, and she wasn't responsible for his actions. He'd made that clear enough to HR and the legal team, hadn't he?

That got a response out of her.

His phone buzzed, and he braced himself as he looked at her text.

"What the…" The words died on his lips. She'd sent him a video—one he very much wanted to watch, based on the still image on his screen. He pushed play, and his every wish and dream came true. "*Zeus have mercy.*"

"What did she say?" Tony asked. "Is she upset?"

His eyebrows jumped when he heard the music that accompanied the video.

"Is she at a club?"

"She's hula hooping," Zane said, the air rushing out of his lungs.

Why? How? The questions hit his brain hard and fast, but he didn't really care. He was watching a video of Emily moving.

And it was a-*mazing.*

She was in a sports bra and leggings, and his gaze was

drawn to the way her breasts bounced. She wasn't showing any more skin than any other woman at a gym, but the squeezing motion of her bare, tight stomach... and the rocking of her hips... *Whoa.* He got turned on fast. And when she switched it up into a body wave thing? His boner nearly broke the zipper in his jeans.

"Let me see," Tony said, stepping closer.

"No way." Zane rolled around so his back was pressed against the bed of the truck. When the video ended, he quickly hit the button to play it again.

Tony grumbled and took another swig of his blue Gatorade. "Why's she hula hooping?"

"I have no idea, but it looks like a class."

"I've heard of that, but it seems pretty daring for her."

It was.

Zane loved it.

His phone buzzed again, signaling another message coming in. He quickly looked to see if she'd sent another clip.

I didn't mean to send that to you, she texted. *Don't laugh at me.*

NOT laughing, he texted back. He didn't have the breath to laugh. She'd knocked the air clean out of him with one rotation of her hips. She didn't look funny; she looked sexy.

Don't watch it, she pleaded.

Ha, fat chance of that. *Too late,* he replied.

Delete it, she typed.

No.

Please?

Not in a million years. No, this baby was being backed up to the cloud.

"They take videos of the students in this class?" Tony asked.

Zane frowned. Good question. Who was with her? At the end of the too-short clip, she'd been talking to somebody. *Who took the video?* he typed.

"A friend," he read aloud.

"Now we're talking."

Zane didn't need to be asked twice. He was more than

happy to lead his brother down a trail away from Emily's video. *Did you take one of her?* he texted.

Yes. Why?

He nodded, and his brother cocked his head with interest. *Tony wants to know if he can watch it.*

YOU SHOWED MY VIDEO TO YOUR BROTHER?

Zane laughed. Oh, he was going to be able to use this for a long time… and for so many things…

NO. That's why he wants to see your friend's. I won't let him watch this one. I promise, nobody else will watch it but me.

He didn't add that he'd be watching it over and over again.

In the next message, Emily sounded more like herself. *Thank you.*

Thank you, he replied. He knew she hadn't intended to send the video; that much she'd made clear. But it stopped with him. She could depend on that.

He didn't know why she was so self-conscious. She looked good.

When are we going to dinner again? he asked.

In a decade. Maybe later.

He was shooting for this week.

He returned a smiling face emoji. *Have fun, Em.*

He liked this little adventurous streak she was on. Seriously. On that video, the thing he'd liked most was the smile on her face. She'd been lit up from the inside. She'd been having fun, and she was happy.

That did it for him, more than anything else.

Although the rocking of her hips hadn't hurt.

"Sorry, T-man," he said. "I tried to get you access, but I was shut down."

"Cock blocker," Tony grumbled. He flipped his empty Gatorade bottle and passed it back. "Well, I'm going to head out. I'll take care of your car."

"Same for your truck. Thanks again."

Zane waited until he heard the familiar rev of his car's engine before he turned to his house. He thought of the video in his back pocket, and the hard-on behind his zipper.

He had an appointment with a warm shower and a handful of soap.

"Ah, sweet Emily," he groaned.

What was he going to do about her?

CHAPTER EIGHT

Zane sat astride his bike and adjusted the fit of his riding glove. It was a beautiful day to be outside. The autumn sky was clear, the air was morning crisp, and the leaves on the trees were starting to turn. Not many had fallen, which could make the trail slick in unexpected ways. It was all good. He wasn't at a desk, and he had steam to blow off.

Lots and lots of steam.

That video of Emily was scorched into his brain. Jacking off in the shower hadn't eased its effect—either time he'd tried.

She hadn't been asleep when he tried to bestow her dreams last night. Again, he'd heard music… Only this time it wasn't Harbingers of Mayhem. It was the same music that had been in the video. Just the idea of her practicing had knocked him out of the dream realm.

He hadn't known that could happen.

His spirit form had slammed back into his body, and his reaction had been acute. He'd had to head right back to a soapy shower and his right hand to get some relief.

There was just one thing he couldn't get around. As much as he was into her, she didn't return his feelings.

Beside him at the trailhead, Pete Larimer took in an appreciative breath of fresh air. "I need to do this more often."

"So you can remember why you put in the long hours?" Wes asked.

Larimer pointed at him. "Exactly."

It had been a good match, putting Wes on the project. Once Larimer heard he was Zane's brother, he'd relaxed more into his decision. Good feedback from his employees was an even bigger feather in Wes's cap. This project was going to do good things for his career, and he deserved it. He was conscientious and hardworking.

Already one step up on him, Zane thought.

Both men were.

He was the loose cannon in the bunch, the wild one. Was that Emily's reservation about him? He liked to work smarter rather than harder, and he tended to go with his gut. She was a cautious planner. They got along great as friends. Were they too different, though, for her to be comfortable taking the next step?

Or was she just not attracted to him?

He jammed his helmet on his head. "We ready to do this?"

"Hell yeah," Wes said.

Larimer tightened his chin strap. They kick-started their engines, and Zane took off. He took the lead down the pathway into the wilderness. It had been deemed a dirt bike trail by the zoning board or park ranger or whoever took care of that kind of thing. All he knew was that they shouldn't be running up on any hikers.

And he was good to fly.

Trees whizzed by on either side as the path wound deeper into the forest. His back wheel spun, searching for traction when the incline became steeper. Once it found it, the bike launched up the trail like a rocket.

Scenery became a blur around him. He kept his eyes on the hard dirt path and went around a puddle. A section that snaked back and forth appeared, following the curvature of the land, and he geared down.

He heard Wes and Pete behind him.

Either one of them would be a better match for Emily

than him.

He gunned his engine, climbing up another hill. The path leveled out, but he took a curve around a boulder way too fast. The momentum swung him off the cleared track onto the grass, and he jammed his foot into the soft mush of leaves and mud to keep from putting the bike down. It continued skidding sideways, and the muscles in his leg clenched as gravity pulled it down the side of the hill.

Dirt bikes were smaller than street bikes, but they were still weighty. He used his body as a counterweight as the bike continued sliding on the long grass. Somehow, he managed to stop from going ass over teakettle, but the bumps jarred him, and the bike flailed. It finally stopped right before a tree, and he wrenched it upright to keep it from falling atop him. His breath came hard in his lungs, and adrenaline gushed through his system.

Letting go of the handlebars, he settled his hands on his thighs and looked to the sky.

What the Hades was he doing?

This. This was why everyone called him unpredictable. This was why nobody depended on him or trusted him with the big stuff. He was the idiot who ran after every thought that entered his head.

The sound of engines became louder on the trail above him and then died off abruptly.

"Zane!" Wes called.

"You all right?" Larimer asked.

"I'm good," Zane said, waving them off.

Wes was already climbing off his bike.

Zane checked his status. Hell, he'd killed the engine, not even realizing it, and he was thirty feet down the hill, away from the main path. What if that tree had been closer? Or another one of those boulders he'd just gone around?

He flexed his foot and tried to stretch out the knotted muscles in his leg.

"Can you get it back up the hill?" Wes called.

Zane jumped on the kick-starter, but the engine didn't

turn over. Damn it. It was going to be a bear walking this thing up that incline if he couldn't get it started. He tried again. This time, the engine growled to life.

Wes began clearing a path up the hill to the dirt trail. He kicked some leaves out of the way, and Larimer joined in. The guy jumped back in surprise, though, and let out a yelp when he moved a fallen branch.

Something slithered away, and he quickly covered his discomfort with a laugh. "Garter snake."

Zane stared at the reptile as it crawled back onto some comfy moss, and his lips twitched. Damn it, he was not in the mood to laugh. A chuckle escaped him anyway, and he shook his head. "Sorry, guys. Let me see if I can get it moving."

Good thing this was a dirt bike. Its tires were designed to grip. He kept the gear low and followed the path they'd cleared for him. It angled up the hill, an easier trek than going straight up, but the grass was still damp with morning dew. Another patch of moss sent his front wheel skidding. Zane planted his foot instinctively, and the muscles in his leg screamed.

"Uhh," he grunted.

Yeah, he was going to be feeling that tomorrow.

At the top, Wes caught his handlebars and helped pull both man and machine over the lip of the incline and back onto the trail.

"You get banged up?" his brother asked.

"Meh, I might have pulled something, but I'm good."

There wasn't assistance out here in the wilderness. Somebody had worried about that…

His mood grew grayer.

"You were riding like your ass was on fire," Larimer said.

Zane's mother had always said he had more heart than head. "Yeah, I got a little crazy."

"Surprise, surprise," Wes said.

Zane sighed. His adrenaline had run its course, and his heart wasn't pumping so hard anymore. It felt way too heavy to race that fast. "Do you want to take the lead, Pete?"

"You sure you're okay?"

"Yeah." Zane revved his engine to stop the questions.

The other two hopped back on their bikes, and then they were off again. Still zipping across the terrain, but not trying to clear cut it.

Zane stayed a safe distance behind Wes. They came upon a split in the path, one direction clearly calling out a jump. For once, he stayed on the straight and narrow. The path most taken. His boys zoomed off to launch themselves, and they met up again where the paths rejoined.

They'd been riding for a good half-hour when the trees opened up into a meadow and then a lake. Comet Tail Park lay before them, with one of those massive boulders thrusting out from the beach into the water.

Larimer stopped in the parking area reserved for bikes, and Wes and Zane lined up next to him. When they killed their engines, the silence was nearly deafening.

"Woo-eee, that was a blast," Larimer said as he took off his helmet. He raked a hand through his dark hair. "Look at that. There's not a ripple on the water."

There was no breeze to be found on this fall day. The sun shone down on a lake that was calm and still. It reflected everything around it like a mirror, showing an upside-down world.

Wes dismounted and took off his helmet and gloves. "Thanks for the loaner, Pete. It rides smooth."

Zane hung his helmet from the handlebars of his bike and sat back.

"You didn't take the jump," his brother said. "That's not like you."

"I took an unauthorized one earlier on the route. I'm good."

Maybe it was time for him to start thinking before he leapt.

He got off the bike and stretched. His right hip protested. Oh yeah. He was going to need some Epsom salts and ibuprofen tonight.

Together, they walked across the rocky beach to the water. They were the only people out and about on a workday. Wes knelt down to scoop water into his hands and scrubbed his face.

Larimer and Zane took the cue to wash up, too.

Dirt biking was dirty work.

Wes rubbed his stomach. "Too bad we didn't bring some lunch."

"I got you," Larimer said.

Zane and Wes perked up when he returned to his bike and dug into his saddlebag. He came up with an insulated bag full of sandwiches from an upscale sandwich place across town. Come to think of it, the eatery was based in the same building as his company.

"Roast beef okay?"

"Oh, man. That will hit the spot." Wes took one of the oversized sandwiches. "Thanks, dude."

"Yeah, thanks, Pete," Zane said.

The guy had planned ahead, unlike the two of them. All they'd brought was water, although Wes found a bag of pretzels in his saddlebag. It was sealed, but the pretzels were mostly broken.

Didn't matter. They all ate the same.

The three of them took over a picnic table at the campsite and enjoyed the tastiest lunch Zane had had in a long time. There was something about being outdoors that made his appetite grow and food taste better.

He thought of the poor shmucks working in an office… or stuck in meetings in a fishbowl of a conference room… He washed down a bite of sandwich with a swig of water. He probably needed to conduct some work out here, even if they were all officially taking personal time.

"How's our software working out for you?" he asked Larimer.

The guy nodded. He'd had to know the subject would come up. "We haven't gotten too far into it, but feedback so far has been good. I've heard the onboarding was helpful."

"Good to know," Wes said. That was his area of business.

That was enough work talk for all of them. Zane finally tossed his contribution to the gourmet lunch onto the table—a two-pack of strawberry Pop-Tarts. He always kept a pack in his saddlebag for emergencies. This was close enough.

"A concession stand lunch, and now this?" Larimer said. "You're spoiling me."

"We'll have to split them three ways." Which was a shame.

"You don't know how big of a deal it is that he's sharing," Wes said. "You don't get between Zane and his Pop-Tarts."

They chomped on their processed pastries and looked at the sun shining off the water. The day was warming up, but fall was definitely in the air.

Larimer cleared his throat. "Uh, I didn't mean to cross the line the other day, asking about Emily."

Zane shrugged, and he could feel Wes staring at him hard. "I'm protective of her."

"Yeah, that's been clear. If you two are an item, I'll step back, but I thought she was nice—and cute."

Zane tensed, and his leg nearly spasmed.

Larimer took another bite of Pop-Tart. "You wouldn't think the money thing would make it harder to meet women, but it has. I never know a girl's intentions these days."

Wes started to perk up, and Zane glared him down. He could almost hear "must be rough" already.

Rubbing his leg, he took a deep breath and watched a fish jump out on the lake. It was there, and then it was gone. All in the blink of an eye.

He had a thing for Emily Hutchins so bad it made him ache, but he'd seen inside her dreams. He knew what she thought, deep down inside.

And he couldn't have her.

But he couldn't bring himself to set her up with Larimer. Everything inside him fought the idea.

But it wasn't up to him, was it? She had the right to choose. She could turn both of them down if she wanted.

But she needed to be given a choice.

Blowing out a lungful of air, Zane gave in to his better side and dug his phone out of his pocket. "Are you doing anything tonight, Pete?"

The guy looked away from where a bird had just taken a low pass over the water, searching for another of those jumping fish. "No, I took the whole day off. Why?"

"Want to come to my house for a barbecue?"

Larimer's forehead rumpled as he tried to figure out how the conversation had gotten to where it was. He quickly put two and two together, showing how he'd become a captain of industry. "Will Emily be there?"

"Give me a minute to invite her." Zane's fingers felt like Edward Scissorhands' as he texted her. It was a spur-of-the-moment idea, and it was as far as he was going to be able to go in playing Cupid. He wasn't going to hand out her number without her permission, and he wasn't going to set them up.

He could, however, put them into the same space and let nature take its course.

It was supposed to be what he did with dreams, after all. Let the dreamer take their imagination where it would, not guide it by his hand.

His leg ached, and he realized his whole body was tensed again as he waited for an answer.

He glanced at Wes. "Want to come?"

"Sure. Are you inviting the others?"

"Might as well. It will make the food situation easier." He glanced Pete's way. "We have a big family."

"It's your party, but it sounds like fun."

Zane's phone dinged with an incoming message. He didn't want to look, but he did. "Emily's coming." His heart squeezed. "She's bringing banana bread."

His favorite.

* * *

Emily parked on the street in front of Zane's house. She didn't feel right parking in the driveway. She didn't want to block anyone in, and she didn't feel she had rank. He'd said his brothers were coming.

She'd met a couple of them. Wes worked with them at High Score, and Tony had joined them for lunch a few times at Hooligan's.

Could she admit that she was disappointed that it wasn't just the two of them? When she'd seen Zane's text, her first thought was that he was cashing in on their second bet.

Not that she was complaining. Not at all. Being invited to a family event made her feel warm inside, and she was hopeful that the awkwardness between them was gone.

She picked up her tote bag from the passenger seat. She wondered who else from High Score would be here. She'd noticed that Daphne hadn't been crowing about getting an invite.

She locked her car with the key fob and smoothed her clothes. She hoped she was dressed okay. She'd tried to hit that midpoint between too fancy and too casual with a short denim skirt and oversized sweater.

"Hey, Emily."

"Wes." She waved when she saw him arriving. He trotted over to catch up with her, and she looked in the grocery store bag he carried. "Chips?"

"And dip." The chips bags crinkled as he searched around them. "Three kinds."

"Easy way out?"

"You know it." He laughed as he guided her up the driveway. "We got back from dirt biking later than I— Uh... *damn*. I probably shouldn't have mentioned that."

She shrugged. "Zane told me you were going. You're all big boys."

He gave her a side-eyed look to make sure she was serious—and seemed satisfied that she was. "I'm glad you were able to come. This might be one of the last times we get to do this before the weather turns."

They passed a couple getting out of their car. They'd parked in the driveway and were unloading something wooden from the trunk.

"Hey, Cael," Wes said. "Devon. This is Emily." He

gestured at her. "Emily, this is my big brother and his girlfriend."

Cael's smile was easy and quick. "Emily. Welcome."

"*The* Emily?" Devon said.

Emily tilted her head. "The?"

"The Emily that works with Wes and Zane," Cael said, stepping forward. He'd wrestled the large wooden thing out of the back end of the vehicle and was balancing it on end. "Do you play cornhole?"

Ah, the bag toss game. "It looks easy enough to learn."

"It is," Wes said. "Do you need help with the other one?"

"Yeah," Cael said. "Devon, where did we put the bags?"

"Here, let me take that," Emily said.

Wes passed her his bag of chips and pointed to the gate. "Zane's probably on the back deck."

"Okay. Nice to meet you both," Emily called to the couple.

She continued on her way, but when she passed through the gate into the backyard, she ran into another brother.

"Emily," Tony said with a lift of his spatula. He was manning the grill. He pointed the spatula at a table that had been covered with a plastic red-and-white-checked tablecloth. "Go ahead and set your things down there."

"Hi, Tony," she said, flushing a little. Wes was a cutie, and Zane made her heart race, but Tony was arguably the most handsome of the bunch. With those muscles and that quick smile, she could always picture him on the cover of a fitness magazine.

He sent a searching look to the driveway behind her. "Where's your friend?"

"Friend?"

"From hula hooping class."

Her face turned hot. "You can't tell anyone about that!"

He grinned, and her knees went a little weak.

"Why not? It's good exercise." He swung his hips in a stiff, tight circle. "Maybe I could join you."

Magic Mike he was not.

Emily moved on him anyway. He was bigger than her, but she could take him. Mortification was a powerful motivator. "Zane said he wouldn't show you."

"He didn't." Tony held up his hands to protect himself. Laughing, he finally had mercy on her. "I'm just teasing you. Hey, I'm the biggest proponent of exercise that there is. If you want to hoop dance, go for it."

She fanned her face. "Really?"

"Really." He slid the spatula under a chicken breast and lifted it to check that it wasn't burning. "It's good for the core... not that you need any help in that area."

She flushed again. It was a compliment, but the fact that he'd noticed? "Um, thanks. Where can I find a knife and a paper plate for the banana bread?"

He pointed at the back door, again using the spatula. He should be an orchestra conductor with the way he wielded that thing. "Zane's inside making margaritas."

Of course he was. She could hear the blender from where she stood.

With a wave, she made her escape into the house. She found herself in a mud room with hooks for coats and a rack for shoes, including Zane's riding boots. He'd taken the time to care for them sometime between biking today and hosting tonight. She looked around shyly. One of his jackets hung from a hook, and his water bottle was on the table by the door. She was in his private space, and she didn't know whether to soak it in or feel uncomfortable.

They were coworkers. Friends—but she'd had a big revelation at that exercise class.

Off in the distance, she heard the blender stop.

"He's your charge; I should have asked you about him first before setting this whole thing up. *Ah, crap*, I spilled. Toss me that kitchen rag, would you?" It was Zane. She recognized his voice, and she headed for it.

"He's a good guy, totally on the up-and-up."

That voice was new.

She followed the hardwood floors into the kitchen.

"Hello?"

Heads snapped in her direction. "Emily," Zane said, righting the jar from the blender in a dramatic swoop to prevent another spill. "Hey. You made it."

"Sorry to barge in. Tony said I could find a knife in here." She grinned when she saw the mess on the counter. "Or a margarita. But maybe not."

"Yeah, yeah." He put the pitcher back in its cradle and wiped down the red plastic cup that was filled to the brim. "Here, take this one."

"Oh, no. I can wait." She turned to the other man. "Hello, I'm Emily."

"AJ. Nice to meet you."

He looked at her steadily, his blue eyes curious. His voice was quiet and smooth, and his very presence was calming. The opposite of Zane, yet… "You two look the most alike out of any of his brothers I've met."

AJ smiled. "Yeah, isn't irony funny?"

"What do you mean?"

Zane tilted his head as he began working on another pitcher of margaritas and let her in on the joke. "He's *quiet.*"

She rounded her eyes. "Enough said."

"Ouch."

AJ's smile slid right into a smirk. "What kind of knife?"

"Butter."

"*Mm,*" Zane said. "Did you bring the good stuff?"

He made it sound like she'd brought something illicit. "Banana bread," she explained to his brother. She'd made two loaves in a rush when she got home from work.

AJ turned, dug into a kitchen drawer like he knew where to find things, and held a butter knife out to her.

"Thank you."

He picked up two margarita-filled plastic cups. "I'll take these to Derek and Shea."

And then, with just as little fanfare, he was gone.

"Here, drink this leftover so I can start a new pitcher," Zane said. He saw the questioning look on her face. "Derek is another older brother, and Shea is his girlfriend. She's brilliant, by the way. A research scientist. You'll feel stupid around her, but she's super cool."

"I'm never going to remember all these names."

"You won't be the first."

Emily stared at him, awkwardly holding a butter knife and half-glass of margarita. She didn't know what to say now that they were alone. She covered her nerves by taking a sip of the drink, and her lips puckered. It was strong.

Silence settled in the room as voices sounded from nearly every direction around them. Zane wiped down the counter, cleaning up crystals of salt and ice, before slyly glancing up at her. "So, hula hooping, huh?"

She knew he wouldn't let that pass. She sloshed her drink and watched it go in circles in her glass. "I'm trying new things."

"I'm down with that." He tossed the kitchen towel aside and leaned his elbows on the clean countertop. Her gaze was drawn to his biceps. They weren't as chiseled as Tony's, but they were nice. Very, very nice. "You looked like a natural."

"I did not."

"Good enough for me."

She started to argue but stopped herself. She could accept that.

"Did your friend come with you?" he asked.

He'd told her to bring along a friend if she liked, and now she was wondering if Tony had put him up to it. As much as she and Hunter felt like friends, though, her life coach had felt that a family barbecue crossed the line. Or an "Oneiroi" barbecue, as she'd put it. Apparently, that was the plural of Oneiros. Dream... Dreams... She was learning so much. "Hunter couldn't make it, but thanks for inviting her."

"A girl named Hunter? Where'd you meet her?"

"At the adventure park."

He gave a slow nod. "That tracks."

Sure, because the park was adventurous and so was hula hooping. Emily wouldn't have gone to either on her own before, but she was liking this new version of herself.

She took another swig of margarita that tasted mostly of tequila. Half a cup might be her limit tonight.

She set the butter knife down because she felt silly holding it. She didn't know why she felt nervous around him. Maybe because, in that video, he'd seen a side to her that even she hadn't known existed. Or maybe because she was in his personal space, and she'd yet to see anyone else here from work.

She looked around the kitchen and eating area. "I like your house."

He straightened. "Do you want a tour?"

Before she could answer, the screen door to the deck suddenly swooshed open. "Zane."

They both stepped back, away from one another, even though all they'd been doing was talking. Emily turned, expecting to find another brother to add to the list. She was beginning to think she should take notes. She was surprised, though, to find a familiar face.

"Pete," Zane said. "Glad you found the place."

CHAPTER NINE

Emily watched as Zane stepped around the kitchen bar and held out his hand. The two men shared one of those tough-guy handshakes that made it look like they were trying to stop the circulation to each other's fingertips. "Glad you could make it."

"Thanks for the invitation." Larimer clapped his hands together—probably to restore the blood flow. "I heard a rumor that you have margaritas?"

"Give me two minutes, and I'll make you a fresh one."

Pete gave a thumbs-up and turned in her direction. "Emily. It's good to see you again."

Speaking of people from work… "Mr. Larimer," she said, lifting her voice when the blender started up again.

"It's Pete," he yelled back.

She nodded and hooked her hair behind her ear, trying her best not to look confused. She'd known that the Oneiros boys—the *Oneiroi*—had gone out dirt biking with him this morning, but were they friends now? It felt odd having a client here. "I didn't know you were coming tonight."

"What?" Pete said, cupping his hand behind his ear.

And she'd thought talking with Zane had been awkward. She decided to charade it out, pointing at Larimer and then circling her finger to indicate where they were.

He smiled, showing the adorable dimple that all the tech

groupies loved, when he interpreted the message. He leaned closer to shout into her ear, and his jacket brushed against her arm. "Zane invited me earlier today when we were dirt biking—OR SHOULDN'T I CONFESS THAT?"

The question came out at full volume when Zane hit the kill switch on the blender. Tony looked into the house with momentary concern, and Emily couldn't help but rub her ear.

"Sorry," Pete said sheepishly.

She smiled and took another drink of her margarita. "I raised my concerns about the two of you riding. I did my job."

Zane's brow furrowed. "Who are you and what have you done with Emily?"

She lifted her drink in his direction. Emily was off taking hula hoop lessons. She was tired of being a killjoy.

"Come and get it, everyone," Tony called from the grill. He was using that spatula like a virtuoso as he moved the burgers away from the high heat and put the hot dogs onto a plate.

Zane flipped over another red plastic cup. It had been dipped in salt, and the white crystals clung to the lip. He filled it generously with the icy yellow mixture and passed it to his latest guest. Emily handed her cup back when he signaled for it, and he topped her off. He poured the rest into a cup for himself, and they began moving toward the door.

Emily turned back to get the butter knife, and she frowned when she caught him walking with a limp. "Did you hurt yourself riding today?"

"No."

Pete let out of bark of laughter. "True. He wasn't riding. He hurt himself falling."

Emily froze and whipped her head around at Zane. He grimaced and hid behind his drink. She rolled her eyes and turned her attention back to the door.

He peeked over the top of his red cup. "Wait. Aren't you going to say I told you so? Chew on me a bit?"

"Why?" She toggled the knife back and forth between her

fingers. "You knew the risks. You can find your own ibuprofen and a cold pack."

He came to a dead halt. "Seriously. Invasion of the body snatchers?"

Emily went out onto the porch when Pete held the door open for her. She was concerned, but she'd be damned if she'd show it.

The deck was full of people talking and laughing and filling their plates. Really good-looking people. That gene pool in the Oneiros family was something else.

"Hey, everyone. This is Pete," Zane called.

On cue, a chorus of "Hey, Pete" came back at them. Devon and a blonde woman who must be Shea lifted their hands to wave, and more than one brother took the opportunity to grab an abandoned serving spoon.

"And this is Emily."

"Emily?" someone peeped.

That announcement made more heads turn, and, for a moment, the line actually stopped.

Emily shifted under the attention. She supposed there were very few women here. "Hey," she said softly. She hurried to put the knife by the bread she'd yet to slice.

"Here," Wes said, passing both her and Pete paper plates.

They got in line, and the scents from the grill made her mouth water. Before her plans had changed, dinner tonight was going to be leftover vegetable soup.

"Burger, chicken, or hot dog?" Tony asked. Surprisingly, he'd switched over to a set of tongs. "I have a couple barbecue chicken breasts left."

"Ooh." She was already over her recommended daily calorie intake—another of those numbers she was supposed to adhere to—but that sounded delicious. "I'll have one of those."

"Here," Pete said, taking her cup. "Why don't I take these out to the table?"

"Thank you." She was a bit disconcerted by all the attentiveness. She wasn't used to just showing up and enjoying an event. She was usually on the planning committee and making sure there were enough ice and condiments.

For being a last-moment thing, they'd managed to put together quite the spread. She saw deli salads and a grocery store vegetable tray, but she didn't care if people had taken the easy way out.

Hadn't she been talking to Hunter about how quickly time was gobbled up?

The line moved along the food table, as everyone sidestepped to choose from the offerings. Folding tables had been set up in the fenced-in backyard and lined up to form one long row. Big get-togethers like this had been rare in her family, but she remembered one time they'd had a picnic with relatives on her mom's side. Zane complained about his family obligations occasionally, but his brothers seemed nice. Apparently, he was the wild child in the bunch.

She felt the niggling need to call her sister.

Emily filled her plate and followed Wes across the yard to the tables. "Do you know which cup is mine?"

"Right here," Pete said from behind her. "By me."

"Oh, okay."

"Let me get your chair for you."

Having Pete Larimer help her get seated on a folding chair at picnic felt bizarre. But things got weirder when she ended up with him on one side of her and Shea on the other. She'd hoped to find time to talk with Zane, but he and Wes were across the table. If she started a conversation, everyone else would hear. What did she want to say to him, anyway?

She listened in as the dirt bikers talked about the day they'd had at Comet Tail and concentrated on her food. She wanted to pick at it, but everything tasted too good. It had been so long since she'd been to an outdoor barbecue like this.

If she remembered correctly, that had been a work function, too.

After dinner, the games began. Dusk was starting to fall, but nobody seemed to care. If anything, many of them perked up. The sun was still up but the moon had risen over the horizon. The half-pie shape glowed brightly against the deepening blue sky.

Mrs. Washington from next door turned out to be a ringer at cornhole, and the Oneiros brothers were fighting over who would be partnered with her. A brother named Mac finally won. Emily found herself paired with Pete as they challenged Wes and AJ. Cael and Devon might have brought the game, but they were engaged in a serious round of HORSE on the driveway basketball court. Emily suspected Zane would have been over there, too, if not for the limp. He was certainly off his game with cornhole.

She tossed a bag. It landed atop the board but skidded and kept going until it fell off.

"Close," Pete called.

But no cigar.

How had she gotten paired with him again?

It felt odd that the two of them were the only ones in attendance who weren't family, a significant other, or a neighbor.

They continued playing, with AJ positioned next to her. He quietly offered her tips, even though they were competitors. She wondered why Zane had declined to play.

"Nice shot," she called when Pete's bag dropped into the hole of the board at her feet, giving them three points.

"That's it. We win!" Larimer said, thrusting his hands up in the air.

Emily clapped in celebration, but she wasn't ready when he hustled over to her side.

"Let's get a selfie," he said, whipping his phone out of his back pocket.

"O-kay." She smiled dutifully for the picture and thanked him for the game. Spotting Devon and Shea at the cooler, she headed over for a cold drink.

"That was fun," Devon said, moving over so Emily could make a choice. "I'm glad we finally got a chance to meet you."

"Me?" Emily straightened with a cold soda in her hand. Icy rivulets ran over her fingers, and Shea passed her a towel to dry off. "You've talked about me?"

"Well, you know, Zane…"

"And Wes," Shea said, jumping in. "You all work together. It's nice to put a face to a name."

"Oh, well, it's nice to meet both of you. I kind of feel like I'm crashing a family thing."

"No, no. You're not. You totally belong here," Devon said.

Shea rounded her eyes at the redhead in a way that Emily didn't understand.

She was just happy for some girl time amongst all this testosterone. She cracked open her soda and heard the familiar sound of fizz that made her mouth water.

"Ah, that sounds good."

The back of her neck prickled when Pete joined them. He was a nice guy, but she hadn't been able to shake him all evening. She hadn't gotten to spend any time with Zane, although she certainly didn't want to follow him around like a puppy dog. Larimer must be feeling like the odd one out, too.

He thrust his hand into the icy water and emerged with another soda. He wiped it down and glanced her way. "Ladies, do you mind if I steal Emily away for a minute?"

Devon's chin snapped up, while Shea's brow lowered. "Uh, no. All right," they said, talking over one another.

Emily immediately got worried. Was there something wrong with the deal his company had made with High Score? Had they run into problems integrating the software? Or had something happened when they'd gone out riding? Had Zane been hurt worse than she suspected?

"What is it?" she asked as Larimer led her deeper into the yard away from everyone. Deeper into the growing shadows. "What's wrong?"

"Wrong? Nothing." He shoved his hand in his pocket and looked at her almost shyly. "I just wanted to tell you…"

The outdoor lights suddenly sprang to life, making her

jump. Zane stood at the back door with his hand shoved inside at light switch level. "That better?" he asked to anyone in general.

Pete bobbed his head and tried to start again. "Yeah, I just... I had a good time tonight, and I enjoyed our concession stand lunch the other day. I was wondering..." He straightened. "Would you like to go out with me sometime?"

Emily froze. Oh, God. He was asking her out? It was the last thing she'd expected, but he stood there, watching her expectantly.

And, suddenly, she felt trapped.

The food she'd eaten sat like a lead weight in her stomach. He was a nice guy, and she didn't want to hurt his feelings. Worse, he was an important client. "I—"

The guy she wanted to ask her out was standing not twenty feet away.

Apparently, she took too much time to respond, because Pete's face took on a reddish cast. "No pressure. I mean... I just thought..."

"That would be nice," she said, the words ripping out of her. Because she was a nice girl. Because she didn't want to hurt his feelings.

Because this was feeling more and more like a setup.

"Really? Great. How does Saturday work?" he asked.

"Not this week," she said quickly. She needed time. "The following weekend?"

"I can make that work, I think." Right, because he was a busy multimillionaire who probably jetted around the world. He dug into his back pocket for his phone. "Can I get your number so we can make arrangements?"

"Ah... All right." She traded her soda for his phone and stiffly typed in her number.

What was wrong with her? He was a really nice man and down to earth. His company had won accolades, but more importantly, he did a lot of philanthropic work. He was a catch.

One she wanted to throw back.

But she was trying new things, wasn't she? And she had no plans with Zane... He'd had no problem going out with Daphne to the Harbingers of Mayhem concert, even though it hadn't worked out well. He'd never tried to hit on *her*. Just because she'd confessed her feelings about him out loud in hoop-dancing class, it didn't mean anything had changed in their platonic relationship.

"Here," she said, thrusting the phone back at Pete.

There was no reason she should shut him out without getting to know him better.

His smile returned, along with that dimple in his cheek.

"Anyone want dessert?" AJ called, somehow getting everyone's attention without lifting his voice. "I brought brownies."

People gathered at the tables again, but Emily wasn't hungry anymore. She clicked her nails as Tony told a story about Zane racing as a kid in a wooden soapbox car that reminded him of the cornhole game boards. When the car had gotten to the bottom of the hill, they found Wes squeezed into the nose of the car with him.

His brothers chuckled at the memory.

"But we won," Wes said.

"And then you were disqualified," Cael reminded him.

Emily's gaze went to Zane when the story turned into how much trouble he'd gotten into that day. He was staring at his brownie, not eating it, but crumbling it up into little pieces.

A phone rang, and everyone checked their devices.

"It's mine," Pete said. He answered, and his expression turned serious as he listened to whomever was on the other end. He was shaking his head when he hung up. "Sorry, that was work. Apparently, my day off is over. We had a server crash."

"Oh no," Wes said.

"Thanks for the evening." He was already turning from Pete the everyday guy into Pete the software CEO. "Zane."

Zane lifted his chin. "Hope everything's all right."

"I'm sure it will be." Pete passed the beanbag he still carried to Emily. "Have a good night, partner." He lifted a hand to everyone at the table. "Goodnight."

A spattering of "See ya" and "Bye, Pete" followed him as he left. Emily couldn't help but feel she'd gotten a reprieve when he opened the gate and disappeared around the corner. But that didn't fix next weekend.

Her attention returned to the table, and she jolted when her gaze collided with Zane's. His blue eyes were deep and stormy. He dropped the look almost instantly. At this point, his brownie was a crumbled mess under his fingertips. He wiped his hands and slouched in his foldout chair with his thumbs hooked in the pockets of his jeans.

Her gaze was steady as she watched him. The sun had dropped below the horizon, and twilight was upon them. The moon sat over his left shoulder, the half-circle tilted like a cup that was about to spill its contents.

"Did you set me up?" she blurted.

Conversation around them died out, and Zane's gaze jumped back up to meet hers.

"What?"

"Did you invite me here to set me up?"

"What do you mean?"

"Pete Larimer." She thrust out a finger, pointing at the gate through which the man had left. She knew she was making a scene. She didn't even know if their client was truly gone, but outrage filled her until she couldn't hold it in.

"It wasn't like that." Zane hung his head in a hangdog way. "I just invited you both to see what would happen."

"Why?"

"He likes you."

"He likes me," she repeated. She threw the beanbag onto the table. It hit heavily, each kernel of corn inside the bag seeming to collide milliseconds apart. It slid across the table until AJ slapped his hand over it. Beyond that, he didn't move. Nobody at the table was moving. Or talking. They were barely breathing.

Zane sat up straighter, and his leg began bouncing. "Are you not interested? I'm sorry. I didn't want you to feel pressured."

Pressured for *what?* "Was this another way to get an in with him? Another creative approach to get him to increase his company's seat subscription?"

"No," Zane said, his voice jumping. "I thought you liked him."

Her head spun. "What made you think that? Because I talked with him once? Because I was nice to him?"

"You don't like him?"

"No, you bonehead," she said, exploding out of her seat and slapping her hands against the table. "I like *you.*"

Leaning in, she did the riskiest, most unplanned thing of her life.

She kissed him. Just planted a full-on lip lock on him with the moon and his entire family watching.

And it made her knees melt.

She heard the short inhale of surprise he took and felt the way he stiffened when she pounced on him. But he didn't pull away. His lips softened under hers, and their mouths meshed. They relaxed into the kiss, and Emily's lips parted. She felt the soft brush of his tongue.

It was everything she'd dreamt.

And... like before, she jolted back to her senses.

She stood upright so fast, her back twinged. Oh God. Oh God. What had she done?

And in front of his family!

Mortification nearly burned her into dust. She could feel the eyes of everyone upon her, and she couldn't bear it. But she refused to run. The old Emily might have. Hell, the old Emily wouldn't have called him out in the first place.

But she was the new Emily now.

"If you're setting me up with other guys, though, I guess that means you don't like me back," she said, her throat tight.

The look on his face.

She couldn't. She just couldn't.

Unable to stay a moment longer, she turned on her heel and speed-walked to the gate that meant escape. She refused to run. She'd already embarrassed herself enough.

"Emily."

She flipped the latch on the gate, catching her finger in the process. "Ah!" The sting added to what she was already feeling.

Behind her, she heard movement. Sticking her finger into her mouth, she tried to numb the pain as she continued walking. She reached for her purse on the other side for her keys but came up empty.

Oh no. Her purse.

"Emily! Wait!"

CHAPTER TEN

The astonished looks on everyone's faces didn't register with Zane, because his brain had just short-circuited. Fizzled, snapped, and flared up in a smoking mess. Emily was attracted to him. She'd kissed him.

And now she was walking away!

He bounded out of his chair to go after her, but his leg cramped up. With a shout of pain, he grabbed the knot in his quadriceps, but he didn't let it stop him. He pulled his leg along, teetering from side to side as he went after her.

How could he have been so wrong? The dream. She'd jumped out of the dream where he'd kissed her.

"Emily, *ow*. Hold on." He couldn't get himself going.

Meanwhile, she was in a royal huff and moving fast.

"Ah, damn it. Slow down." He gritted his teeth as he hobbled along. The gap between them was growing until she suddenly stopped. She patted at her side and then her hands were fluttering over her pockets as she looked down and around and behind her. Keys. Thank the gods, she'd forgotten her keys.

He took to hopping on his good leg to get to her before she took off again.

"Emily," he huffed. She flinched when she realized how close he was, and he looped an arm around her waist when she would have stormed away. "Wait. Please. Talk to me."

She faced him with her arms wrapped around her waist and her face downcast. She looked angry and embarrassed.

And hurt.

"I'm sorry," he said. "I didn't know."

His heart was racing, and his breaths were coming fast. What he said next could make him or break him, and so far, he'd bungled things up good.

He brushed back her hair that she was trying to hide behind. They were on his driveway, standing in the spotlight coming from the light on his garage. The moment called for careful thinking. A delicate approach. Consideration.

So he did what he always did—he went for it. "Em, I like you too."

Her gaze sprang up to meet his, and his heart clanged against his ribcage.

"So much."

He leaned in, hesitated just in case, and then covered her mouth with his. Kissing her back. Softly... reverently... And it was so good. He tightened his hold around her waist, and she stepped into him. Their bodies brushed and then pressed flush. Gods, it was like heaven here on earth. He slid his other hand into her hair and deepened the kiss.

But then she was batting at his chest like she was trying to put out a fire.

He dropped his hold on her, and she stepped back. Her chest rose and fell as she looked at him with equal amounts of confusion, frustration, and, he hoped, arousal. Her cheeks were pink, and her brown eyes sparked.

"If you had feelings for me, why did you invite Pete Larimer tonight?" she demanded. "Why did you try to put us together?"

"Because I'm an idiot. You just said so."

Her eyes narrowed. "Only when you want to be. You knew what you were doing."

He'd thought he did. "I was trying to do the right thing."

"By *pimping me out*?"

"Gah! No." He pulled back in revulsion and ended up

putting too much weight on his bad leg. "Son of a bitch. Don't even say that."

"What am I supposed to think?"

"That I want you to be happy… That I think you work too much to meet someone… That you deserve a nice guy…"

She batted out another apparent flare on his shoulder. "*You're* a nice guy."

"I know!" He caught her by the waist and moved back into her space. "I told myself that, too."

"Then why didn't you ever say something?"

"Why didn't you?"

Her face screwed up, but she didn't have an answer for that. "You don't look at me the way you look at other women."

"You're right about that."

Her hair swished around her shoulders as she shook her head. She didn't understand.

"I was looking at you, Em. I see you—and you're special."

The pink in her cheeks turned brighter. "So special you paired me up with someone else?"

Zane let out a frustrated growl. Was she ever going to let that go? "I made a mistake, but how was I supposed to know? You never let on that you wanted to be more than friends—and *work friends*, at that."

He'd been stuck in the stinking work friend zone for so long. How had he missed this? Was she that good at hiding her feelings?

That dream. That stupid, mind-boggling dream.

He drew back. Wait a minute. He'd thought its meaning was crystal clear. If his kiss hadn't made her bolt upright in bed, what had? Fear? Was she afraid of getting involved?

Or was it the shock of it all?

Christopher. Zane felt almost dizzy when the pieces suddenly clicked together in his brain. Christopher had stayed in his football dream, hanging in there as his heart raced and his skin grew clammy. Fear hadn't snapped him out of the reverie. He wanted to play football, and he'd hung in there as the bigger defensive back chased him. It had been a jolt, the shock of seeing the lion on his tail, that made him wake up.

Emily stared at him, her eyes big and round. They were both at fault here, neither being upfront with the other. They'd been ships passing in the night when they really, really wanted to crash into one another. At least, Zane knew *he* did.

"So we like each other... *that way*?" she finally whispered.

"Definitely *that way*."

She bit her lip. "It's not weird?"

He could practically see the gears in her head seizing up as she calculated the risks and possible drawbacks.

"Not if we don't make it that way."

Excitement sizzled through him—greater than a jump on the motocross course, more thrilling than a heavy metal concert, and better than the best dream ever.

Because this was real.

"Come on, Em. Live dangerously for once."

Their gazes locked, and the night air pulsed. There was no shock this time, no element of surprise. He stepped up to her, leading with his good leg. It put him in her space and her in his—and he loved it. Leaning down, he brushed his mouth over hers. When her lips trembled beneath his, he groaned and kissed her the way he'd always wanted to kiss her.

Hungrily, consumedly, and with laser focus.

Sensation buffeted him, and when she let out a hum of pleasure, it caught him right in the groin. Damn. If she didn't believe he was telling the truth, that should convince her.

Instead of pulling away, she wrapped her arms around his neck, and he gathered her in close.

Zane heard movement behind him, and he waved on whichever brother was trying to sneak by them.

Emily wasn't as bold. She heard the twig snap, too, and she broke the kiss. She spotted one of his brothers... The one who'd partnered with... that neighbor lady at... that game.

Ugh, she couldn't think.

She pressed her hands to her hot cheeks. He was tiptoeing down the driveway, trying to get away from the crazy woman who yelled at his brother one moment and tried to kiss his lips off the next. "Oh my gosh, I—"

"Sorry to interrupt," the brother said. "We're getting out of here."

As if she hadn't already caused enough of an uproar. "No, don't leave on my account."

"Leave, Mac," Zane said.

Mac. That was his name.

He gave a salute and trotted off to his car. "I've got to go to work anyway."

The commotion coming from the back of the house indicated that the rest of Zane's brothers were packing things up quickly. Emily bit her lip. If they were still talking about a soapbox derby from years ago, she could imagine how long they'd be talking about this.

Zane rubbed her sides. "Come back?"

She'd already taken the plunge. This step was smaller, but it seemed almost more significant. She could leave and never show her face again. Or...

"Okay."

He wrapped his hand around hers, their fingers twined, and she caught hold. She couldn't believe this was happening. If this was a dream, she didn't want to wake from it and lose him again. She'd pull him right into the real world with her.

Someone on the deck dropped a pan, and Emily's face flared even hotter. "Do you have a bag I could put over my head? Where's your riding helmet?"

"You look beautiful."

The tips of her ears tingled. Not the point, though. "What they must be thinking," she hissed.

"They already knew."

She looked at him sharply. They knew?

The looks. The odd comments, like she was some kind of old friend. Butterflies fluttered in her chest. Zane had talked to them about her. His family knew how he felt about her before she did.

He squeezed her hand and led her back up the driveway to the gate into the backyard. His limp wasn't as pronounced, but it was still there.

"You hurt yourself out there today."

"Baby, trust me, I am feeling no pain."

They turned the corner, and Emily winced when she saw the chaos. His brothers were scrambling around, grabbing food off the table, bagging it up or rushing it inside. They were obviously trying to give the two of them some privacy. To talk or whatever...

Whatever.

She tucked her head into Zane's shoulder. She didn't know what had come over her at that picnic table. She hadn't thought about it; everything just exploded out of her.

Then she'd kissed him.

She hadn't thought she had an impulsive bone in her body, and now she was riding scooters, taking hula hoop classes, and kissing Zane Oneiros in front of people.

Shea saw the two of them, and she smiled before returning her attention to the veggie tray she was wrapping up.

Derek called to her from the doorway, "Plastic wrap."

She tossed it to him, and the long, thin box flipped end over end. He caught it and disappeared like the next runner on a relay team.

"You don't need to rush off because of me," Emily said. Her voice had gotten so much quieter now that she wasn't yelling.

"Don't listen to her," Zane said, waving them along. "You're doing good."

"Zane!"

"We didn't realize how late it had gotten," Cael said as he hurried by with one of the cornhole boards.

"It's way past my bedtime," Mrs. Washington said. She held on to AJ's arm as he accompanied her down the walk toward her house.

Tony looked up from where he was cleaning the grill. "Don't worry about tonight," he said to Zane. "We've got you covered."

Emily stopped in her tracks. "You have plans?"

"It's nothing," Zane said. "Just a family obligation."

"A family obligation?" She moved away. "I should be the one leaving if you have something you need to do."

She tried to let go of his hand, but he hung on.

"No, he doesn't," Tony said, closing the grill lid with a definitive bang. "I've got it."

This time, Zane was the one who stopped. "Unless you want to leave?"

"No." She did a weird little half-pirouette and then turned back into him. "Oh, this is so awkward."

"Too awkward?" He bent his head down close to hers, and his blue gaze was steady. Guarded.

He'd asked her if she wanted to live dangerously. If she couldn't even take this… "Not for me."

He kissed her cheek. "I can tough it out, too."

The kitchen was abuzz with activity when they entered.

"There's your purse," he said, pointing at the counter where she'd taken her first drink of margarita.

She'd known those margaritas were strong, but what had been in that stuff?

Emily caught more than one curious glance and happy grin directed her way. They'd definitely known. They'd all known how Zane felt about her. Her stomach gave a squeeze. How much time had she wasted by not wanting to take the risk of putting herself out there?

The brothers passed the plastic wrap around. Leftovers were being shoved into bags or the refrigerator or the garbage. She winced when she saw the haphazard way Wes was loading the dishwasher. What they lacked in orderliness, though, they made up with speed. It took only minutes before people were saying goodbye.

"That was so awesome," Devon said, touching her shoulder as she walked past with Tupperware filled with burgers and potato salad. "I wouldn't have missed that for the world."

Shea caught Derek's hand and tugged him toward the door. "You've got a good one, Emily. He might be a bonehead, but he helped me when I really needed it."

"Hey," Zane said indignantly, but then he whispered in Emily's ear, "I really did help her."

Wes was shoving the ketchup, mustard, and horseradish bottles into the fridge. "Do you want the banana bread in here, too, or should I leave it out?"

"Goodbye, Wes."

"*Zane,*" Emily said.

Wes wasn't offended. He shut the refrigerator with a whomp and shuffled backward to the door. "You kids have fun."

"Lock it," Zane called.

Wes left and closed the door between them and the rest of the world.

Emily's heart began to thud so loudly she could hear it.

Zane looked at her and grinned. "Now this is more like it."

His grin was infectious, and she smiled back. She hoped it didn't come off lopsided. Her skin felt tight, and the ball of nerves in her chest made it hard to breathe.

What now?

Did they talk? Did they kiss? Did they do more than that?

She'd held her attraction to him in for so long that she wanted to revel in it, but they'd leapt so quickly from friend to something more that she wasn't quite sure how to act. She hadn't planned for this. She hadn't thought through all the angles. She'd gone from making banana bread to being asked out by another guy to kissing her dream man. She wasn't prepared for this.

Well, she was *prepared.* She was on the pill, and she was one hundred percent certain he'd have condoms in this house.

Oh, God. She was not good with spontaneity.

Zane laughed softly and rubbed her arms. "Stop thinking so hard. You'll blow a gasket."

Her skin tingled as he slid his fingers across her elbow, down her forearm, to the palm of her hand.

"Want that tour?"

The coil of tension inside her relaxed. "Yes."

Taking her hand, he showed her around the place, starting with the kitchen. It was top of the line and modern, with pots and pans hanging over the center island where everyone had joined forces in the mass cleanup effort. The counters looked spotless, but a pot was hanging amongst the pans, and the edge of a storage bag stuck halfway out of a cupboard door. She wasn't about to judge.

The eating area by the back windows was cozier than an old-fashioned dining room, but it could still seat six easily. Her banana bread sat on the kitchen table, wrapped in so many layers of Saran wrap, it looked like a Frisbee. "Do you even cook?" she asked.

"I make a mean breakfast burrito." He winked at her. "Maybe someday you'll experience one."

Someday. That put her more at ease, making her think this tour wasn't a roundabout way of getting her to his bedroom. But then again... why not?

He led her into the living room, and she saw the expected man cave with electronics, a large TV, and surround-sound speakers. His style was minimalistic and sharp, which appealed to her. "People always think I like country style with ruffled pillows and knickknacks on all the tables, but I prefer this."

"Thanks." He patted the back of the leather sofa. "But I like comfy, too."

They continued around the house, and Emily discovered she was insanely curious. The things he owned and the way he chose to display them gave her more insight to him, like a private view inside his mind. What would that be like, to have that superpower? She didn't think she wanted to know. She'd be afraid of finding out things she didn't like.

She looked around his office where he often worked from home. It felt right that it should be the one place that looked like an exploded mess.

They moved up the stairs to the second floor. Zane grunted every time he pushed off with his right leg, and finally, he gave up trying. He stutter-stepped, using his uninjured leg for the rest of the climb.

Emily spotted the bathroom and directed him toward it. "Enough. Where's the ibuprofen?"

"Snooping in my medicine cabinet already?"

"It's not snooping when you're right here." Without waiting for permission, she opened the mirrored door—and found herself face to face with a package of condoms.

"I warned you."

It wouldn't be like him to let her pretend not to see them. The fiend. Her face felt so hot, she worried she'd break out. Keeping her focus on the shelves, she finally spotted the pain reliever. She offered two tablets to him, and he filled the glass by the sink with enough water to wash them down.

"How bad did you wipe out?" she asked.

He turned and leaned back against the sink. "Not bad."

She lifted an eyebrow.

"Honest. I stayed upright." He shrugged. "It surprised me more than anything. I went off course and down an embankment. When the bike tilted, I jammed my foot down. I must have strained something."

Emily did it again—she acted without thinking. She laid her hand over his leg where he was hurting, and his blue gaze jumped up to hers.

Things went from friendly and comfortable to intense and sexual within the span of a second.

"Emily," he said gruffly. Reaching out, he caught her by her hips. He pulled her within the spread of his legs, and then he was kissing her again. Only this time, the contact was hard, hungry, and deep. Their tongues tangled, gliding against one another, hot and wet.

Her hand tightened on his leg. It felt so good.

He felt so good.

They made out like horny teenagers hurrying to get some time in before an adult came home. Kissing and touching and rubbing all at once.

"Oh my God, Zane." Emily let her head fall back when he skimmed his hands up under her skirt. Skin on skin.

"Not a god," he joked, "but close to it."

He had to be.

She swore she felt sparks coming from his touch.

She wanted to touch him. She clawed at his T-shirt and tugged it up, twisting and fighting with it when it didn't fall off him.

"Hold on, give me a second." He let go of her long enough to cross his arms, grab the shirt, and pull it over his head.

Emily watched as his abs, his ribcage, and then his chest were exposed, and her breath came out in a whoosh. He was ripped, all the way from his six-pack to the slabs of muscle crossing his chest.

"Touch me," he said, his voice like sandpaper against her ears.

She let out a whimper. She could touch him. She could indulge herself the way she'd always wanted to. She spread her hands wide and placed them on him. Her pinky unintentionally brushed across one of his male nipples.

He came right to his feet and caught her sweater in his fists. "Tit for tat," he growled.

Emily couldn't help it—she laughed.

"I mean…" His color was already high, but he flushed when he realized what he'd said… and what he was doing…

"I'll show you mine," she whispered.

The laughing stopped quickly.

He helped her pull off her soft sweater, and he stared as he tossed it aside. "You're beautiful."

As if in a trance, he ran his thumbs over the slopes of her breasts above the demi-cups of her bra. She curled her fingers against his chest, and white lines appeared on his skin as she dragged them downward.

"Hell yeah." He came for her then, dipping his head and squeezing her breasts.

Emily tilted her head back under his kiss. Off balance, she stepped back.

"Mm," she murmured when she came up against the towel rack.

"Shit. Sorry." He slapped his palm against the wall and straight-armed it to keep her from getting hurt. Looping his other arm around her waist, he rolled them around the doorjamb out into the hallway. Emily found herself plastered against the wall as he took possession of her breasts once more. The way he hovered over her and leaned...

She had to squeeze her thighs together, arousal hit her so hard.

He undid her bra, and it loosened around her. She watched him with her pulse thrumming.

He cupped her again, and she arched hard against the wall. He rubbed his thumbs over her nipples, making her squirm, and she felt the evidence of his arousal against her stomach. His cheekbones looked hard in the dim lighting. Dusk had fallen, and here in the hallway, they were back in the secrecy of the night.

"I need to know where you are, Em," he said in a low voice. "We just decided we wanted to be more than friends."

She laid her hands against his chest. Now that she was finally allowed, she couldn't stop touching him. "Right. We don't want to go too fast."

"Are you saying we should stop?"

No! But maybe they should... She tried to get her head screwed on straight. "You're right. We probably shouldn't go all the way tonight."

He let out a shuddering breath and rested his forehead against hers. "Okay. I don't want to screw this up."

"No, I meant your leg."

He pulled back sharply to look at her.

"You're already limping," she said.

He let out a snort and then began to laugh… to the point that she had to laugh with him. She was so happy that they could still do that even when they were doing *this*.

"Now you're just daring me," he said when he could finally catch his breath.

Emily giggled, but then she saw the wicked glint in his eye. Her giggle turned into a groan when he deliberately slid his hand back under her skirt—and kept going. She clutched at him. "Oh! Zane!"

His fingers weren't under her panties, but they were doing dangerous things. "Yes?" He rubbed more specifically, stretching the gusset of her panties. "Or no?"

Over his shoulder, she saw an open door to what had to be the master bedroom. His bedroom. The moon glowed there, a perfect half-circle outlined by the window. Its rays were already starting to slant across the bedroom floor. It looked mystical. Magical.

She wanted the magic to keep going.

"Yes," she cried when he started to pull the touch away.

It was like the starting light turning green on the motocross course, and things sped up fast. He kissed her as he pulled her panties down to her thighs. He put his feet between hers, widening her stance and stretching the material into a tight rubber band of fabric as he pressed his hand between her legs once again.

He stroked her carefully as his mouth came down on hers in a hot kiss. Emily rocked her hips forward and clenched the nape of his neck as she kissed him back. She was barreling toward something she'd never experienced before, but knew she wanted.

And then he was penetrating her with a thick finger. She sucked in air so hard, she feared her ribcage might burst. He rolled her clit with his thumb, and she cried out.

Her body arched, and he held her tightly, trapped between him and the wall as he drove her deeper and deeper into pleasure. She moaned, and the sound echoed off the walls of his second-floor hallway. She ground herself onto his plundering hand. She wanted this. She wanted—

"Zane!" she cried when he licked at her breast. The orgasm just hit, consuming her whole body in one luscious, overwhelming wave. Another ripple went through her when he circled his thumb again and lashed at her nipple with his tongue.

He held her through it all until, at last, she sagged against the wall, stunned and amazed.

He smiled. "Dare met."

Emily looked at him through her lashes. He was going to be hell on wheels to keep up with, but she'd be damned if she wasn't going to try. With a soft touch, she traced the lines of the muscles on his chest, along his abs, and all the way down to the waistband of his jeans. His head snapped up, and his eyes went as dark blue as the sea.

She held that look as she deliberately moved her hand even lower.

He slapped his hands against the wall on either side of her head, and his hips swung into her touch. "You don't have to," he said tightly.

Yes, she did, for both of them.

"You don't like it?" she asked.

"Fuck, you know I do."

Then she was going to return the favor. His gaze locked on to what she was doing as she undid his jeans and pulled down the zipper.

"Emily," he groaned when she pushed her hand inside.

She swirled her thumb around the sensitive head of his cock, and his hips bucked.

Then things got a little out of control.

She pushed at his jeans, and he was quick to help her yank the denim down. Her hand was hot on him as she pumped him, but the heat was only building. She needed… *lubricant.*

Even the idea made the tips of her ears heat.

His thoughts must have matched hers, though, because he was suddenly pulling her back into the bathroom again and into the bright light. He walked her right back into the shower, lifting her over the lip when she would have tripped. He crowded her up against the shower wall, slapped a bottle of liquid soap into her hand, and then began kissing the lights out of her.

Emily got to work. When she wrapped her hand around him again, the glide was slick and fast.

The groan he let out was guttural.

She pumped him, surprising herself at the confidence she felt, but he was giving all the signs that she was doing it right. She worked him fast, and the sounds they both made were sexual, but when she got greedy and cupped his butt with her other hand, he jerked away.

She caught her breath, but when he turned, it wasn't to get away from her.

He let out a shout and ejaculated all over the wall of the shower. The act was shockingly private and sexy and beautiful—and she'd brought him to that.

He slumped against her. His breaths were damp against her neck as she wrapped her arms around him.

"Remind me again why we haven't been doing this for the past three years."

"Because we're both boneheads."

He laughed. "Well, we didn't technically go all the way."

"Close enough."

He pulled back to look at her. His hair was rumpled, and his eyes were soft. "Emily, want to be my girlfriend?"

Her heart melted. She'd never thought it would happen.

"What do you think?" she said with a silly smile.

"I think you'd better spell it out, because we've crossed signals before."

"Yes, Zane. I want you to be my boyfriend."

CHAPTER ELEVEN

"Don't leave me hanging," Hunter said. "What happened after you fooled around?"

Emily winced and glanced about the juice bar. Could she have said that any louder? The place wasn't quiet, by any means, but private questions always carried. Nobody seemed to be paying any particular attention, but she did her best to hide behind her hair. It had been more than fooling around, but she wasn't about to share such private details—not even with her life coach.

"I stayed over," she admitted, keeping it low.

"You *did*?"

Okay, that squeak wasn't any better. Emily caught the questioning look of a juicer at the next table, and she knew she had to get this conversation under control. Although maybe her response hadn't helped… Staying over sounded like a longer-term version of fooling around. "It was no big deal. We watched a movie, and I fell asleep on his couch."

Technically, they'd cuddled, and she might have fallen asleep in his arms. In the morning, she'd woken up from the best dream ever to find a pillow under her head and a blanket covering her. As much as she was downplaying it, the whole night had been a very big deal to her.

"Did he make breakfast for you?" Hunter asked.

"Yes."

"Cold cereal or hot meal?"

"Hot."

"Microwave?"

"Stove."

"Ooh. He likes you."

That was what had woken her, the sound of Zane cooking and the scent of something delicious. He hadn't been lying—he did make a mean breakfast burrito.

Hunter took a drink of her strawberry-watermelon combo. "So, are you two an official couple now?"

"Mm hm." They'd made sure they were on the same page about that. Emily stirred the tiny umbrella round and round in her drink. They'd jumped right past the dating stage from work friends to a couple who fooled around.

Was it hot in here?

After hula-hooping class, Hunter wanted to go out for drinks, and they'd ended up here at the Night and Day. Emily had gone through the drive-up before, but she'd never been inside. There was a lot going on. The place seemed to be having an identity crisis of sorts. It was known as a juice bar during the day, but, apparently, it turned into more of a club at night.

Wait… Night and Day. Opposites… She got it now.

Everyone was dressed super casual. Although she'd seen alcoholic drinks on the menu, they were all tropical and fruity. Juice seemed to be the common theme, and her drink was a tasty, healthy option after the gym.

She decided she liked it. The place had character—and karaoke.

They clapped as the next singer climbed up to the tiny stage at the opposite end of the room.

"What made you finally tell him how you felt?" Hunter asked over the opening chords of the song.

"I don't know," Emily said. "Maybe the work you and I have been doing? Or maybe the panic that I felt when he was pushing me into a relationship with some guy I'd barely met."

That still irked her on so many levels.

The singer was good, and Emily looked to the stage. Half of the club was lit in warm yellowish light, and neon-colored centerpieces sat on the tables. Here on the night side, the walls were painted black, and the lighting was cool. Reflective stickers of stars adorned the ceiling, but her attention homed in on the mural that showed a full moon over a forest pond. "Now that I think about it, after Zane had set me up, the moon was grinning over his shoulder at me. I remember looking at it and thinking that there was nothing funny about the situation. I sort of lost it after that."

"The moon was grinning at you?"

"It was a perfect half-circle, sitting on its side. Like one of those emoji smiles." She shook her head. "It's stupid."

"No, no," Hunter said. "It makes total sense."

"It does?"

The life coach turned in her chair. They'd chosen a high table with stools since the club was busy, and a table wasn't available. Apparently, karaoke night was popular with juice drinkers. "The waxing half-moon is a pivot point. It's a time for facing challenges. You faced yours head-on."

"What does waxing mean?" Emily asked, lifting her voice when the singer hit a high note.

"It means that more of the moon is becoming visible. Gibbous is the next stage."

"Gibbous?" Emily held back a snort, and her nose tickled almost painfully.

"Rounded out on both sides."

It didn't matter what it meant; it was a funny word. Hunter didn't seem to react, but Zane would get it. *Gibbous.* Emily took a sip of her drink to hide her smile.

"And then it's the full moon." Hunter lifted her arms and chair-danced along with the song. "You know what that means."

"I'm not dancing naked under the moon with you."

"Why not? That's when the Moon Goddess comes into her full power. It's a time to release things and bring your true nature out into the open."

"The Moon Goddess doesn't need me to release my clothes."

"Spoilsport."

"That's me." Although wasn't she trying to change that about herself? "How do you know all this stuff?"

"What?"

"Greek mythology, the Moon Goddess…"

"And juice," Hunter said, lifting her glass. She sighed when Emily lifted an eyebrow. "I… well… I use the stages of the moon to coach people sometimes. It's powerful and meaningful and feminine."

Emily noticed the way her life coach was toying with her napkin. Interesting. She wasn't as free-spirited as she'd thought. There was a method to her madness, unconventional as it might be. "So what does a new moon signify?" Emily asked.

Anyway, she thought that was what it was called when the moon went dark in Earth's shadow.

"New seeds… new dreams." Hunter gave a shudder. "Ugh, don't even talk about that energy drag."

Emily paused with the stirring tip of the umbrella caught between her lips.

"Anyway, that's what they say." Hunter clapped when the singer finished his song, and then changed the topic. "What's Zane doing tonight?"

Emily grimaced. She'd been watching her phone for an update on that. "He's meeting with Pete to tell him that I won't be going out with him."

"Did you make him do that?"

Emily began rubbing the tip of her ring finger with her thumb. "He volunteered, since he set the whole thing up. He said he's used to being in trouble."

He was protecting her, and she knew it. Her fingernails began clicking. They'd actually argued over it. She didn't know how Pete was going to react. She knew how it was to be caught in the middle—because the two of them had put her there. He might get angry or be hurt or embarrassed.

Honestly, she felt bad for the guy.

But not enough to make her go out with him.

"Your boyfriend is a brave soul."

Emily didn't think Pete was a hothead, but she was worried about the ramifications. "I'm afraid we might lose his account."

She'd already changed the status of the Larimer account from green to yellow because of the risk—not that she'd communicated her reasoning behind it to her superiors. That was one discussion she didn't want to have until it was necessary.

She picked up her phone and checked again for messages. "Maybe I should send Pete a text, too, apologizing. I shouldn't have accepted. I knew I didn't want to go out with him." A light bulb popped on in her head. "Do you want to?"

"Do I want to what?"

A new song came on through the speakers, and Emily's ears perked up. *Harbingers of Mayhem! Nice.*

"You," she said, pointing at her friend. "Are you dating anyone?"

"I really don't think I should get caught up in your love triangle."

"Next up," the karaoke host said, purring into the microphone. "Hunter and Emily."

Emily stilled.

"Oh, that's us," Hunter said. She waved her hand. "Over here."

Emily's eyes rounded. "Why are they calling our names?"

"Because we're singing 'Storm Cloud.'" Hunter popped off her chair and began dancing her way toward the stage. "Come on."

Emily groaned. How had she not seen this coming? It was so obvious. Her life coach had wanted to go for drinks at a juice bar on karaoke night. It was right there in the invitation.

Hunter skipped up the steps to the stage and pumped her fist to the driving beat of the song's intro. The crowd was getting into it, especially the men. She took the two microphones the host gave her and held out one.

"Hurry up," she called. "You're singing the high part."

Of course she was.

Emily stared at the stage. It was a combination of night and day. The walls were dark, but the lighting was that multicolored neon. Hunter's white T-shirt was variegating from blue to green to purple.

Sighing, Emily climbed down from her stool. The crowd roared in approval, and the grin on Hunter's face turned electric yellow.

Seriously, the neon lighting made her teeth neon yellow.

Emily began laughing. Giving in, she marched to the stage and grabbed her microphone. "On one condition—I get to play air guitar, too."

* * *

Zane pushed open the door to Hooligan's and looked around. It was early on a weeknight, and the bar was starting to get busy. It wasn't a place with a "happy hour," but it was a good spot to get a cold beer after putting in a long day. He headed for the bar, got a draft from the tap, and turned to evaluate his options.

The booths were nearly full, but a table seemed better anyway. There were more avenues for escape if Larimer hauled off and tried to punch him. It was a possibility he had to consider. It was why he'd chosen Hooligan's anyway. If Pete wanted to kick his ass, a bar fight wouldn't draw as much attention as if they'd met in his office.

Although thinking on it now, that might have been the smarter thing to do. A CEO wouldn't get into a fistfight in front of his employees.

But that would have been chickenshit.

Zane chose a table and swept the peanut shells onto the floor. Pete was a decent guy, and he hated that he'd gotten him tangled up in this mess. He'd been trying to do a good thing, but *man*, he'd screwed things up royally. He needed to accept the repercussions.

Hector stopped by on his route around the room.

"Meeting your pretty friend?"

"Girlfriend," Zane said. It felt good to be able to draw that line now, especially with this smooth operator.

"Good for you. Made your move, huh?"

"Yeah—but no. I'm not meeting her. It's a work thing." Kind of... Actually, food was always a good way to offer penance. "Why don't you bring some loaded potato skins?"

"Coming right up."

The waiter grabbed an empty basket off the next table and headed for the kitchen. Zane had no time to think through his approach or to come up with a plan, because Hector nearly ran into Pete Larimer as he came in the door. The software tycoon scanned the room, spotted him, and gave a head bob toward the bar.

Okay, Zane had about three minutes to come up with something. It wasn't like he hadn't been mulling things over all day, but nothing seemed to work *Hey, Pete, you know that awesome girl you asked out at the barbecue I put on just so you could talk to her? Yeah... Take backsies...* or *Hey, Pete, you know that date you have next Saturday? Not gonna happen. Or Hey, Pete, you know that girl that you asked out last night? I kissed her after you left.*

Hell. This was why he was going to get punched—and why the guy deserved to take a swing at him.

Zane downed half his mug of beer before Pete made it to the table.

"Hey."

"Hey. Thanks for meeting me here on such short notice. I know you're a busy guy."

Pete stretched his legs out and rubbed his neck. "It was a good time for a break."

Ah, shit. The server crash. Could he have timed this any worse?

"Did you get things back up and running?"

"We were never fully down. We re-routed to other servers halfway across the country. Hopefully, our customers didn't notice a blip."

"Good. That's good." Zane braced himself with another

drink of his beer.

"Thanks for inviting me over last night." Pete glanced up when Hector arrived with the potato skins. Pulling his feet back under the table, he sat up with a little more pep. "I had a good time."

"Yeah… you might want to hold that thought," Zane said. He worried at a chip in his mug's handle with his thumbnail.

Pete glanced up from the potato skins he was loading onto his plate. "Why? What happened?"

The best way to do this was like pulling off a bandage, Zane decided. Fast and straightforward.

"I have bad news. I'm sorry, man, but your date with Emily isn't going to happen." *Because I'm going to be dating her instead.* No, definitely don't go there. "I messed up big time, Pete."

"She doesn't want to go out with me?"

"No… Yeah… I mean, it's not that she doesn't think you're a great guy."

Larimer's shoulders dropped, and he did a head roll as if he'd heard it all before.

"She caught on that I was trying to set you two up"— Zane stopped to take a deep breath—"and she felt pressured to say yes because you're a client."

Pete's eyes bugged out. "No, it wasn't like that."

"I know, but she felt she was being offered up as some part of the deal." *Do not say pimped out. Do not.*

Pete dropped his potato skin like it was a hot potato. "Oh, God."

Gods, but yeah. "I felt like a total heel."

"We're both stupid."

"So stupid," Zane agreed. He dragged a hand through his hair. "She let me have it."

"I don't blame her. I never even thought about it from her angle. I mean, I just thought she was nice."

"Because she is." Nice, pretty, and sexy as hell.

"I feel awful."

And he didn't know the half of it. Zane had to tell him.

He was going to find out one way or another. It wasn't like they didn't work in the same circles. "And damn it, there's one more thing. You were right... about her and me... Apparently, there is something between us."

Pete leveled a look on him.

"She called me out on it, in front of all my brothers."

Time moved on, tick by tick.

"You're even more oblivious than I am," Pete finally said.

"I know. She called me a bonehead." Leaning both elbows onto the table, Zane met the guy head-on. He led with his chin, because the situation sounded even worse out loud. He deserved to have his ass handed to him. "Look, if you want to pull back on the agreement with High Score, I understand. This has been totally unprofessional, at every level. If you want to talk with our CEO, I'll set up the meeting."

The look in Pete's eyes hardened, and a muscle in his jaw bulged. Hector was nearly to their table to check on them, but when he caught the tension that had suddenly risen, he veered away.

"Do you seriously think I'd buy software for my employees to use just because of a woman?"

Ouch. Talk about glacial. "A great woman," Zane said.

"An exceptional woman," Pete agreed. He rolled his eyes, clearly put out, and sat back in his chair. "I'm sold on High Score's product, but switching over to new software and integrating it into the system is a whole other thing."

"Oh. Yeah. Right." Zane wasn't a technical guy, so he left those details to others. "Wes can probably help you with that side of things."

"I know. We're working through it, but I've got other issues to think about. We're heading into a new market, and then that server crashed."

Zane felt like crap. The guy had a lot on his plate. "I'm sorry, Pete, about the whole thing."

Pete shook his head, but instead of heading for the door, he returned his attention to the potato skins. "She really thought you were offering her up as part of the deal?"

Zane winced. "Yeah."

"Okay, you're in enough trouble that I don't need to pile on."

Zane nodded and finally reached for a potato skin of his own.

"What am I supposed to say if I run into her again?"

"You got me." Zane sat back and watched the Satellites football game on the big screen as he thought about it. "Maybe we need to find you someone else to date for cover. I'll put my brothers on the job."

Pete coughed and reached for a paper napkin. "I've seen your brothers. No woman is going to look past them to me."

"Come on. You're one of the most eligible bachelors in the country."

Pete's cheekbones reddened. "Don't remind me. That's part of the problem."

Problem? Zane would have ridden that kind of publicity for all it was worth.

He snagged another potato skin. They were pretty tasty, and he'd concluded he'd be leaving tonight with all his teeth. "Let's put another dirt-biking day on the calendar before the weather turns. You don't happen to snowboard, do you?"

"No, but I've always wanted to learn."

"Wes is a total shredder. The Adventure Park opens up their half-pipe once we get enough snow."

"We could always go snowmobiling, too," Pete said.

Zane grinned. Emily might not want to date the guy, but *he* would.

"Are we good, man?"

Larimer held out his fist. Thankfully, not to punch, but to bump knuckles. "We're good."

Pete stayed for another twenty minutes or so until he headed out. They kept their discussion on dirt biking, snowmobiling, and other motorsports—well away from women. The guy seemed to crave normalcy. All the money and power hadn't gone to his head. AJ had been right when he reported that his charge was on the up-and-up.

They'd been talking about that when Emily walked in on them at the barbecue, come to think of it. Next time Zane planned one of those things, he needed to use one of her spreadsheets to assess the risks. But who could have seen this coming?

Emily was into him. The concept still made his heart skip a beat.

"Everything all right?"

Zane glanced up when Tony approached the table. For a big guy, he moved like a cat. "All copacetic. I saw you come in. Did Wes send you?"

"No, I dropped by for takeout. When I saw you and Pete, I decided to eat here and watch the show." Tony pulled out the abandoned seat and considered the one remaining potato skin. "Is he chapped at you?"

"No. Maybe." Zane knew his big brother would have stepped in if things had gotten out of hand. That was Tony, the peacemaker. With his size, one way or another, things were always settled when he was around. "He took it pretty well when I explained Em's point of view and how she felt cornered."

Tony let out a snort. "Yeah, not your best idea."

Zane drained his mug of beer. When Hector started over, he declined another. One and done was a good policy for a while. "And maybe it was the best move I've ever made."

Tony considered that. "You did end up with the girl."

His dream girl. The one he'd been crushing on forever.

A roar went up throughout the bar. The Satellites must have scored, and Zane pumped his fist. He could cheer for more than one win at a time.

"That was something with her last night," Tony said. "I've never seen her act like that before. First, she called you out in front of everyone, and then, you know, *the kiss*. It was bold."

Zane's jaw set. "Yes, Tony. I remember the kiss."

It had seared him down to his toenails. They'd done a lot after that, too, that had generated an even more enthusiastic response from his body.

"She must have been feeling that way for a while. You finally pushed her too far."

"I guess."

She'd been doing a lot of unexpected things recently. Had the motocross meeting with Pete been the last straw for her? Was she tired of being the responsible one? Or had it been Daphne? Zane began worrying that chip in his mug's handle again. He still felt bad about that. He'd been thinking about the concert when he'd accepted, not the redhead.

He glanced across the bar to the pool table. He and Emily had come here to sort that mistake out, too.

Wait. Was he that dense?

"What?" Tony asked. "You look like you swallowed a bug."

"Em and I came here the other night for dinner and some pool."

A guy at the next table booed at a bad call, and Tony leaned in so he could hear. Zane was not going to tell him about the bet or the dream ride he'd taken with her.

"It might have been a date."

"You don't know?"

Zane scrubbed his hands over his face. "I don't know up from down right now."

Tony chuckled and signaled to Hector for another beer. "Women will do that to you."

They'd never done that to him. Zane thought he knew women and that he'd somehow cracked their code.

Had Emily been trying to get his attention? Was that what the hula hooping had been about? She'd been behaving in a lot of unexpected ways, but if that was her intent, she didn't need to go to the trouble. He'd liked her all along. She didn't have to do outgoing, un-Emily things to make him want her.

His phone suddenly pinged, and he pulled it out of his pocket.

"Emily?" Tony asked.

"Yeah, she wants to know how it went with Pete." Zane texted her back, letting her know he was still in one piece.

They'd gone back and forth trying to figure out the best way to handle the situation, but there'd been no way he was going to let her take the lead.

I'm still going to text him, she wrote.

He didn't think it was a good idea to rub salt in the wound, but she felt responsible because she'd said yes. He doubted she'd ever broken a promise in her life.

"Where is she tonight?" Tony asked.

"Taking another hoop-dancing class, I think."

His brother sat up straighter. "With the friend? Is this a permanent thing?"

"I don't know," Zane said. The football game seemed to be getting interesting, but he was getting the itch to get out of here and meet up with her. They hadn't planned on anything, knowing they had to get over the Pete hurdle before they went much further. But that impediment was out of the way now.

How was class? he typed.

His eyes popped open wide when he saw her answer.

"They learned how to do something called chest hooping," he read aloud.

Tony went deathly still. "Any videos?"

"Unfortunately, no."

"Damn."

Want to meet up? Zane typed. His head bobbed when he read her next message. "They went to a juice bar after class."

"Night and Day? I love that place."

"They're doing karaoke." Zane stared at the phone, unable to picture that. Talk about taking a risk. Who was this wild woman and what had she done with his Emily?

Tony was leaning forward on the table now, trying to see the iPhone's screen. "Have you met this friend? What's her name?"

"Hunter."

"Is she single? I've got to meet her, Zane. Seriously."

Zane smiled when the next message came in. "Emily's asking me out."

She was settling up the bet they'd made right there beside the pool table, the one he made just to spend more time with her.

"I'm happy for you, man," Tony said. He sat back in his chair, rocking it onto its hind legs. "You're a pain in the ass, but she's good for you. Maybe you're good for her, too."

"You think she's getting more outgoing because of me?" Zane said.

"It's not unheard of for opposites to attract. It's called magnetism."

Yeah? Well, he and Emily had that in spades. Zane typed his acceptance with his thumbs, punched send, and then got serious.

"Okay, I can't mess up again. Help me plan a date at someplace nice."

CHAPTER TWELVE

Emily pressed her hand to her stomach to settle the butterflies when she heard the knock on her door. Zane was here for their date. She didn't know why that made her nervous. They'd known each other for a long time. They were good friends.

But now they were more than friends.

That changed everything.

Another knock snapped her out of her stupor. Grabbing her handbag, she hurried to the door. She opened it—and she and Zane stared at each other.

"Wow," he said. "You look fantastic."

"So do you." He was wearing a crisp gray suit with a deep blue shirt and a dark tie. The blue matched his eyes, making her want to stare into them until she drowned. Even his notoriously mussed blond hair had been combed and tamed.

A thrill went through her when his gaze took a slow slide over her from head to toe. She hadn't been sure about the dress—she didn't know if she dared—but that look told her that her risk had paid off.

For the first time in her life, she was showing cleavage.

Her air left her in a rush when he stepped up close to her and dipped his head. He paused, and their gazes connected. Their breaths merged, and he slowly pressed his mouth to hers. The kiss was sweet, with an edge of restraint that was exciting.

"Ready?" He held out his hand.

For a moment, Emily's mind was blank. She gave her head a little shake to get it started again. That's right, they were going out. "Yes, let me lock the door."

His hand settled on the small of her back as he led her to his car. It was a sleek, powerful black Camaro... the newer, updated model. He opened the door, and she carefully settled into the passenger seat. The skirt of her dress was flowing rather than tightfitting, but that could be just as dangerous when climbing into or out of a low-slung muscle car. She became more conscious of the dress's low-cut neckline when she bent over. She swung her legs in and checked that everything was situated as Zane circled the car to the driver's seat. The dress wasn't as scandalous as she was making it out to be in her head, but she couldn't help but tug at the bodice to try to cover more of her side boob.

"I still don't know why you're driving," she said when he sat down behind the wheel. "I'm the one who lost the bet."

"I'm driving because this is a date." He clicked his seatbelt into place. "We're going to a nice restaurant, where I will be paying, too, just so you know."

"Wait, now..."

He looked at her, and in the confines of the car, he was close. "Let me take you out, Em."

She felt a tickle in her stomach. "Okay."

He started the car, and the engine let out a low purr as it woke up. He pulled out of her driveway and headed for the highway. She stroked her hand over the armrest, loving the tough-guy car. By the time they hit the highway, she was ready for him to open it up and show what it could do. She wouldn't admit it aloud, but the sound of the engine and the power of the car was a turn-on.

He covered her hand on the console. "I think fall is officially here."

Patches of yellow, red, and orange were beginning to pop amongst all the green of the trees. They painted unexpected splashes of color as he took the two-lane road up into the hills on the edge of town.

"The days are getting shorter," she said. "Soon, it will be dark at this hour to see how pretty the drive is."

"The dark can be pretty, too." He rubbed his thumb against her pinky finger. "I'm kind of partial to it, actually."

The car climbed the hill on the northern side of Solstice easily. They took the first exit, and the variegated trees pressed in more tightly around them, making it seem like they were entering another world. Darkness would fall quickly once the sun dropped behind the hill. They were going to The Chalet, an upscale steakhouse with a fantastic view of the city.

Not only was this a real date, it had all the hallmarks of a romantic one, too.

The sun was a halo outlining the pitched roof of the restaurant when Zane parked the Camaro and came around to help her out. The golden rays caught the warm strands of his hair, burnishing them gold. Emily took his hand and managed to exit to car onto her heels. It had been a while since she'd had the occasion to wear them, and the shoes made her feel feminine and sexy.

The whole night so far had made her feel that way, and they hadn't even made it to their table yet. She tucked her hand into the crook of Zane's elbow, still a little dazed at the turnaround in their relationship. It was like a switch had been flipped.

Their host gawked at Zane when she laid eyes on him, but for once, Emily didn't feel irritated. He was with her tonight.

And yes, he was hot.

His grin might even have gotten them a better table. The server bloomed like a flower under that grin, but the moment she turned away, Emily caught Zane's wink. He knew the power he had over women.

Did he know the power he had over her?

Uncertainty tried to niggle through her layer of confidence, but then she remembered the way he'd shuddered under her touch in the shower the other night… the night when the veil of friendship had fallen.

She had power over him, too.

He pulled back her chair for her, and she took in the view when she sat. "Look at that sunset."

The Chalet looked out over the city. The entire wall of the building was made up of glass windows, and the seating arrangements were strategically placed to take advantage of it. The two of them sat side by side at their circular table, facing the view. Beside them, others were similarly situated, while tables behind them were offset to allow unobstructed views for everyone. There really wasn't a bad table in the place, but here in the front row, it felt like they were the only couple there.

And nature was putting on a show for them. Wispy clouds lit up as pink and purple streaks against the deepening blue sky. It was a skyline an artist would paint to capture forever.

The swanky establishment realized the value of its surroundings, and it showed up in the prices on their menu. Emily didn't know if she made a sound or her eyes simply rounded, but Zane let out a grumble.

"Remember that bonus I got? Order whatever you'd like."

"Hm." She pursed her lips. "I *was* the one who tattled on you and got the attention of the CEO."

"Hey, I sold fifty seats to Pete Larimer. *I* got the attention of the CEO."

She grinned. There they were. That was the old Zane and Emily.

He was grinning back at her when the server appeared. The woman had nearly the same reaction as the hostess, doing a stutter step when she caught a look at him. "C-can I take your order?" she asked.

"Emily?" he said, letting her go first—and reminding the woman that he wasn't the only one at the table.

"I'll have the sirloin with the baked potato," she said. "The six-ounce cut."

"Same for me," he declared, handing over their menus.

"But make it the ten-ounce. Rare."

"Oh, medium for me," Emily said. She so rarely ordered steak, she forgot you needed to tell them how to cook it. But it sounded good, and it was the restaurant's specialty. She'd be missing out of if she ordered anything else.

"What would you like to drink?" the server asked. This time, she asked the question of them both, but her gaze kept darting to Zane like a magnet.

"Feel like wine?" he asked.

Emily relaxed. His attention was fully on her. "Sounds good."

They chose a red vintage from a local winery that was growing in popularity, and the server reluctantly headed to the kitchen to place their order.

Emily spread the linen napkin over her lap. "It's like she never met a Greek god before."

Zane's head snapped toward her so fast, it was a wonder his neck didn't crack.

She laughed softly. "I looked up your last name. You're a god of dreams."

He looked at her almost speculatively. "Daemon, actually. Not a full god."

He knew about the mythology. She loved it. "Demon? I didn't read anything about the Oneiroi being evil."

"Daemon has an 'A,' as in spirit god… the personification of a natural phenomenon."

She leaned forward, entranced.

"Like my mother, Nyx." He gestured at the window. "The night."

The sun had set, and dusk was darkening the sky before them. Houses down below were becoming defined by the lights shining from their windows, and streets became the dotted lines of their streetlights. Downtown high-rises looked like checkerboards with some offices and apartments lit, while others had gone to sleep for the night. Prettiest of all was the dome of the courthouse, glowing gold under multiple soft spotlights.

"It's lovely," Emily murmured. The twinkling of the lights only became more magical as the darkness deepened.

"You're lovely," he said, taking her hand in his.

She blushed and felt the warmth spreading down to her chest—right into that darn cleavage. She fought the urge to tug at the neckline again. "Thank you."

"Did you have a good day?"

She perked up. She'd wanted to tell him about that. "I did. I took your advice and spoke with the engineering manager. I'm going to embed with my team full-time."

"Will it be quieter there?"

"Like a monastery with a vow of silence compared to sitting next to Double-Talk." She didn't want to bring up the name of that woman. Not now. "And I'm hoping we'll be able to figure out that navigation bug faster. Astrid is going to see if she can move out of the project manager pod, too."

"See?" he said, leaning closer. "I have good ideas every once in a while."

"With crazy ones the other ninety-nine percent of the time." She felt bad the moment it came out. She'd only meant to tease him. "Are you sure your talk with Pete went all right the other day?"

Zane straightened the fork next to his plate. "I think we're square, and he's sorry he put you in that kind of a situation. We both are."

"I know."

"You and I should play it low-key around him, though." He glanced at her slyly. "Like making out on the motocross course... That would probably be a bad idea."

His blue eyes glittered with deviltry. Her dream. That had been her dream, and he was reportedly a dream god... daemon... whatever.

And he was just making a lucky guess.

She swatted at him. "Stop it."

He caught her hand and kissed her knuckles. "So, you're doing karaoke now, huh?"

Emily's breath caught, and she almost missed the change

of topic. "Someone had to carry the tune."

"Hunter can't sing?"

She grimaced and shook her head. "That didn't stop her, though."

"First hula hooping, now karaoke. What's next for you two?"

"I don't know." Emily shrugged, and the neckline of her dress moved, showing a quarter inch more of her breast. She fought not to reach for it and bring even more attention to it. "Although I did see a place at the mall today." When she'd been clothes shopping and deciding to go bold... "Have you ever tried axe throwing?"

His jaw dropped. "You want to go axe throwing?"

"Maybe." She almost gave another shrug and stopped just in time. "It might be a good way to vent the frustration I'm feeling at work. This latest project is driving my team into burnout."

"Em," he said, getting serious. "I don't know if throwing axes is such a good idea."

"Why? Lots of people are doing it these days."

"I know, but what if your grip slips? Or Hunter is as bad at axe throwing as she is at singing? You could cut off a toe."

Emily pulled back. "Thanks for the support."

"No, I don't mean it like that." He shifted in his seat. "If you want to go, then go with me."

She snorted. "Like you'd never cut off your toe."

He winced. "Ouch."

"You've only just stopped limping," she reminded him. She laid her hand on his thigh under the table, only realizing how intimate that was once she touched him.

And felt the muscles in his leg clench.

And her belly squeeze, way deep down.

She started to pull her touch away, but he covered her hand with his, keeping it right where it was.

"Seriously, though," he said. "What's behind all the changes? Why are you pushing the envelope these days?"

"I'm not pushing. Singing and hula hooping aren't that

outrageous."

"For you, they kind of are."

And that, *right there*, was why she was doing them. She took a deep breath. How could she make him understand? Being outgoing was just what he did. "I've discovered that I like trying new things. My life has gotten stale. It's time to mix things up."

"Does it have anything to do with this new friend of yours?"

Maybe. Hunter had certainly gotten the ball—or scooter—rolling. Emily felt safe with her. She forgot to worry about repercussions or feeling awkward when the two of them dove into a new adventure. "She's helped me see there's more to life than following rules."

He lifted an eyebrow. "Yeah, so when do I get to meet her?"

Emily fidgeted with the napkin in her lap. "You're probably not."

His forehead furrowed. "Why not?"

"Because she doesn't think it's appropriate."

"What the hell does that mean?"

"Well, she's not really my friend…"

"What happened? Did you two have a falling-out?"

"No. It's not that. I think of her as a friend, but… Well, she's my… life coach."

"Your *what?*"

"Life coach."

Zane stared at her blankly. "I heard you. I just don't understand why you would need one. Em, you don't need someone to tell you how to live your life."

Her fingernails began clicking underneath the table. "She's helped me break out of my shell."

"You're telling me."

Emily started feeling defensive. She liked this new version of herself. She'd liked the old one, too, but she'd pushed too many things down deep inside. Like interests she wasn't brave enough to explore on her own… or feelings nobody knew she had… "She hasn't forced me to do anything. She just listens and offers suggestions."

"And suddenly you're throwing axes?"

"And suddenly, I'm telling you that I like you!"

The façade of seclusion slipped when her raised voice drew the attention of nearby diners. The woman at the next table's eyes danced with delight as she whispered something to her date, and the man at the table slightly behind them gave her a thumbs-up. Emily blushed and swung her attention to the window before them.

Her gaze collided with Zane's in their reflection.

Just like that, the intimacy returned to their table.

"I think we're both happy you did that," he finally said, his voice gruff. He raked a hand through his hair, mussing it up. Handsome, suave, attentive Zane was something, but add the dash of rogue back in, and he was irresistible. "If she had anything to do with your stepping out on that limb for us, then I'm in her debt. But Em, you don't need to change a thing. I like you the way you are."

Emily felt a sting in her eyes, and she had to clear the tickle in her throat. "She's unconventional, but she's gotten me… *me*… to explore my wild side. I get it now, Zane. It's liberating."

"Is that what you think of me? That I'm wild?"

It was the label his brothers had put on him, deservedly or not. She knew it didn't always sit right with him. He was an extrovert, but he wasn't out of control. "No, I think you're a free spirit who cares about others, and I admire that."

He still had that concerned look on his face, the one that said they'd switched places. She was following her instincts now, while he was the one worried about the consequences.

Impulsively, she leaned closer and kissed him. "Stop thinking so much," she said softly.

He lifted a hand to cup the nape of her neck. "That's a first, you telling me not to think."

"Yeah? Well, you tell me that all the time, and it's good advice."

He grinned. "I love when you get lippy."

Zane had waited a long time for this—for Emily to see him as more than her work buddy—but her comment about exploring her wild side bothered him. He knew that was what his brothers thought of him. He was the reckless one, the one who leapt before he looked. Was that what she thought, too? She didn't need to be a live wire to get his attention, and he really didn't like the life coach thing.

But she was here, and they were on a date. They'd deal with all of that later.

He leaned in to deepen the kiss, but she pulled back.

"Our food's here."

He draped his arm over the back of her chair as the waitress served their food. The woman finally seemed to clue into the fact that he was off the market, and her professionalism took over. She checked that they received the right steaks, topped off their water glasses, and made sure they had enough bread. "Is there anything else you need?"

Zane cast Emily a glance. "I have everything I want."

The lighting in the restaurant was dim, but he saw her cheeks turn a pretty pink.

"Thank you," she said to the server, "this looks delicious."

He gave her a nudge as the server drifted away, silent as a ghost. "Novel. A woman who orders steak at a steakhouse."

She armed herself with her fork and steak knife. "I'm tired of chicken and salads."

She tried her first bite, and her eyes rolled back into her head. The look of pleasure had Zane freezing in his seat. Oh yeah, it was going to be a good night.

She looked at his plate when she saw he hadn't started. Without waiting for him to ask, she passed him the pepper. "Here you go."

She knew him too well—and he hoped she was about to know him even better.

He doctored up his baked potato, and they settled in to enjoy the meal. As the night moved in, Nyx really put on a show. The city lights were dazzling, but the stars overhead gave them a run for their money. The clouds had moved out, and, with light pollution at a minimum, the sky was thick with twinklers.

Emily pointed at the moon. "Gibbous."

He cocked his head. "Say what?"

Her eyes sparked. "Gibbous. It's my new favorite word. It means convex on both sides."

He knew what it meant. "Where did you learn that?"

"At the juice bar, Night and Day. Have you been there? Half of it is decorated as if it's daytime, and the other half is night."

Ah, that made sense. He relaxed. "Gibbous," he repeated.

A dimple dented her cheek.

He caught on and pointed at the sour cream on his baked potato. "Dollop."

A giggle erupted from her, and she pressed her napkin to her lips. She was too cute, and in that dress, almost too sexy for him to stand.

"Dollop," she repeated when she gathered herself.

The music piped over the speakers was subtle, and conversation around them was at a low murmur. The overall feel was one of privacy and intimacy. It could have made things awkward, given their background as friends, but their friendship made everything so much easier.

Zane was so damned happy she'd yelled at him that he was a bonehead.

"Would you like dessert?" the server asked when she came by to check on them later.

"What do you think?" Zane asked. "Crème brûlée?"

"I've never had it," Emily said.

"We'll take two," he told the waitress.

As he'd hoped, she brought a torch with her when she brought the ramekins to the table. Emily's eyes rounded when the woman fired it up to caramelize the sugar atop the custard.

"Ooh, I don't know if that's a good idea," she said, her

entire body stiffening.

The server immediately stopped. "Do you not want them?"

"We do. Go ahead," Zane said. He caught Emily's hand where she'd squeezed it into a fist atop the table. "There you are—I was afraid my Emily might have disappeared with all your new adventures."

"Well, it's fire," she whispered as the server turned to light his. "And this old building has a lot of wood."

"I'm sure she's been fully trained."

"I have," the waitress said, with a reassuring smile.

They watched as the sugar turned crispy and brown, although Zane was pretty sure Emily was ready to jump into action with her glass of water and cloth napkin if any flames got out of control.

He watched as she carefully tasted the finished product.

"Mm," she said.

"Worth the risk?" he asked.

She thought about it. "No, it could have easily been prepared in the kitchen, where I'm sure they have sinks with water and fire extinguishers."

He chuckled. It had been worth the look on her face now that she was enjoying it.

"What do you want to do next?" he asked. The night was still young, and he wasn't ready for it to end. "Is there any place you want to go? Drinks? A movie?"

She looked at the view and then around the restaurant. "I almost wish they had a dance floor here."

"You want to go clubbing?"

"Absolutely not." She looked horrified. "Slow dancing. You and me. Together."

"Huh." He looked around for an open patch of flooring. "I could be down with that."

Getting her into his arms faster? Yes, please.

"I don't know if there's a place in town. It's kind of an old-fashioned thing." She took another bite of her dessert. "Mm, that is good."

The look of pleasure on her face sealed the deal. He needed to take her dancing. "I've got an idea."

"Do I dare ask?"

"Don't worry. It's perfect."

CHAPTER THIRTEEN

Zane pulled into the driveway at his house, right up to the garage.

"I thought we were going dancing," Emily said.

"We are." Getting out of the car, he rounded it to help her. The Camaro rode low, and her heels were high. He was graced with the view of long, sleek legs as she put her hand in his.

"The only slow dancing I've done has been at weddings," he admitted. "I figured it might be less embarrassing if you teach me here."

She tilted her head back to meet his gaze, and the moonlight made her skin look dewy. "Okay."

Zane took a cautious step back. He needed to be careful, or he'd leapfrog right over the dancing to something even more intimate. Catching her hand, he led her through the gate to his backyard and onto the deck.

Inside the house, he turned on a light, and she set her purse on the breakfast bar in the kitchen. He didn't have the right kind of music in his collection, so he turned on the radio and flipped through channels until he found an easy listening station. "Will this do?"

"Sounds good to me."

He turned up the volume enough for the music to make it to the deck, but not bother Mrs. Washington, and took her hand. "Let's go back outside."

The deck was the perfect size of open space that they needed, and it took advantage of the perfect autumn night sky. He left the exteriors lights off, so they were bathed by the light of the moon.

"What?" she asked when she saw the smile on his face.

"Gibbous."

She was laughing when he pulled her into his arms and began to sway.

"Dollop." Looping her arms around his neck, she felt into rhythm with him and the slow beat of the music.

"Did I tell you how beautiful you look tonight?"

"It's the dress."

"It's a good dress, but it wouldn't look half as good without you in it."

She smoothed her hands over the lapels of his jacket. "You look dashing in a suit."

"The tie is strangling me."

"So, take it off."

Their gazes met. He was tempted, but he didn't challenge her to do the same. Instead, he held still as she loosened his tie and pulled it over his head... and then carefully unbuttoned his shirt halfway down his chest. It was more than enough so he could breathe, but not enough to feel her skin against his.

"I think, technically, you're supposed to hold one of my hands."

He was fine with his hands right where they were, on the small of her back, venturing close to the rising curve of her backside. But she wanted to dance, and if it would keep her close, he'd hold her any way she wanted him to.

"Left or right?" he asked.

"Right," she said. "No, your left, I think. I can never remember."

"Makes no difference to me." He took her right hand in his left and spread his other hand wide across her back. Her leg brushed against his as he attempted a turn.

Oh yeah, slow dancing had been a good idea.

The music turned sultry as their bodies aligned and got into sync. Soon, moving with her became as natural as breathing. The stars glittered overhead as the moon lit their little private dance floor.

"You lied," she said. The words were close to his ear. "You're a good dancer."

"You're a good partner."

In so many ways…

The rest of the world slipped away as they danced from one song into the next.

At one point, she shivered, and he stopped to give her his jacket. It was way too big on her, but it still showed that amazing dress with its dipping neckline and the swell of her breasts. He tried not to stare, but the lure was damn near impossible. Her curves were small, but firm. Perky enough to drive him crazy.

He caught her to him again, and their bodies bumped. She let out a murmur that sounded an awful lot like a sigh of pleasure, and he couldn't stop himself from bending his head to kiss her.

They kept dancing, their feet moving them around in a random, circling path as their mouths clung to one another's. Off in the distance, an owl hooted in response to the music. A soft breeze swept through, lifting her hair and making it brush against his face.

The languorous song was a contrast to the way Zane's heart was slowly beginning to thud harder. She was so soft. So sleek.

She had to feel his erection brushing against her stomach, because the dance hold had degraded again. He still held her hand, but their knuckles were now brushing against his chest and the side of her breast.

He kissed his way down to her neck. "Do you want to stay over?"

She slid her hand into his hair. "Yes."

Emily hadn't danced naked under the moon, but she'd danced with Zane. To her, that was better. When he took her hand and started walking toward the house, she followed. Her heart was fluttering, and butterflies were flying in her stomach. She'd wanted this for so long. Were they really going to take the next step? It seemed so fast... and yet so slow in coming...

"I'm nervous," she said.

He locked the door behind them, closing out the world.

"So am I." His blue gaze locked with hers. "Want to stop?"

"No." She squeezed his hand tighter. "But what if it doesn't work?"

He glanced down at the front of his dress pants. "Pretty sure it's going to work."

She rolled her eyes, even as the temperature in the room heated by at least ten degrees. "No, I mean... what if it's awkward?"

"Kissing has been pretty hot."

True.

"And practice makes perfect."

He had a point there.

"Okay."

"Yeah?"

"Yeah."

He kissed her fast and began leading her through the house to the stairs. He turned on lights to guide the way and turned them off as they moved by, until they were back in the second-floor hallway where things had gotten hot and steamy between them before. Instead of the shower, this time he led her into the master bedroom. His bedroom. The moon shone through that same window, and he went to pull the shade.

"Wait." The cool blue light softened the edges and made everything easier. It was enough light to see by—and she definitely wanted to see him—but it eliminated the need for a bedside lamp. "Can we leave it that way?"

He paused. "I'm fine with that, but if we turn on a light,

Mrs. Washington will get quite the show."

"I like it like this," she said softly. Less pressure. More sexy. No fumbling around in the dark.

"Then this way it is." He approached her slowly, as if he didn't want to spook her. Reaching out, he caught the lapels of his jacket that she was still wearing. "We don't have to do this tonight, if you're not ready."

"I'm ready." She was so ready.

Moving into him, she slid her arms around his waist and nuzzled against his neck. She felt the swivel of his hips. They'd been dancing. She'd known she affected him, but this embrace was different. Her nipples hardened against his chest, and she felt his erection press against her stomach. He fisted his hands in the lapels of the jacket, and then he was pushing it off her shoulders.

He circled behind her to draw it all the way off. The jacket hit the chair that she could barely see in the corner, and then he wrapped his arms around her from behind. He felt warm and solid as he pulled her against him, and his mouth found the side of her neck. She let her head drop back onto his shoulder.

"You feel as good as you look," he murmured, nipping at her ear.

Her body arched when he slid a hand into the neckline of her dress and fondled her breast. The demi-cup provided little coverage, and the heat of his hand was shocking. The moment he discovered the bra had a front closure, he popped the tab open, so he could touch her skin to skin. Her nipple pinched tight as he held her possessively, and he rubbed his palm against her until she moaned in pleasure.

"Tell me what you want," he said. "Tell me what you like."

"Ah," she cried.

"This?" he asked, kissing her neck as he molded and shaped her.

"This!"

He crossed his arms to cup both her breasts, and Emily's head spun. If she'd known he was a breast man, she would have bought the dress sooner. Heck, she would have sewn it by hand. She cupped her hands over his as her nipples throbbed, and her pussy squeezed. She'd never been aroused so fast. She wanted to touch him back, but all she could do was grind her bottom against his stiffening erection.

It was enough.

He let out a sound from the back of his throat, and then he was turning her in his arms to kiss her and pull her dress off at the same time.

Emily hurried to catch up. It wasn't fair that he'd jumped out to a head start. His tie was somewhere out on the back deck, so she worked on his shirt, pulling it out from his pants. The moment she had access to his chest, though, she lost her train of thought. He was lean and muscled. Opening her palms wide, she touched all that strength and heat.

He inhaled deeply, and his ribcage expanded. "We need to move this horizontal, and fast."

She agreed.

She rolled her shoulders to get out of the dress and pushed it over her hips. He shrugged out of the shirt and had to fight with the cuffs when it didn't come off. She reached for his belt to undo it, but she gasped when his fingers snagged in her panties. He pushed them down, and then his hands were cupping her bare bottom.

Molding and shaping her there, too.

She let out a whine of urgency. "Horizontal. Faster."

They tumbled onto the bed, pushing at clothes, tugging at zippers, and toeing off shoes. Emily found herself naked long before he was, and she managed to pull down a corner of the comforter and fold back the sheet.

Zane chuckled, and the sound was full of intimacy. "Always the planner."

"On top of the covers? No." She wiggled underneath the sheet, sending him a look that dared him to come after her. "The cleanup."

"Just what I'm saying."

He rid himself of his pants and boxer briefs. Bathed fully

in the moonlight, he did look like a Greek god. He had a finely honed, perfect masculine form… with an erection to match…

He lifted the covers and slid into bed with her. Emily caught him, gliding her hands up his muscled back and then down again. All the way down. The muscles in his butt tightened when she stroked him there.

"I've wanted to do this for years," she said as she teased him with her fingernails.

He pushed himself up on one knee and settled atop her more heavily.

"Baby, if we're talking about fantasies, you're about to be shocked." He rocked down, and suddenly his mouth was on her breast as he plumped it up with his hand. The hot lick of his tongue *was* shocking, but it was nothing compared to the explosion of heat that went through her when he closed his lips around her nipple and began to suck. She cried out, and her entire body went taut. She slid her fingers through his hair and scored at his scalp, but he kept at her until she was nearly out of her mind.

He stopped to inhale deeply. "You are so unbelievably sexy."

Before, it wouldn't have been a word she used to describe herself, but now?

"I want you, Zane."

Arousal hummed through her veins. His breaths were coming hard, and his erection felt hot tucked between them. His weight pressed her into the mattress, and she shifted to bring him closer to where she wanted him… to where she needed him…

He flung his hand out and smacked it against the nightstand. "*Ow. Shit.*"

He gave it a shake and yanked the drawer open. Leveraging himself up onto his knees, he ripped open a square piece of foil. The way he straddled her gave Emily a prime view of his body and that erection she was about to feel inside her.

Her eyes rounded. Oh God.

Deliberately, he settled his knee right where she was rubbing her thighs together. Emily's heart began to thump in her ears as she spread her legs. He pushed his knee high between them, and her hips rocked. Heat flooded her face as she humped his leg, but then he was working himself between her thighs and locking her knee around his hip.

Her neck arched against the pillow when he tested that she was ready with his fingers. She was wet. She'd been ready when they were dancing outside on the deck.

She trembled as he swirled a finger inside her. Finally, he lined his cock up with her opening and pushed into her slowly... inexorably... She let out a cry as her inner muscles stretched to take him, but then he settled in to the hilt.

"Yes!" she cried.

His hips bucked when she caught at his shoulders. He kissed her in a rush and then began moving, pumping into her and pulling back, only so he could push in again. The slide, the grind... Emily locked her right leg around him, not wanting to let him get away, wanting him to continue what he was doing forever.

"Zane," she gasped.

His breaths were coming in sharp, rhythmic pants, as she let out soft cries and groans. He was fucking her like a man who'd waited for three long years. Three years of denying themselves. Three years of pent-up desire for one another.

His thrusts became more jagged, with him driving in more than he was drawing back. Emily clung to him as the coiling inside her got tighter and ready to spring. The way their bodies moved together was mind-blowing. Their chests rubbed, their stomachs grazed, and the heat grew deep inside her where they were so intimately connected.

Zane. She was finally with Zane.

With that simple thought, she came. She let out a cry as the orgasm rolled through her. She clamped her thighs around his hips and dug her fingertips into his shoulders. He let out a yell when he felt her come, and his hips pumped a fast rhythm, juddering her on the bed. It didn't take but a minute until he joined her, his body going rigid in her arms.

The moonlight bathing them was dimmer than it had been, and the night closed in around them. Vertebra by vertebra, Zane's spine relaxed until he was lying half-atop her. His breath was hot against her ear.

"Holy damn, Em," he said.

She stroked her hand down his back. It was the best she could do at the moment. She felt as limp and dazed as he was acting.

"Tell me that was as fantastic as I think it was."

She let her fingers glide over his sweat-slickened skin. "It definitely worked."

He lifted his head, and he let out a bark of laughter when he saw the teasing in her eyes. He pulled out of her carefully, dealt with the condom, and rolled onto his back. Wrapping an arm around her, he pulled her snug against his side.

Emily relaxed against him, loving the intimacy they were finally finding. "I'm glad your leg loosened up."

"You're telling me." He pulled the covers over them, even though the entire room had heated with their exertion. "Sleep, sweet Em. I'll watch over your dreams. We can practice more later."

* * *

It didn't take Zane long to fall asleep. He was tired, satiated, and happy. So damn happy. His spirit form rose from the bed, and he looked down at the two of them from the dream realm. They were tangled together on his bed, naked under the covers, and his heart jumped. He'd wanted to be with her this way for so long.

They *had* this.

Any concerns about awkwardness had been blown out the windows. They were meant to be together.

He looked at Emily. He was ready to give her the best dreams ever, but she was still awake as she snuggled up beside him. He could understand that. As zonked as his physical form was, his spirit manifestation was juiced with energy. That had been... *wow*. Just wow.

His Dream Weaver powers were surging.

He waited, but she showed no signs of nodding off. She might not be ready to sleep, but he needed to bestow dreams before he blew a metaphysical gasket. As much as he didn't want to leave her or the privacy of his bedroom, he let himself disperse into the night—and promptly did Dream Weaver zoomies around Solstice.

Finally, he settled down enough to hear the calls of would-be dreamers.

His charges were getting the royal treatment tonight. Good dreams for everyone. Yeah, yeah, some of them might need a bad dream to work out an issue or two, but that could wait. Tonight, happy dreams ruled.

"Christopher, my man," Zane said as he materialized beside the boy's bedside. He could feel the kid's slow delta waves as they crested and fell. It was the perfect time to rev up that brain activity. Laying his hand over Chris's forehead, Zane led him up into REM and the dream realm. He let the boy choose the setting, and soon they were right back on the football field.

"Excellent," Zane said. He had the energy to run some plays, and it had been a while since he'd loosened up his throwing arm.

Screw his brothers and their random rules. This was the way he did things. It turned out it didn't hurt—he just had no clue how to interpret the dreams his charges had. Hell, there might not be any real meaning to them at all, or they might only make sense to the person having them. That didn't mean he couldn't help their dreams along. It might help them get to the solution faster.

At least, that was how he saw things.

He clapped his hands as the team formed a huddle around him. "Christopher, go long."

The pint-sized boy nodded. With his helmet on, he looked like a bobblehead.

Zane clapped again. "Let's do this."

He lined up behind the center, and his old quarterback days came back. He had some actual experience with this dream, at least. He looked over the defense and then into the stands.

With a crook of his finger, he added Christopher's dad halfway up the bleachers. Satisfied that everything was in place, he called out the play. On the count, the center snapped the ball, the players went into motion, and Zane dropped back in the pocket. Oh yeah, Christopher had learned that playbook. The kid juked to the right and then cut around the defensive back to his left. He took off down the field, and Zane let the football fly.

The crowd went wild, jumping to their feet when Christopher caught the pass and gathered it to his chest as he raced down the field. The boy was fast. There was no way that defensive back going to catch him.

Zane took a hit as the defensive line broke down, but the ten-year-old that tackled him felt like a puppy jumping on him. Playing the part, he fell to the side and let out a dramatic grunt. From his fetal position, he looked through the grass on the field and saw Christopher take the ball into the end zone.

"Yeeeeah!" Zane roared.

"Atta boy, Chris!" the kid's dad yelled from the stands.

Seeing his dad cheering him on, the boy cracked a grin as big as his face mask. He broke out in an end zone dance before he was mobbed by his team.

Zane rolled onto his back and gave a fist pump. Yeah, baby, he still had it.

"My work here is done."

He jumped out of Christopher's dream and went in search of Marilee. He took a dream ride with her, too, taking the form of her grandson as they rode horses across an open prairie. He was surprised when the older woman spurred on her horse, but he accepted the challenge. Soon, they were racing like their hair was on fire. She beat him, fair and square, and he gave her a high five when they arrived back at the corral.

Tamika, Shea's administrative assistant, came next. She was getting her business degree on the side, so he decided to practice his selling technique on her. "So, Tamika, what do I have to do to get Biodermatics into High Score's performance software?"

She sat behind a big wooden desk, wearing a sharp blue suit with killer shoes to match. "Honestly, I don't think we're big enough for performance review software."

"But with the direction the company is going, a smart chief operating officer like you knows you need to plan ahead."

The way she perked up at the title made Zane fight a smile. That was the problem with dream riding—he had to stay in character. But damn, it was fun to give his charges a boost. People's goals and wishes might not come true in real life, so why couldn't he spin a little magic here in the dream realm?

What was so bad about giving his charges a thrill every now and then?

He was as exhilarated as they were as he went about his route. He rode a rocket into space with a geeky teenager who'd need LASIK if he ever wanted to do it for real. He had a tea party with four-year-old twins, and he broke another Dream Weaver rule when he let the two of them share the dream. He handed out an A on a math test. He netted a prizewinning bass for a fisherman who was struggling to get it on the boat alone. After that, he turned around to play with a different kind of bass when he backed up a singer on stage who'd never performed outside his shower. And they killed it. The stadium crowd went wild, dancing and singing along.

Zane was about to lead them into a second encore when an odd sensation ran through him.

It wasn't bad, but it was unusual.

Was it his charge? Was his heart rate getting too high from the excitement of finally being a rock star?

Zane backed off the stage and sent out another bass player so his charge wouldn't notice when he hopped out of the dream. When he formed again, he knew immediately that it wasn't his charge that was experiencing something unusual.

It was *him*.

He lifted a hand to his chest, but it wasn't his spirit form that was experiencing the unfamiliar sensation. He cocked his head as he tried to determine what he was feeling.

Going with his instincts, he went back to check on Emily and his corporeal form. Dream Weavers were vulnerable when they slept, for precisely this reason. When he manifested in his bedroom, though, he skidded to a stop. His particles literally bumped into one another as he discovered why his heart rate had jumped so high.

Oh yeah. That was a good reason to get back here, and it definitely wasn't something he experienced every night.

Emily hadn't fallen asleep yet because she obviously had something else on her mind. Her attempts to get the attention of his sleeping form were low-key, but he could feel her lips on the side of his neck as he watched from his vantage point at the foot of the bed. Her curves were warm as she pressed up against his side, but her hand was downright hot as it glided down his chest. She traced her fingers along his ribcage and then down his abs, ever so gently to—

Zane leapt back into himself, and his spirit form crashed into his body with a jolt. She flinched when he came awake with a start.

"Oh, I'm sorry." She snatched her hand back. "I didn't mean to wake you."

"You didn't?"

His gaze met hers in the moonlight. Catching her hand, he put it right back where he wanted it. Her touch stilled, low on his abdomen, but she didn't pull it away.

"Touch me," he whispered.

Hesitantly, she wrapped her fingers around his erection, and, suddenly, Zane realized how awesome it was to have your dreams come true.

CHAPTER FOURTEEN

It was Sunday, Oneiros family breakfast day. Emily braced herself when Zane opened the door to IHOP for her. It had taken a lot of convincing on his part to get her here, and she still wasn't quite sure what she was going to say when she saw his brothers. She'd made a spectacle of herself the last time she met his family.

To the point where they'd all run away...

She cringed and did a quick sweep of the restaurant. Zane caught her hand, probably because he knew *she* was the flight risk today, but she couldn't avoid the Oneiros brothers forever. She and Zane were a couple now, and she was bound to see them often.

She needed to apologize.

She caught his hand tightly. A couple. They'd gone from friends to lovers so quickly that her head was still spinning. They'd even been together in her dreams. The past few nights, her nighttime meanderings had been crystal clear: the two of them sitting on a cloud over the city of Solstice, him filling her arms with rambunctious puppies, her showing him the latest moves she'd learned at hoop-dancing class...

Now, he was taking her to breakfast.

She knew how big this step was. She knew about this weekly breakfast with his brothers. She felt uncomfortable about intruding today, but his winning argument had been that she could sit at the girls' table.

She waved shyly when she saw Devon and Shea sitting at a table and having coffee.

Zane dipped his head close to hers. "Are you sure you'll be okay? They're great, but I realize that you don't know them well."

"I'm more comfortable with them than sitting down with all your brothers." She clicked her nails nervously. "Besides, I'm hungry."

He chuckled. "You should be. We worked off enough calories last night."

She shushed him, but he just kissed her cheek.

"Can I drop my girl off with you two beautiful ladies?" he asked when they arrived at the booth.

"Don't try your charm offensive on us, Zane Oneiros," Shea said. "We're still going to talk about you."

Devon nodded over her cup of coffee. "It's the only reason I rolled out of bed."

"Talk all you want," he said as he hooked his thumbs into the pockets of his jeans. He lowered his eyelids to half-mast and tilted his head like a pouty boy-band singer. "Only the good stuff, though, right?"

Devon's eyes glittered. "Of course, only the *good stuff*."

He froze, and Emily had to hide her smile. Feeling more comfortable, she slid into the booth next to Shea. "Go. Enjoy your time with your brothers."

He seemed uncertain about leaving her alone with them, but he turned when Devon shooed him away. He kept looking over his shoulder as he walked to the back room where Cael and Derek were already seated.

"I'm glad you came today," Devon said. "We didn't get a chance to chat much at the barbecue."

And they all knew why that was.

Emily winced. "Thank you, but I need to apologize for my behavior the other night."

"Why?" Devon said. "You stood up for yourself."

"It was spectacular," Shea agreed.

"I embarrassed myself," Emily said with her head down as she smoothed a napkin over her lap.

"You did not. You voiced your opinion on something that affected you," Shea said, "and you went after what you wanted."

"I'll say. That kiss!" Devon fanned herself. "Whew."

It was not how Emily wanted to be remembered.

She clicked her fingernails together underneath the table. "But I ruined the night."

"Ruined it? You made it." Devon gave a dismissive wave. "If it makes you feel any better, his brothers have seen us at less than our best, too."

"They have?" Emily couldn't help but glance at Shea. The woman seemed so graceful and put together.

"Trust me," she said, "in this family, you fit right in."

Somehow, that was exactly what Emily needed to hear. She flexed her hand and settled it against her thigh.

Devon smiled. "I'm happy for both of you."

"Me too," Shea said. "Zane's a free spirit compared to my Derek, but he's got a really good heart."

"And you make him happy," Devon said. "I can see it. He seems much more... I don't know... *settled*."

The description surprised Emily, but as she thought about it, she realized he *had* calmed down. If anything, she was the one who'd gotten more rambunctious. Who'd have thought it? Her, rambunctious? She cleared her throat. "So, do you two always get your own table?"

"I usually sleep in, to be honest," Devon confessed.

"We came today because we wanted to have breakfast with you," Shea said.

"How'd you know I'd be here?"

"Zane called Cael," Devon admitted. "He was going to pass on the family meeting today to spend the morning with you until I offered us up as a trade."

Emily blinked. When had he done that? She hadn't heard him make a call. "I didn't know he did that. I'm sorry. You didn't have to come for me."

"Are you kidding? I've been dying to know what happened after everyone cleared out like a hurricane was coming."

"A hurricane named Emily?" She sighed and patted her flushed cheeks. Oh well, she supposed there were worse things to be known for than kissing a guy in front of his family. "Zane took me to The Chalet for dinner the other night."

"Oh, I love it there," Shea said. "It's so pretty."

"He even dressed up in a suit."

"Wow," Devon said. "That shows you right there how much he likes you."

Emily didn't tell them about dancing on the deck under the moon and stars. It seemed too private. "We've just been friends for so long…"

"It only makes it better," Shea promised. "Derek and I were business colleagues, but the connection was always there beneath the surface."

"You already know his quirks," Devon said. "Don't go looking for problems. Just enjoy the new turn in your relationship."

The server arrived at their table to take their orders, and Emily was happy for the reprieve. She was known for getting too deep inside her head. She'd thought she was getting better about being more open and adventurous, but it was easy to slide back into old patterns. Maybe it was time to set up another meeting with Hunter.

They'd just put in their orders when two more Oneiros brothers arrived. They stopped at the table to say hello.

"We have a girls' table now?" Tony asked.

"Today only." Devon jerked her thumb over her shoulder. "No boys allowed."

"Why not?"

"We wanted a chance at the muffin basket."

He scratched his chin. "It *is* a contact sport with us."

"We'll catch you later?" Wes asked.

"Sure, our rides are at your table."

Zane's brothers continued on their way to the back room, and Emily saw how the table there was filling up with good-looking men. "I like that their family gets together every week like this. The Oneiroi. It's nice."

Shea's foot banged into the wall, and Devon coughed when her coffee went down the wrong pipe. "What did you say?"

"Oneiroi. It's the plural of their last name. They're dream gods in Greek mythology."

"We know," Devon said as she patted her mouth with her napkin.

"We're familiar with the story." Shea uncrossed her legs and then crossed them the other way. "But what do you know?"

"Only what I've read. The Oneiroi were dark-winged spirits who'd fly up from the shores of Erebos to bestow dreams on sleeping humans. Zane calls them daemons, but I don't like to think of them that way."

"And... what do you think of all that?" Devon asked. "The *mythology*?"

"It's an interesting coincidence." Emily smiled. "Zane teased me, saying that's what they talk about at these Sunday breakfasts, their job of dream weaving."

Shea stared at her. "He told you he's a Dream Weaver?"

"Sure." All the talk of muffins had Emily's stomach growling. She peeked into the muffin basket to see what was there. "Did Derek tell you about the mythology, too?"

"Well, yes, he did."

"I love that they're staying in touch with their heritage."

"Their *heritage*. I suppose you could put it that way."

Devon smiled from across the table. "I am *so* glad I came today."

* * *

Zane hitched up his jeans as he left Emily in good, if mischievous, hands and turned toward the boys' table. Only Derek and Cael were here, which made sense given that their girlfriends were, too. His big brothers. Sucking it up, he went to sit down with them.

He saw the grins on their faces when he was halfway there. "Yeah, yeah," he muttered.

He pulled out the chair across from Derek and parked himself. He wasn't expecting the clap on the shoulder he received from Cael, though, and it nearly sent him sideways.

"Congratulations, Zane. I'm happy for you."

"Me too," Derek said as he held out his hand.

Zane looked at it, a bit stunned. These two were the leaders of their small Oneiroi group. He respected the hell out of them, but they were both usually so serious and responsible. He liked to keep things light and fun, which often put him crossways with them. But this? This was a first. He wasn't used to the warm sensation spreading inside his chest.

He shook Derek's hand. "Thanks."

"She's a great gal."

"Looks like you two worked things out?" Cael asked.

"Yeah, we decided to give it a go."

"Which is what you always wanted."

"Uh, yeah." Zane cleared his throat when it suddenly tightened. There'd been no hiding that—at least from everyone other than her.

Cael chuckled. "You didn't mention she was so feisty."

Zane let out a snort. "She usually isn't. That's why she made it as far as the driveway before my brain kicked into gear."

Derek laughed and rubbed his side. "Damn, I think I pulled something trying to vacate the premises so quickly that night."

"I know what you mean," Cael said. "Hey, you didn't happen to find a stray cornhole bag in your backyard?"

"Two," Zane said, "only one was in my refrigerator."

That got them going.

"I blame AJ," Derek said with a straight face. Poor AJ, so quiet and unassuming. He ended up taking the blame whenever Zane had an alibi. "What did you end up with for food?"

"Mainly burgers," Cael said.

"Hm, you must be missing the buns."

"Why?"

"Because that's what Shea and I both grabbed."

"Just buns?"

"Just the buns."

They were still laughing when Wes and Tony showed up.

"What's so funny?" Wes asked.

"What did you end up with after the grill-out?" Zane asked.

"Enough potato salad to stop up a horse," Tony bitched.

"Better than a bowlful of baked beans," Wes said. He pulled out a chair. "Frickin' AJ."

That doubled them right back over.

Sally moved in efficiently and poured them both glasses of orange juice, their usual. Bobby wasn't far behind, and AJ showed up last, which was rare. He flopped down into the chair next to Tony, and Cael started laughing all over again.

AJ looked at them in confusion. "What?"

"Nothing," Derek said, wiping his eyes.

"What did you take home from the picnic the other night?" Tony asked.

"Steak. Why?"

The uproar was instantaneous.

AJ held up his hands. "The plate was sitting right there. Any of you could have grabbed it."

"But I got beans. Do you know what a week of eating them does to a guy?"

Tony shook his head. "Not cool, man."

"Why are you coming for me?" AJ pointed at Zane. "He's the one who had us running out of there."

Heads turned, and Zane sat up straighter in his chair. "Hold on, now. I didn't chase you out."

"Yeah, you did," AJ said, holding his ground. "I believe your exact words were 'go' and 'hurry up.'"

Zane grinned. "Okay, maybe I did, but you've got to

admit, I had a good reason."

They looked to the girls' table, and Emily flinched when she realized they were talking about her. Her blush was visible from across the room, and she lifted her hand to give a little wave.

"All right, that's enough, guys," Zane said. "She's still flustered about how it all went down."

"She's not the only one." Seeing that their attention was diverted, Wes made a play for the muffin basket in the center of the table. "She's usually steady as a rock, but she called you on the carpet that night. I've never seen her so worked up."

"And aren't I happy she did?" Zane said.

Derek shook his head. "What were you thinking, setting her up with another guy?"

"Yeah, man. What the hell?"

A chorus of "*dude*" echoed around the table.

Zane accepted the criticism. "I admit, it wasn't my best move."

"How did Pete take being dumped?" Wes asked. He had a vested interest in keeping the billionaire happy. It was his most important account.

Zane shook his head. "Better than I would have. I was upfront with him about everything. I think he still wants to punch me, but he feels bad for the way we set up Emily." He narrowed his eyes. "Come to think of it, though, *you* were there when I came up with the idea. Why didn't you stop me?"

"*Me?*" Wes said. "Now it's my fault?"

"You're my wingman. You're supposed to stop me from doing stupid shit."

"Like that's possible." Licking muffin crumbles off his thumb, Wes pointed at everyone around the table. "Besides, every one of us has told you to man up and ask her out."

"*Man up?*" Zane repeated.

Tony kept him in his seat with a bar arm. "All right, settle down."

"The cookout was a good idea, though," Cael said, for

once looking on the bright side. "We should do things like that together more often."

"I agree," Derek said.

"But days are getting shorter," AJ noted. "Cornhole by candlelight isn't really fair for your girlfriends."

Cael looked out the window. The sun was lower on the horizon than it had been only a few weeks ago. It was rising later and setting earlier as autumn deepened, but they were Dream Weavers. They navigated the dark with ease, but there were other implications. "You have a point there. Nighttime is coming into season." And just like that, Cael reverted into his role as leader. "We need to remember that some sleepers go by darkness rather than the time on the clock."

Like Marilee, Zane thought.

"Mom's coming into her power with these longer nights," Wes said.

"She's not the only one. The full moon is coming, too," Tony reminded them. "We need to be on the lookout for Lunatics and their tricky little games."

"Shit," Bobby said. "Is it that time of the month again already?"

"Wait. I know that Lunatics make people behave goofy, but how do they affect sleep?" Wes asked.

"It's subtle," Cael said. "People mainly tend to fall asleep later or have trouble getting to sleep, because the brightness of the full moon affects their body clocks."

"Which makes it impossible for us to deliver dreams," Tony said.

Derek leaned forward and braced his elbows on the table. "It's called lunar insomnia. It affects a lot of people, but the Moon Goddess's daughters, the Lunatics, take it further. They mess with people's heads and their inhibitions. That's why there's so much more activity on police scanners during a full moon."

"And at the hospitals."

"And on the roadways."

"And bars." Tony ran a hand through his hair. "Ugh.

Hooligan's.''

"They're tough to spot, though," Cael said, "because they're not in the dream realm."

Wes pulled back. "Not in… What the hell?"

"They evolved like us."

"Only they play with people's minds in the wakened state," Tony said. "We affect their thoughts when they're sleeping."

"We do *not* play with people's minds," Cael said sternly.

Tony lifted an eyebrow. "Some of us don't."

"Hey now," Zane said. Although given his recent spate of dream rides, his brother might have a point…

"We open their minds to the dream realm," Cael said, "and let them choose their own paths."

"And Lunatics don't?" Wes asked.

Derek flicked the cloth napkin off the muffin basket and searched the offerings. "We're not quite sure what they do, exactly. We don't know how they pick their targets or how they influence them."

"But we know it's not good," Tony said. "Lunatics bring out the crazy, and people sometimes get hurt."

"Be on the lookout for changes in the ordinary: escalating behavior, strange dream choices, reduction in deep sleep— that kind of thing." Cael looked around to make sure everyone was clear on that. "All right. Let's go through reports."

Derek leaned back in his chair and crossed his arms. "I have a teenager who's showing some escalating behavior that could be caused by a Lunatic. It's either that, or the crowd he's fallen into. He's a freshman getting used to high school. I'll watch him closely this week."

Hm, Zane thought. Maybe he should keep a closer eye on Christopher.

"AJ?" Cael said.

"Nothing unusual to report."

"Bobby?"

"I found the Sandman for my gamers. It's definitely screen

time that's screwing up their sleep patterns. He's pretty hacked off about it, too."

Cael rubbed his chin. "There's not much we can do about that."

"Unless one of us tried to get information about the effects of blue light out in the physical realm," Derek said.

Zane caught on. "Like, say, a newspaper editor?"

Heads swung in Cael's direction, and he grimaced. "The *Sentinel* may be part of the problem. We've got more online subscribers now than paper delivery. Still… that's a good idea for a story."

Taking out his phone, he left himself a note.

Zane nudged the phone with his fingertip. They had a strict rule for no phones at the table on Sunday mornings. "You're not being an upstanding example for us today, big brother."

That got him the look that he was used to, and Zane laughed.

"What about you?" Cael said. "What's going on with your charges?"

Zane shut down fast. Shit. He should have come better prepared. *Do not report the zoomies… or the countless dream rides… or the dream sharing…* He'd broken so many rules this week, but weren't they really just rules for rules' sake? "Lots of happy dreams in my world," he said.

Lots and lots…

"Is that your sleepers' work or yours?" Derek asked, his dark gaze drilling into Zane across the table.

Zane went still. There was no way Derek could know. It was that investigator inside him. He'd scented something, though, and Zane knew he had to evade and quick.

"My bedwetter is getting better," he said. Shoot, he should have led with that. "He's starting to hear the call of nature. He hasn't had an accident in two weeks."

"Hey," Tony said. "That's good news."

"Even better for the kid."

"All right. Good report," Cael said. "Wes, how about

you?"

They barely made it around the table when Sally arrived with their food. The conversation switched to football, and Zane glanced over his shoulder to see how Emily was doing. He smiled. She was deep in conversation, and she'd stopped clicking her nails underneath the table.

Nodding to himself, he dug into his biscuits and gravy, but he saw Derek check on the girls' table, too. It got him thinking.

"Hey," he said quietly to his older brothers. "Mind if I ask you two a question?"

Cael stopped buttering his toast. "Why the whispering?"

"Because you're the only ones with significant others," Zane said, waggling his eyebrows to get his point across.

Derek paused with his coffee lifted halfway. "Oh, hell. Where's this going?"

"I'm just wondering," Zane said as he leaned closer. "How do you balance out your nighttime *duties*, if you know what I mean?"

Derek's eyebrow rose, and Cael stared. For such smart guys, they weren't picking up what he was laying down.

"You know," he said, "the dream weaving and *the sex*?"

Cael pulled back, while Derek dropped his chin to his chest. "Shit, we should have known."

"Yeah," Tony said, hopping into the conversation. "I've wondered about that, too."

As always, the quietest discussions attracted the most attention. It didn't take a moment before the subject of football was dropped, and all his brothers were looking to the head of the table for answers.

"*Zaaaane,*" Cael said as he rubbed his hands over his face.

"I'm serious. I really want to know."

"We all do," Tony said.

"See," Zane said. "This is the kind of important stuff you should be teaching us. How do we take care of our charges *and* our partners? Sexually, I mean. Well, dreams for the charges. Sex for the other."

"We understand the question," Derek growled.

Zane grinned. Maybe, just maybe, this was why he had the reputation he did. Still... "Come on. If it's a need-to-know thing, I qualify now. I've got Emily, and *I need to know*."

CHAPTER FIFTEEN

Zane held Emily's hand as they walked to the car in the parking lot. All in all, it had turned out to be one of the better Sunday family breakfasts for him. He'd sufficiently tormented his older brothers, hidden his night of dream rides from them, and earned kisses on the cheek from both their girlfriends when he picked up the tab for their table.

Best of all, Emily seemed more relaxed after spending time with everyone.

"Bye, Em," Wes called as he climbed into the passenger side of Tony's truck. "See you at work tomorrow."

Tony rolled down the window where he was already behind the wheel. "You're doing a good job keeping that one in line."

Zane flipped him the bird. "I'll keep you in line."

"Zane!" Emily pounced on him to make him drop his hand and smiled at his brothers. "Bye, guys. See you soon, Wes."

His younger brother stood, his feet planted inside the cab, as he talked to her over the top of the massive truck. "Hey, when's your product owner going to have them fix that navigation glitch?"

"Soon, I hope. I've been warning him it's a risk."

"It's starting to irritate Pete's team," he warned.

"And you're all starting to irritate me," Zane said.

"Enough work talk."

He nuzzled his face into Emily's neck, and she wiggled away. "That tickles."

"And that's our cue." Tony slapped his hand against the door of the F-150. "Get inside, Wes. I don't want to watch these two get mushy again."

Zane laughed as they pulled away fast, and he gathered Emily into his arms. "So that was Sunday breakfast. Did you have a good time?"

"Yes," she said as she melted against him.

"Good." He gave her a peck on the cheek and opened the door of his Camaro for her. She nimbly climbed inside. He'd really liked that green dress on their date night, but the jeans she wore today had definite pluses, too.

He closed the door once she was settled and hustled around to get in on the driver's side. She waved when they saw Shea and Derek exit the restaurant.

"What did you girls talk about?" he asked as he fired up the engine.

"You."

"Excellent."

"And axe throwing."

His head snapped around. "Say what?"

"Shea's company did it as a team-building exercise."

"And I got my ass dragged for going dirt biking?"

"Different company, different rules." She clicked her seatbelt into place. "You didn't tell me that she owns Biodermatics! I use their skin cream."

"Shea went axe throwing." He couldn't get past that vision. It just didn't fit. "Shea?"

"Apparently, Derek went with them."

Zane shook his head. "Still not computing." He turned out of the restaurant's parking lot and headed north to take her home. "I'm glad you got to know them better."

"They're nice," Emily said as she rested more deeply in the bucket seat. "What did you and your brothers talk about?"

"The full moon tomorrow night."

"Really?"

"And how it will affect sleep."

"Of course." She grinned. "I told Shea and Devon about the Oneiroi."

He stopped a little short at the light. "You did?"

"They looked at me like I was crazy, but they admitted that Cael and Derek had told them about the mythology, too."

Oh, his brothers and their ladies knew all about the so-called mythology of the Oneiroi. He'd seen Emily reading up on it. There was just one difference—she didn't believe it was real.

He shrugged. He'd done his part; he'd been honest and upfront with her.

"Got any plans for the rest of the day?" he asked as he drove down the main drag. The house she rented was closer to High Score's offices than his place. It was an older neighborhood with rentals popping up on every other corner now that the tech company was catching on. "Half the weekend is still left."

"Not really," she said.

"Playing it by ear?"

"No, I'm trying to decide."

He itched to ask if he was in any of those prospective plans, but he held back. They'd spent a lot of time together the past few days, and she'd just survived an Oneiroi breakfast. He'd understand if she needed space to do her own thing, even if he had no desire to go home alone.

"What are you going to do?" she asked, turning the tables on him.

His brain momentarily went blank.

"Probably watch the game," he said when he remembered what his brothers had been talking about before he'd sidetracked the discussion with his question about sex. "The Satellites are playing this afternoon."

"Sounds fun."

He pulled into her driveway. "Yeah."

He kept his foot on the brake and the motor running, but waited for her to give him a sign... like mentioning that she owned a TV.

The click of her seatbelt sounded loud. She simultaneously raised his spirits and dashed his hopes when she leaned across the console to kiss his cheek. "Thanks for taking me to breakfast."

"Anytime." Seriously. Anytime she wanted him, he'd come running.

She opened the door and got out.

"Oh," she said, turning back around. "I think I know what I want to do. Do you have time to come inside? I want to show you something."

His heart took off like a racehorse. "Sure, I've got time."

He killed the engine and hopped out of the car. He thought he saw a tiny grin on her face, but he didn't care. She needed a picture straightened? He was on it. She needed a drain unplugged? Not so fun, but he'd do his best at playing plumber.

"This is me," she said as she unlocked the front door and led him inside.

They'd been spending most of their time together at his place, and, he had to admit, he was curious. He visited her here every night in her dreams, but he'd been stricter about following the rules with her than with his other charges. Snooping on her from the dream realm felt like it would be crossing a line, so he'd never done it.

"Nice place," he said, meaning it.

The house was small, with one or maybe two bedrooms, but their tastes ran along the same lines. The house was older, but the interior looked crisp and tidy. Modern, even.

Moving deeper into the room, she used her shin to push the coffee table out of the way.

"You need to move furniture?" he asked, hurrying to help.

"No, I'm good."

She pulled out her phone and wandered over to the entertainment center in her living room. He wasn't expecting it, but he wasn't surprised when she started playing the latest Harbingers of Mayhem release. "Oh yeah," he said, nodding in time with the beat.

"Sound okay?" she asked. "Enough bass?"

The speakers must be new. "Sounds good. Where'd you get them?"

He started to wander closer, but she held up her hand. "That's not what I wanted to show you."

He stopped. "Okay."

She propped her phone up on the little holder on the shelf and then reached behind the couch.

Zane stopped dead in his tracks when she pulled out a hula hoop.

Next thing he knew, she was pulling her High Score T-shirt up... and off. His eyes nearly bugged out when she tossed it on the sofa. He stayed put as her shoes and socks went next, but he took a step back when she gave the hoop a twirl around her waist and started moving.

"Zeus save me," he whispered.

"You said you wanted to see what I learned in my class."

"I did... *I do.*"

She moved in fluid, hypnotic lines to the heavy beat of the music. She was half undressed, and it was sexy as hell. The combination shouldn't have worked, but it did—and it was glorious.

He watched as her body moved in long, rhythmic waves. Her breasts bounced in a plain white bra, her hips swung forward and back in low-riding jeans, and he got hard. Rock hard and fast.

Her confidence grew as she watched him watching her.

Zhh-zhh-zhh. The hard-driving beat of the drums was expressed in her hips and the sound of that whirling hoop.

"This is the vortex," she said, catching her breath as the exertion got to her.

She wasn't the only one sweating.

Zane knocked into the breakfast bar off her kitchen when the hoop began to climb. She was amazing. Standing in a swath of sunlight, her body was rhythm itself.

"That's good," he said, "damn good."

Too good.

He suddenly realized that sunlight meant no curtains, and his gaze snapped to the window behind her. It opened up to the backyard. Still… He spun around to look behind him to make sure he was the only one witnessing her performance.

Her hands did some flowy, circular thing that got his attention right back. The hoop had moved all the way over her head, and she was controlling its movement around her wrist like a lasso.

"Fuck, Emily," he said, barely able to breathe.

She brought the hoop back down and turned in a circle. The swinging motion of her hips nearly brought him to his knees.

Zane's body felt tight. He was clenching muscles he didn't even know he had. "You're a quick study."

"Am I?" she asked as she somehow traveled toward him, keeping up that circular motion of her body.

Her jaw-dropping, lithe, sexy body.

"Emily," he said, reaching for her.

He caught her by the waist, and the hoop smacked into his arm. It came to an abrupt halt, crisscrossing her and keeping them separated as he tried to pull her closer.

She wrangled it over her head. "Have I gotten better since that first video?"

"I'm not deleting it," he growled.

And then he couldn't hold back anymore. He pushed himself away from the counter, their bodies bumped, and he kissed her. His mouth consumed hers, and she rocked her hips forward one more time.

And flat-out owned him.

The Harbingers of Mayhem filled the room and Emily's head. She moaned when Zane kissed his way down to her neck. Dropping her head back, she splayed her hands wide over his chest. He stroked her bare torso, making her skin tingle and her blood heat.

"I want you," she whispered.

Their gazes locked, and time was suddenly of the essence.

"Sofa." He took a step toward it, but it was blocked by the coffee table.

"Bedroom," she said, catching on quick. "This way."

They tried to rush but moving together slowed them down. They nearly tripped over the hula hoop, but then they were in the bedroom. Sunlight streamed through the window, and she hurried to pull the shade. When she turned back to him, he was *right there*. He pulled her into his arms, and the kiss they shared was as fiery as the music that spilled into the room.

He reached for her bra with one hand and slid his other down to cup her bottom. Her hips instinctively swung forward, and they ground together.

He popped open her bra and pushed down a strap. He kissed his way over to the other one, and Emily wiggled her shoulders to make it fall to the floor. Once free, she began tugging at his T-shirt.

"I was really hoping you'd ask me in," he said.

"I was trying to think of something interesting enough to get you here."

"I was ready to do plumbing for you."

Their jeans came next, and Zane pulled away to take care of his own. Emily sucked in air when he carefully worked them down, and she saw how stiff his erection was. Her belly squeezed, and they scrambled, naked, onto the bed together. She scooted until she was lying against the pillows and reached for him.

He crawled up the bed on his knees. "Atop the covers?"

Ew... But she could deal. She didn't like the aftereffects, but she needed him *now*. "I have a washing machine."

He braced his forearm beside her head on the pillow and pushed a knee between hers. "Sexy talker."

"Hurry." She was ready. Hot and wet and oh so ready.

He pushed into her. In the brightness of the morning, the

act felt blindingly intimate. Shockingly tactile. Zane stared at the place where the two of them were connecting, and Emily rolled her head on the pillow when he began to move in and out. In and...

"Shit," he said, yanking out of her. "Condom. *Condom*."

"*Ah*. Don't stop." She caught at his shoulders and swung her hips toward him, trying to connect them again.

"Emily," he said harshly. "I'm not wearing a condom."

A little red flag rose deep in her mind, but need had consumed her. What were the chances? That sensible part of her brain tried to calculate the days. They were both clean. They'd discussed it. Wildness rose inside her. "Let's risk it."

"*What?*" His brow furrowed in deep lines for all of two seconds. "I've got one. My jeans. Where are my jeans?"

He clambered off the bed and ripped his jeans off the floor to search the pockets.

Emily let out a sound of frustration, but then she climbed onto her knees. He was right, about it all. Returning to form, she yanked back the comforter and pushed it away. Zane rolled the condom onto his straining cock and put a knee back on the bed.

She was already coming for him. He met her halfway and, still kneeling, pulled her onto his lap. She lifted herself high on her haunches, they got back into position, and she lowered herself onto him. Taking his hard cock into her.

They both shook when she settled down to the hilt, straddling him.

She kissed him, and he fisted a hand in her hair. It swung back and forth as they began to move.

"Oh God, Zane."

They found a rhythm with him thrusting up and her sliding down to meet him. She let out a cry of pleasure and speared her fingers into his hair. She squeezed her knees tighter around him, and he fucked her faster. Her cries jumped into a higher octave. She was close. They both were.

He wrapped his arms around her and caught her bottom with both hands. Lifting himself up onto his haunches, he locked her into place and shafted her deeply. Her body arched, her fingernails bit into his shoulders, and then she was coming.

And so was he.

He let out a final groan, and after a long, suspended moment, they slumped against each other. The Harbingers of Mayhem were still grinding out their song, "Chaos Coming," as Emily slid down his chest and leaned against him heavily.

It certainly had.

Zane lowered them to the bed. Reaching over him, she found the comforter and pulled it over them both.

"You have a washing machine?" he said groggily.

She let out a bark of laughter.

He slid a hand into her hair and cupped the back of her head. "*Let's risk it?*"

She ducked her head when he stared at her hard. "I blame hormones."

"You don't risk anything."

Her gaze went soft. "For you, I might."

"Aw, Em." He dropped his head onto the pillow next to hers.

She rolled onto her side to face him and settled a hand on his chest. The connection was beginning to feel natural. Needed. "We can watch the game here, if you want."

He smiled at her. "It doesn't start for another two hours."

She blushed. "I knew that."

He grabbed the Solstice Satellites jersey that she used as a sleep shirt from where it had gotten jammed against the headboard. He crooked an eyebrow as he showed it to her.

"See," she said. "Big fan."

She tossed it aside, out of the way, as he laughed at her. She was happy, she realized. Without qualification. For the first time in a long time, she felt like she didn't have to hold on tight to make sure things went right. She didn't have to manage everything. She could let go and trust in life… and in Zane.

Their knees knocked, and she decided to drape her leg

over his. She was still on a high, the adrenaline gone, but satisfaction made her feel like she was soaring.

Look at her, having wild sex with a man in the middle of a sunny day. And not just any man, but Zane Oneiros.

Her Zane.

She combed her fingers through his blond hair, loving the feel of it.

"What are you thinking?" he asked. "I can see the wheels turning."

"That I'm happy."

His eyes sparked. "I'm happy, too."

"And I like your family."

He coughed. "You've caught them on their good days."

"Did you really talk about the full moon at breakfast?" she asked.

"Yeah, why?"

"I didn't know that it happens tomorrow."

He pushed himself up onto his elbow. "Why is that important?"

She traced the lines that suddenly rumpled his forehead. "Because I won't be able to say it's *gibbous* anymore."

He grinned, and his forehead smoothed. "I love the way your mind works."

"Don't tell anyone."

Honestly, she didn't share the random things that went through her head with anyone else.

"Don't worry. It will be gibbous again afterward," he said as he rolled onto his back, "only it will be waning. Then it turns crescent. Hey, that's a good word."

"No, crescent is cool. Gibbous is funny."

"Agreed." He thought for a while. "Dollop is still available for use."

"That's your word."

"There's got to be other words out there." He drummed his fingers on his chest in time with the current song. "How about... mogul?"

She frowned. "Like Pete?"

His head snapped up off the pillow. "What? No. Too soon. I meant like skiing. Moguls."

"Where did you come up with that?"

"Wes was talking about snowboarding this winter."

"Modules is weird-sounding, now that I say it out loud."

"Modules. Yeah, that's better. Modules. No, *nodules*."

"Ew," she said.

"Too late. That's the one."

She shook her head. "We're the ones who are weird."

"But we're weird together." He looked at her suddenly. "Undulate."

"What?"

"That's my new word. You *undulate* when you hoop dance."

She blushed. She still couldn't believe she'd performed for him like that. "Was it okay?"

"Okay?" He pulled her closer until she was drowning again in the blue of his eyes. "Baby, you're incredible."

"I'm a beginner."

"But you're good. I can see it. You weren't just doing the moves, you were feeling them."

"Our instructor said that we're not supposed to think. We should just listen to the music."

"Why do you like metal, Emily? I mean, I love that you do, but what is it about it that you like?"

"I don't know," she said quietly. But she did. Inside, she knew. "I like the energy and the power, the drive in it." It was a good enough explanation, but she found herself continuing. "It's like your Camaro. If I were driving, I'd always hold it back, rein it in, because that's what I do—but I love the idea of letting all that energy out... giving in to the drive and ambition and just going for it."

He was watching her so intently she got a little self-conscious.

"Does that make any sense?"

"Is that why you like me?" he asked, turning her concerns upside down.

"In a way, yes," she answered, being truthful, "but I like that you accept me for the way I am—a four-door sedan with a high safety rating—even if it's not as exciting."

"You excite me," he said. "I like that I don't always have to be 'on' with you. I don't have to sell you on anything, and I don't have to explain when I just need to let the crazy out."

"Well, that's not always true," she said, thinking of the motocross course.

"We get each other, Em. We always have. The fact that you're super-hot only makes it better."

She let out a snort. "Super-hot?"

"Did you see me tearing my pants off?"

And forgetting a condom? That important detail hung in the air.

He rested his forehead against hers. "I like being with you like this even more, Em."

"Me too," she whispered.

"And you undulated."

She giggled. "Devon wants to take a class. I told her she could come with Hunter and me."

Zane's eyes popped open wide. "Cael will flip."

Emily went still. "So, no?"

"So, hell yeah. He'll flip in a good way, and that's one brother I could use indebted to me."

"The top Oneiros?"

"We call ourselves Dream Weavers these days."

"Who's my Dream Weaver?" She combed her fingers through his hair. "Or do you hand out dreams willy-nilly?"

She expected him to latch on to *willy-nilly*, but he surprised her by going serious.

"Me," he said, no sign of teasing in his voice. "Only me."

He waggled his eyebrows, finally breaking. "How do you think I got you on that motocross course?"

She swatted at his shoulder. "You don't stop, do you?"

"Never." He kissed her so fast, she never saw it coming, but when he slowed it down and kissed her soundly, her toes curled. Rolling her onto her back, he rose over her.

"I thought you wanted to watch football," she said.

"We've got time. Right now, I want to make all your dreams come true."

CHAPTER SIXTEEN

Talk about a bad sales call. Zane loosened his tie as he walked to the entrance of High Score. He'd known it wasn't going to be easy. The guy had a reputation for being old school—and a hard-ass—so he'd prepped for their face-to-face meeting. Unfortunately, there was no getting around stubbornness and a refusal to leave the Dark Ages.

"Who needs software to tell an employee to get off their ass and do their job?" the CEO had asked.

Zane could have turned that statement right back around on the guy, but he knew how to pick his battles. At least, when it came to his job he did. There was another approach he could take, and he knew how to bide his time. The company owner was getting up there in years, and his daughter was next in line for succession. She got it. He'd just start working with her instead of her pain-in-the-ass father.

He could wait. He just hated wasting time.

And wearing a suit.

He swiped his badge over the security reader and yanked open the front door. He didn't plan to stay long. He had a few things he needed to take care of here in the office, and then he was going home to change. Hell, he'd landed more sales wearing a T-shirt and sitting in Zoom meetings.

Or riding on a motocross course.

He headed to his office, thinking about *moguls* and how he

never wanted to be one, but a clump of High Scorers standing in the old project management pod got his attention. From the flurry of low whispers, he could tell something was happening.

He spotted Wes and went to get the scoop. "Hey, what's up?"

"There you are. I've been looking for you." Wes bobbed his head. "Emily's in the fishbowl. Looks like things are getting heated."

Zane's attention zeroed in on the glass-walled meeting room, and his heart sank when he saw Emily seated at the table with her arms crossed and a fiery look on her face. "What the hell?"

He quickly scanned the players and saw the product owner for her team, the engineering manager, the engineering VP, and...

"Shit."

All he saw was the back of the woman's head, but the red hair gave her away. *Double-Talk Daphne.*

"What's the meeting about?" he asked.

"Nobody's sure, but I'm afraid I might know."

"The navigation problem in the software?"

Wes nodded.

Zane transferred his weight to the balls of his feet. He didn't like the look on Emily's face or her body language. She was known for being cool-headed. She was an experienced facilitator who helped teams work through differences, but it was clear she wasn't a facilitator here. She was a player.

And she looked ready to blow.

Work things had been getting under her skin recently. She didn't talk about it much, but it had been affecting her sleep.

His gaze settled on Daphne. He hoped she wasn't the reason why.

He raked a hand through his hair. "Give me the lowdown."

Wes tilted his head closer and lowered his voice so nobody else would hear. "Baseline, Emily's team is getting squeezed.

Their product owner is burning out the engineers with priorities that aren't as important as that navigation bug, if you ask me."

"And Daphne?"

"No clue why she's in there."

Unless they were asking her team to pick up the overload. Zane gritted his teeth. Em would not be happy about that.

The scene in the conference room became more heated, with the product owner leaning into the table and jabbing his finger at something on the wall display.

Zane held back a snarl. Another leaner.

Emily kept her cool as she said something, but then Daphne crossed her legs and swiveled in her chair. She toyed with a strand of her long red hair as she said her piece, and Emily came right to her feet.

Zane immediately started to move in, but Wes caught his shoulder and jerked him back.

"Whoa. You can't go in there."

The hell he couldn't, although… *Shit*. He couldn't. Just because they were dating didn't mean this was any of his business. It wasn't his fight, and, more so, it would undermine her.

Besides, it wasn't the first time Emily had gone through one of these kinds of meetings. She could hold her own.

But she didn't usually do it while standing and yelling. He yanked on his tie. Whatever the argument was about, this wasn't the way for her to make her point. Even a hothead like him could see that.

"Oh, hell," Wes said. "Here comes Kevin."

The company CEO. Their mogul.

"Fuck." There wasn't anything Zane could do but watch the train wreck as it happened.

"Damn, I can't tell whose side he's on, can you?" Wes asked.

"No," Zane said. Nobody looked happy.

As the hand waving from the boss grew, the subordinates in the room became more subdued. Emily crossed her arms and retook her seat. Zane tried to see if she was clicking her nails, but he was too far away.

He'd lay odds on it, though.

Finally, the door to the conference room opened, and the CEO marched out. Everyone in the bay outside suddenly became engrossed in other things. Including Wes, who leaned down to pretend he was looking at something on Priya's screen.

Zane was the only one who didn't hide his interest. He planted his hands on his hips and watched as the others spilled out of the room. His body was coiled, ready to jump into action.

He wasn't built for standing on the sidelines.

Emily walked stiffly out of the room, clutching her ever-present laptop to her chest. The line of her mouth was flat, and color flushed her cheeks. Her eyes flashed when she spotted him, but she said nothing. He dropped into step with her as she headed back to her desk.

"You okay?" he asked.

"Been better."

"The navigation thing?"

She nodded. "I don't want to talk about it here."

Eyes were on them as they entered her pod with the engineers. They looked at her hopefully, but she shook her head. Cursing arose, but she remained silent, her moves crisp and contained as she pulled her bag out of her desk drawer.

Zane frowned as she started to pack her stuff. "Em?"

"I wasn't fired," she said. "I'm taking the rest of the afternoon off."

The band of tightness around his chest loosened. "Good idea. Where do you want to go?"

"No," she said, stopping what she was doing. "You can't come with me."

"We can talk."

She pressed her lips together and glanced around the pod, side-eyed, to see who was watching them. They'd kept their new relationship status quiet. The engineers were too involved in bitching about the results of the meeting, though, to pay attention to them.

The meeting which Zane still didn't quite understand.

"You need to blow off some steam," he said. "I can help. We could go to Hooligan's... or Night and Day... wherever you want."

"Not this time," she said as she reached for her phone. She began texting rapidly, and he looked at her closely. She was barely holding it in.

"Em," he said with concern.

She nodded at whatever message came back. Hooking her bag over her shoulder, she caught his arm and dragged him away with her.

"Emily," he said, trying again. "You're worrying me."

She stopped around the corner in the hallway by the exterior windows. It was mercifully empty. "Zane, I know you want to help, but I need to talk to someone else... to Hunter. You can walk out of a meeting like that with a bonus, and I... I just need to talk to her, okay? A professional."

He took the words like a gut shot. "You're mad at me?"

"No. Not you." She blinked fast, and his concern intensified. She was close to crying. "Please," she said. "I love you, but I need to clear my head. Hunter helps me do that. Do you understand?"

He looked at her, dumbfounded. When his world turned right side up again, he reached for her... and immediately did the "hand sweeping through his hair" move when someone turned the corner and started walking down the hallway toward them.

Shit. He cut off what he was about to say and nodded. "Okay."

She spun around and headed for the door. She was gone before they were alone again and he could make another try. Standing with his hands on his hips, he watched her exit the building. His gaze trailed after her, through the wall of windows, as she walked double time to her car in the parking lot.

Did she realize she'd told him that she loved him?

His heart was beating so loudly in his ears, he didn't hear Wes come up to stand beside him. His brother spotted Emily's car as she pulled out of a parking spot. "Is she okay?"

"Honestly, I don't know." Zane turned to face his brother. "What do you know about this navigation bug? Is it really that big of a deal?"

"It's a pain in the ass, yeah," Wes said, "but to this extreme? I don't know. There must be more to it. What has she said to you?"

"That she's frustrated, but not like this." Zane raked a hand through his hair for real this time. "She was just telling me yesterday how happy she is."

It had been such a good day. He'd seen nothing like this brooding.

"Zane, I'm worried about her," Wes confessed. "This isn't like her… Neither was the way she acted at the barbecue."

He held up his hands, ready for Zane to take a swing at him for that, but Zane dropped his chin. "I know. Fuck, I'm worried, too."

"What's going on?"

"I don't know. She's been doing a lot of things that are out of character."

Wes shook his head. "You need to go after her."

"I tried." Hell, everything inside him was still pushing him toward the door. "She didn't want me to."

"I thought that things between you were good."

"They are." Zane forced out a breath. She'd told him so with three very important words. "She just wants to talk to Hunter."

"The gal from that exercise class? Well, okay, I guess. As long as she's talking to a friend."

"That's just it," Zane snarled. "Hunter isn't a friend; she's a life coach."

"A *what?*"

The outburst was loud, and Zane caught Wes's shoulder to direct him into an empty conference room—a tiny one with windows only to the outdoors. Seeing a life coach was Emily's prerogative, but it was her business and nobody else's.

"Keep that quiet," Zane said, making sure the door clicked shut.

"A life coach? Emily? Why in the world would she need one? She's the most put together, capable, organized person I know."

Zane agreed. He'd only recently come to understand the pressure of that, especially the pressure she put on herself to keep to those standards. "She's a rock star, but she's been wanting to get out of that box and try new things. Hell." He locked his fingers behind his neck, so filled with confusion, irritation, and worry that he could hardly stand it. "I shouldn't be sharing any of this with you, but you're my brother."

Wes sucked in air until his chest puffed out. "I've got you, bro. Nothing goes beyond us."

Looking at his younger brother, Zane realized that the promise was good as gold. Wes was his wingman, his partner in crime. He'd followed him around everywhere when they were little, usually into trouble, but now the tables were turned.

Zane moved his locked fingers to the top of his head and wandered over to the window.

Emily loved him.

He'd loved her for years, but his heart was aching when it should have been soaring.

"She's been working with this life coach, Hunter something-or-other. First, it was little things, like trying spicy food and moving her work desk, but I swear it's been escalating."

"Like the hula hooping?"

Ahh, the hula hooping. Zane worked to keep his train of thought on the track. "And karaoke and… you're right, the kiss."

"You think that this life coach is pushing her to do these things?"

"I think she's inside her head." Zane turned away from the window. Dropping his arms, he planted his hands on the table. He needed stability. Logic. For once, he had to look before he leapt.

"When did it all start?" Wes asked. "Where did she find this gal?"

Zane let out a snort. "At the adventure park when Pete and I were trying out the motocross course."

"What was a life coach doing there?"

They looked at each other, the answer hitting their heads at the same time. "Coaching someone else?" Zane said.

"Is this a theme with her? Pushing people to do things beyond their comfort zone?"

"Seems like."

Wes pulled out his phone. "What's her name again?"

"Hunter…" Zane racked his brain. "I don't know if Emily's ever told me."

"Shouldn't be too many female life coaches in Solstice with that first name."

Good point. This was why Wes was good in times like this. He was always down for some fun, but he was curious about everything. The when, why, where, and what. Zane always thought about that stuff later. Basically, he flew through life by the seat of his pants.

"I don't know, maybe it's a valid approach to getting people on the right track." Hell, he'd never looked into life coaches before. He hadn't even known it was a thing, but he was beginning to have concerns. "She's getting to be too big of an influence on Emily."

He was starting to lose sight of the woman who'd turned his head in the first place. She was eating Tabasco sauce on her breakfast burritos now. "She's escalating."

She'd gone from trying to pull him off his dirt bike to telling him "let's risk it" in bed. It was almost as if she wasn't the one in control anymore…

Zane never saw the two-by-four that hit him upside the head when the pieces fell into place. Hunter… exerting growing influence over people… making them do things they normally wouldn't…

"Mahina," Wes said. "Here she is. Hunter Mahina, life coach. Wow, she's a looker."

Zane circled the table. "Let me see."

The woman on Wes's phone screen was drop-dead gorgeous. Big brown eyes, long, dark hair, and sun-kissed skin. Her beauty was otherworldly… *goddess*-like…

"Mahina," Zane said. "Look it up."

"What do you mean? You think she's got a record or something?"

"Or something." Zane pulled the phone out of Wes's hand and began punching buttons himself. He nearly dropped it when the answer he'd been expecting—but not wanting to see—popped up on the screen.

"What is it? What did you find?"

"Mahina… It means 'moon' in the Hawaiian language."

Wes's expression showed he'd just gotten clobbered by that invisible two-by-four, too. "You're saying—"

"Hunter Mahina is a Lunatic."

"Fuck." Bending at the waist, Wes let out another f-bomb. "It's been there right in front of our eyes."

"She got her claws into Emily," Zane said, feeling sick. How had he missed it? Lunatics worked during humans' waking hours, but he'd been right there for everything. Worse, he'd been supporting it. "That's why Em has been doing these things and getting more extreme. It's the rhythm of the moon."

Oh, gods. *Gibbous.*

A jolt went through him. "Shit! The full moon is tonight." He grabbed Wes's shoulder and shoved the phone into his chest. "We've got to find them. We've got to get Emily away from her."

Zeus only knew what stunt this Lunatic, Hunter, would put her up to next.

Moving fast, Zane nearly mowed Wes down as he headed to the door. He wrenched it open and went barreling back into the hallway. He hadn't made it five steps before he came to a screeching halt.

He didn't know where to go. He didn't even know where to start.

Wes caught him by the scruff of the neck and pulled him back into the conference room. He slammed the door shut, drawing more than one concerned gaze from other High Score employees. Zane was ready to fight when Wes shoved him up against the wall, but he couldn't see when Wes shoved his phone back in front of his face.

"You can't go off half-cocked," Wes said, "because it's even worse. It's October. It's her moon, the *Hunter's Moon*. She's at full power, Zane."

Zane stared hard at the screen... and then his brother... This was bad. Really bad. Emily was in danger.

The cold that swept through his veins numbed his brain. What were they supposed to do? "We've got to find her, Wes."

His brother glanced to the window. "It's still daylight. That's on our side. Where did she say they were going to meet?"

"She didn't."

"Damn. Okay, we can figure this out. Where have they met in the past? The adventure park, we know."

Zane nodded. He tried to think, but the gears in his own head were working in jerks and starts. "The community fitness center... and Night and Day..."

Wes flipped his phone around. "That's good. We can cover those. Let me tell my boss I'm taking a few hours off."

Zane nodded. None of those places were that wild or dangerous—other than the adventure park. Oh gods, they needed to start there. Emily hadn't liked it there, but it was the riskiest place—

"Axe throwing," he said, the words jumping out.

The color drained from Wes's face. "You've got to be kidding me."

"She's been talking about it a lot." Zane's voice sounded

like rocks over glass, but he knew he was onto something. His gut told him so. "They haven't been there yet, that I know of, but now would be the day to start."

This time, it was Wes who was pushing him out the door. "Why would Emily, of all people, want to throw an axe?"

Zane flung a hand toward the fishbowl as they walked by. "Oh, I don't know," he said sarcastically.

He wanted to hurry, but Emily would not be happy if people started talking about him running after her.

Wes was on his phone again, looking for axe-throwing venues. Zane dug into his pocket to find his keys.

"There are three of them," Wes muttered as they hit the door. "Who knew?"

Zane gritted his teeth. "We'll have to go to them all."

This was it, though. She'd want to go somewhere she could get the frustration out.

Wes shook his head in disbelief. "What is she thinking? She could cut off a toe."

"That's what *I* said." Zane threw up his hands, although he now knew why his cautious little project manager was laughing at risk. She was under the control of a powerful night creature—albeit one who had assimilated into the daytime world.

A light bulb went on. "Wait, text Shea. Ask where she went."

Wes took a stutter step. "Shea went axe throwing? What is the world coming to?"

"No. Derek. Text Derek and let him know what's up." Zane hit the button on his key fob to unlock his car, and he dove inside.

Wes was just as fast. "How much do you want me to tell him?"

"Everything. Send out the message to everyone." The tires of the Camaro squealed as Zane peeled out of the parking lot. "My girlfriend is under the control of a Lunatic. I need every Dream Weaver we can find."

CHAPTER SEVENTEEN

Emily liked the weight of the axe in her hand. She looked at the target at the end of the stall ahead of her. Each throwing lane was walled off for safety purposes and had mounds of hay cushioning the floor. It was like a private lane at a bowling alley, only the axes were sharper, and the targets didn't fall down.

They could improve on that, she thought.

But it did sound nice and loud when the blade lodged into the wood with a solid *thunk*. When the axe made it to the wall, that was... and when it stuck instead of bouncing off and falling into the hay...

She and Hunter were still trying to get their technique down.

"*Humph*." She grunted as she let the axe fly. It tilted forward, top heavy, and the toe of the blade pierced the pockmarked wall and froze. "Yes!"

It was like playing darts, only the pointy end was much bigger and harder to aim than she'd expected. She'd hit outside the target, somewhere around knee level, but it didn't matter. That wasn't the goal here today.

"So why was Daphne, with the flippy red hair, even in the meeting?" Hunter asked.

"Good question." Emily turned away from the throwing mark and returned to their table. They were drinking soda.

No alcohol was allowed on site.

Someone here thought about risks.

"My product owner—the idiot—was asking if her team could do some of the work." Emily kept the explanation vague. She was ticked off, but she knew better than to talk outside the office about confidential things. "Of course, Daphne said yes. She wants to play the savior, but her team isn't familiar with this part of the code base, nor do they have access. We wouldn't need them, though, if my product owner could do his job and prioritize the work correctly."

"That's the job you want, right? The product owner role."

"Yes," Emily said, finally admitting it aloud. She wanted that job. She was a project manager because that was where she'd been pigeonholed. It obviously fit her skill set, but she'd done it for so long now that she was bored. She was more interested in what they were building than how they were building it.

"Have you told your boss any of this?"

"No... but I might have said it very loudly to the company CEO when he came in the room."

"He gets involved in minutiae like this?"

"He does when it involves our most important client."

"Ah, that makes sense." Hunter chose her weapon—literally—and moved up to the throwing line. "So how did that go?"

"I don't know." Emily flopped down onto a chair. "I got lots of shocked looks, and then I left and came here."

Hunter took aim, rocking her forearm back and forth like a windshield wiper over her elbow before letting loose on the forward motion. "*Woo-haa.*"

The people from the next lane looked over at them in surprise. The axe hit and stuck, but it was only about a foot from the ceiling.

"A little more follow-through," the instructor/safety monitor said as he passed by.

Hunter gave him a thumbs-up. "I'm going to hit that target before we leave here today."

Emily had had more success, but she was still amped up from the meeting. Her throwing arm had more purpose.

Although Hunter was practically vibrating with energy today. Emily watched as she took a drink of soda. "How much caffeine have you had?"

"It's not the caffeine," her friend said with a skip in her step. "It's my day today."

"Your day?" Emily's eyebrows jumped. "Wait, are you saying it's your birthday?"

"In a way."

It must be an anniversary or something. Emily wanted to ask, but she was the student, not the coach. That didn't stop her from feeling bad about dragging Hunter out on a special day. "Why are you here listening to me whine?"

"Are you kidding me? We're throwing axes," Hunter said with glee. "Get back up there and tell me more."

Emily chose another axe. She thought about the short training session they'd had and decided to try the two-armed toss this time. She approached the throwing line. "More like what?"

"How did it feel, letting all that frustration out?"

"Awesome as I was doing it but terrifying a moment later." She closed one eye and focused on the center of the bull's-eye ahead of her. "And humiliating as I walked out of the room, realizing how unprofessional I behaved."

"Was it really that bad?"

"Yes." She wound up and threw the axe, using her legs for energy, and it hit the wall with a thud. Unfortunately, not the good kind. She jumped as the axe hit wrong and bounced. It only traveled backward a foot or two before tumbling to the ground like a lead weight. For a split second, though, she was worried about her toes.

She scurried back to the table.

"Somehow, I doubt it was that horrendous." Hunter swung her arms like she was making a snow angel. She'd tried various techniques to loosen up since they'd been here, but none seemed to be helping her. "I bet you just woke them up."

Suddenly, she froze with her arms straight overhead like a high diver before yanking them back down. "Uh oh. Time to go."

"What? Why?" Emily twisted around in her seat to try to see what had caught Hunter's attention.

Make that whom. Zane was here, along with Wes.

Hunter was already gathering up her things. "Sorry, Em. I'm a life coach, not a relationship counselor."

"No, don't go." Emily stood quickly, but Hunter was already swinging her bag over her shoulder.

"I've got things I need to do. Big day today." She gathered her hair over her other shoulder so the bag wouldn't pull it. "Call me later if you need to blow off more steam. Seriously, I'm okay with that."

"Can't I at least introduce you?"

"Sorry, gotta bail." Instead of exiting the way they'd come in, Hunter made a beeline for the back.

Emily frowned. She hadn't realized it was such a conflict of interest.

With a sigh, she turned to face the two handsome men who were now creating a bit of a commotion. She'd had quite enough of that today, thank you very much. She waited for them with her arms crossed and her fingernails clicking.

"Emily," Zane said, sounding winded. He practically pounced on her, pulling her into a bear hug. "There you are. Are you okay?"

"I'm fine. All toes intact." She drew away. They were making a scene. "What are you two doing here?"

"Where's Hunter?" he asked, looking around the venue.

"You ran her off. Why?" He caught her shoulders. It was like he couldn't stop touching her, and Emily became concerned. "What happened? Why did you follow me here?" She sucked in a sharp breath. "Kevin didn't change his mind about letting me go, did he?"

Certainly, HR would tell her first.

"No, it's nothing like that." Zane saw the rack of axes and

gently pulled her away from them. "We just need to talk, babe."

"*Babe?*"

Wes cleared his throat and held up his phone. "I'll update everyone."

"Update who on what?" Emily demanded. Zane led her to the table to sit, but she dug in her heels. "What's going on? I told you I needed a session with Hunter."

"Yeah, about that... I don't think your friend is giving you good advice."

Emily lifted an eyebrow. "She's not a friend, she's my life coach. She's trained in giving advice."

"But do you really need it?"

"Apparently, I do." She began clicking her nails faster. "Are you trying to tell me who I can and can't spend time with?"

"*No.* Shit. No." Others looked their way, including some very big guys from the next axe-throwing lane. "I'm not trying to be controlling, Em. Hell, I can't even manage my own life. You just haven't been acting like yourself since you met her."

"That's the point. She's been helping me try new things."

"You're getting reckless."

Reckless? *He* was calling *her* reckless? Emily turned away to take a long drink from her soda. It didn't cool her down. She'd told him why she was working with Hunter. She'd shared some of her deepest, most sensitive secrets. She didn't appreciate him barging in like this to stop her. In fact, she didn't like them swapping roles at all.

"So, you can go dirt biking on company hours, but I can't come here?"

His forehead furrowed. "Emily, you yelled at our CEO."

She was concerned about that, and the poke stung. "Just because I don't have an urban alligator to blame..."

"Fuuuck." He rolled his head and, finally, pinned her with a deep blue gaze. "Yesterday you said *let's risk it* to me in bed."

Fury bubbled up inside her like a junior high chemistry experiment gone bad. Her jaw muscles clenched, and the lobes of her ears burned.

"Hi there, folks." The instructor/monitor appeared again, placing himself directly between the two of them and the axes. "I think it's time you moved this outside."

Emily looked at him, dumbfounded. "Are you asking us to leave?"

"Yes, I am. No fights allowed on the premises." He swept his hand in a calming wave that directed them to the door.

Emily was flabbergasted. She was getting kicked out of an establishment? *Her?*

She picked her jaw up from off the floor and looked around. All eyes were on them. They were causing a stir at a place where people really needed to keep their focus.

"Our apologies." Zane came to her side at once. "We'll be going."

Emily tried to hide behind her hair as she snagged her purse. Her balloon of indignation had been popped. She was horrified and embarrassed. She moved with Zane out of the throwing area, past the concession stand and ticket booth, and out the door.

He rubbed her back. "It's okay."

"Okay? I got thrown out of a place that lets people toss axes at things."

"You've got to admit, that's kind of badass."

She gave a hiccupping laugh. "Don't try to make me feel better."

He gave her another pat anyway.

First the work blowup and now this. Emily wrapped her arms around her middle. She didn't know about her own actions, but the day was spiraling out of control. "Hunter isn't a bad influence. She's just unconventional."

"Can we compromise?" he asked. "Could you get a second opinion? Maybe meet with someone else a time or two?"

Emily didn't want to talk to anyone else. She liked Hunter, and she liked the person she'd become during their adventures together, although she could see how those that knew her might think she was getting irresponsible. It was all about expectations, apparently. Some people could get away with crossing a line, and others couldn't. "I guess."

She was so tired of being staid and boring, nitpicky and nervous.

He swung his arm around her shoulders. "You're just having a bad day, and you didn't sleep well last night. Let's go to my place and have a quiet night in."

Sleepy and quiet. Safe and humdrum. Apparently, that was who she was supposed to be. "All right."

He led her to his car, where she was surprised to find Wes waiting quietly. He had the same expression on his face as Zane when he looked at her. The frown, the lines on his forehead… Had she really gone that far around the bend? She'd heard stories about the two of them that would curl a person's hair. What about that soapbox derby with Wes stowing away in the racer?

She'd sung some songs and learned how to hula hoop.

"Want me to take your car back?" Wes asked.

The two of them must have come running out of High Score after her.

The fight drained out of her, and she opened her purse to find her keys. Wes took them and left.

Emily sighed and rested her head against Zane's shoulder. "I'm so tired, Zane."

He kissed the top of her head. "One more night, and then it will all get better. I promise."

CHAPTER EIGHTEEN

Emily moaned as Zane made love to her from behind. They lay on their sides, spooned together with her back tucked up against his front. He was in no rush as he moved inside her, but every stroke lit the fire a bit brighter. She threaded her fingers through the hand he had splayed across her stomach and held on. The deep thrusts were driving her crazy, but his breaths were steady against her ear as he drew out the pleasure.

Moonlight snuck through the cracks in the curtains. She wanted to run in that night. She wanted to soar.

He ran kisses up her neck, leaving goosebumps behind. She squeezed her eyes shut as she tried to last for as long as he did, but then his thrusts slowed down, and she felt his lips against her ear as he seated himself deep.

"I love you too," he whispered.

She let out a surprised cry as she crested, and he followed right along with her.

Warmth and energy suffused her, unlike any she'd ever felt. Zane leaned against her more heavily, and he nuzzled his face in her hair. She reached up to cup his cheek, and they lay that way quietly, satiated in more ways than one.

Emily's heart felt too swollen to fit inside her chest. She'd let her feelings slip out earlier today in a way she hadn't intended. She hadn't known if he'd heard. She'd wanted a second try at something, she should have said with more care.

The hazy blue light of the moon lit up the room, smoothing out all the rough edges, making the words easier to say and to hear.

She rolled over in his arms to face him.

"I love you so... much... Zane?"

He was asleep.

Her eyes stung with tenderness. His lashes brushed his cheeks, and his chest rose and fell in rhythmic waves. She laid her hand against him and felt his heart beating.

"You tell me that and then you fall asleep on me?" she whispered. "You *dolt.*"

She considered the word. Not her best, but her brain wasn't functioning on all cylinders.

He loved her.

She smiled as she brushed back his mussed hair. He slept on, his body warm and relaxed. When he went under, he slept hard. He might shift and turn, but it would be morning before he roused again. She knew his habits well enough now.

And he knew hers.

She lay down next to him as she watched him. With three little words—and some really good sex—he'd turned her day completely around. What had started out bad had turned to very good.

She closed her eyes and snuggled into the pillow. This was what she'd always wanted. This quiet closeness... to sleep safe in one another's arms...

It should be enough, shouldn't it?

She didn't need more than that.

She tried to drift off. She tried to sink into the warm contentment, yet the sleep that had come so easily for him was elusive to her. She felt like her battery had been recharged, and the room was lit up like a spotlight. Slipping out of the bed, she walked to the window and parted the curtains.

"Wow," she whispered. The moon looked huge as it sat low on the horizon. She spread the curtains wider and looked at the way it lit up the backyard. The moonlight let nothing hide, exposing the nighttime world and all its secrets. Putting a light on all that was scary…

She lifted her face to the luminous rays.

She'd scared people by trying to become something she wasn't. She realized that now. They didn't like her playing against type. It confused the people who thought they knew her best.

She rested her temple against the window frame. She didn't want to scare them anymore.

"But you get it, don't you?" she whispered to the moon.

She regretted none of her adventures: the karaoke, the scooters, the hula hooping, or even the meeting this morning. She'd raised her voice, but she said some things that needed saying. The only thing she felt bad about was Hunter taking the rap for her self-exploration.

Hunter.

Emily spread her hand against the windowpane, trying to catch the moondust. There had to be a way they could keep spending time together. She'd learned so much about herself. She couldn't let this be how the experiment ended, with her life coach running out the back door.

"No." Her breath clouded the window. She needed to fix this.

At the very least, she needed to apologize.

The way Zane and Wes had rolled into the axe-throwing place, you would have thought Hunter was a mortal enemy.

And her life coach's resistance to meeting them?

Emily frowned. Hunter had been familiar with the Oneiros family from the beginning. Did they know each other? Was there some kind of rivalry there? Some kind of feud?

Emily looked at Zane sleeping on the bed and felt a moment of uneasiness. They loved each other, but this Hunter thing could stand between them. He didn't want her meeting with the woman; he'd made that clear. She still had an issue with that—a big one—but maybe he would compromise. Maybe she could arrange for them all to meet, not for couples counseling, but life coaching.

The more she thought about it, the more desperate Emily became. There had to be a way to meet halfway. She didn't want to lose her boyfriend, any more than she wanted to lose her friend.

She looked to the moon for guidance and, suddenly, she felt the overwhelming need to straighten things out, to reduce the risk and find a path forward.

Tonight. She had to fix it tonight before it was too late to fix it at all.

She looked for the time. It was late, but Hunter had told her to call her. Looking back, she'd been adamant. She must be dying to know what had happened with Zane.

Trying to be quiet, Emily retrieved her phone. Zane slept on unaware, but she didn't want to disturb him. She moved back into the moonlight to see.

Are you awake? she texted.

She waited for an answer. When one didn't come, she started reconsidering…

Yes! Hunter replied. *Is everything okay on your end?*

It's fine, Emily answered, *but I'm sorry about what happened.*

No apology needed.

Yes, it is.

We're good, Hunter assured her.

Emily blew out a sigh of relief. She was happy Hunter was still talking to her, but she didn't like that it had come to secret texting in the middle of the night. She wanted her boyfriend and her best friend to get along. *I want to discuss something else with you.*

I'm up, and the moon is full! Want to meet somewhere?

I'm not dancing naked with you.

Hunter sent a grinning emoji in return. *I need to talk to you, too.*

Where are you? Emily was wide awake now, and they needed to talk in person. What she wanted to propose was tricky.

Home, but Night and Day is still open, I think.

That sounded good. Emily started to agree, but then she let out a groan. She clapped a hand over her mouth when it came out too loud, and she shot a look at Zane. He didn't stir, but that didn't solve her other problem. Her car wasn't here. Wes had dropped it off at work.

Shoot. She wasn't going to borrow Zane's beloved Camaro without asking. Maybe she could call an Uber or Hunter could pick her up?

Or...

Her eyes rounded when a better idea came to her, one that made her pulse jump. But did she dare?

The full moon winked at her.

Did she remember how? Was any of it right?

She *had* been dreaming, yet the temptation was strong to see if any of it was real.

Everyone seemed to want staid and boring Emily. Safe and secure. This might be the last time she'd get the opportunity to explore her wild side. Who knew what Hunter wanted to talk about? She might want to stop working with her.

Emily made the decision fast, ignoring the risk. *I'll meet you there.*

* * *

Paraphysics always won. As much as Zane wanted to stay in bed with Emily, mentally *and* physically, the pull of sleep was too strong. He'd been so worked up about the whole Lunatic thing, and so relieved to get Emily out of that sleep raider's clutches, that he felt like he'd run a marathon.

Not to mention the sex.

It all pushed him over the edge. He needed to get into the dream realm to recuperate, but damn if it didn't come at the most inconvenient time. He'd barely told her he loved her when he felt the yank. He tried to resist, but he couldn't stop his spirit from astral-projecting out of his body.

He managed to stay in the bedroom to watch her reaction from the dream realm.

"I love you so... much... Zane?"

He winced. "Sorry, babe. I'm here."

He sensed a tingle at the back of his neck. A sleeper was calling for him, but he brushed it off.

"You tell me that and then you fall asleep on me?" she whispered. "You *dolt*."

"*Dolt?*" he choked out. He nearly doubled over with laughter.

That was a good one.

From the physical realm, she couldn't hear him. She settled down next to him, resting her head on the pillow. Burrowing into it, as she always did.

The last bit of tension inside him unkinked. There was his Emily. He was so happy he was getting her back.

He *had* been a dolt not to recognize what was happening to her right in front of his face. The Hunter's Moon had latched on to her early, and its effect on her had grown over time, getting more extreme. He was so relieved they'd stopped things in the nick of time.

Axe throwing. He shuddered.

And felt another tingle run down his spine.

He lifted his chin. It was Christopher calling for a dream. One of his brothers should be getting to the boy shortly. They'd agreed he should have light duty tonight after the close call with Emily.

Unfortunately, the kid's calls kept coming louder and stronger.

Zane was tuned into him, while his brothers weren't.

"Come on, *someone*."

Christopher had made so much progress. He hadn't had an accident in a long time, but Zane still had to prompt him every now and then with water signals in his dreams. A sudden rainstorm, a backfiring drinking fountain, or even a water balloon.

The calls kept coming, and they had a tinge of desperation that Zane recognized. He didn't want the kid to have a setback.

He looked at Emily on the bed. She'd rolled onto her

back, and his hand was on her stomach. She wasn't nodding off, but then again, he'd just told her how he felt about her. He knew how hearing her say "I love you" had woken him up this afternoon.

He felt pulled in two different directions. Emily was safe in his bed, *a Dream Weaver's bed.* The curtains were closed against the full moon. The Lunatic hadn't reached out to her all evening, not by phone or even text. He and Wes had run Hunter off earlier today; she was surely on to another sleeper who was unguarded and restless.

Not that he wished Hunter Mahina on any of his brothers' charges.

"Damn it," Zane said, reaching for his temple when Christopher's call became nearly a wail.

The kid needed him.

He shot one more look at Emily. She was running her fingertips over his hand on her stomach.

He could get to Christopher, take care of him, and be back in minutes. Emily was safe and sound, and he couldn't let the kid suffer.

He dispersed to go weave some dreams.

When he returned, he found a half-empty bed and heard his dirt bike peeling out of the driveway.

CHAPTER NINETEEN

Zane sent out an emergency call for help over the family group chat. He needed anyone who was still awake. He needed them all.

He scrambled to get dressed and rushed out to his car. Emily was under the influence of a Lunatic on the night of a full moon. It didn't get much more serious than that.

A cold shiver ran down his spine.

She'd taken his dirt bike out on the road. Dirt bikes weren't street legal. He hadn't made any of the modifications that would even bring it close, like a headlight, taillights, or a turn signal. The full moon was out, but other cars and trucks would be on top of her before they saw her—*and she didn't even know how to ride the thing.*

He sat at an intersection, his Camaro rumbling, as he tried to figure out which way to go. He'd walked her through the controls once in a dream. She obviously remembered enough to get the bike moving, but riding was about balance and coordination, too. All that came with experience, and this was the first time she'd ever sat on a real bike.

Gods, don't let me find her in a ditch somewhere.

His phone rang, and he hit the answer button on his steering wheel. "Tony, talk to me."

"I'm out looking. Which part of town do you want me to cover?"

"East," Zane said, throwing out anything. Wait, his brother was right. They needed to be more strategic about this. "Cover the Morningside area. I'll take Sunset Ridge."

At least now he knew which way to turn. He took a left, heading for the western side of Solstice. Traffic was light, which made it easy to spot anything that was moving. The less traffic, the better… although the bars would be closing soon. He didn't want to think about that. Hopefully, Emily's destination was somewhere close, and she wasn't riding just to ride.

He did that sometimes.

His phone did that stutter-tone thing, and he added another caller.

"Any idea where she might be headed?" Wes asked.

"Do you think she's going to see the Lunatic?" Tony's voice was cold.

"Strong possibility." Zane scanned the road, cross streets, and parking lots, and he realized that might not be enough. She could go off-road if she wanted. The dirt bike would perform better if she did, but could she handle it?

"What are some of their spots?" Wes said, bringing him back on task.

Shit. Zane tried to concentrate. "The fitness center."

"Closed."

"The axe-throwing place."

"Should be closed, but I'll check," Wes said.

"I think they get coffee someplace, and then there's that juice bar."

"Night and Day?" Tony asked.

"Yeah."

"I'll take that one."

Zane's brain squeezed as he tried to remember more. "I can't think. Wes, can you take over coordination?"

"On it."

Zane couldn't strategize as well as his little brother anyway. He was better at taking action.

"I'll call back if I find anything," Tony said. "I'm going to roll down my windows to listen for the bike."

Good idea. Why hadn't he thought of that? Zane shut down the call and jabbed the control button for the windows. His muscle car wasn't exactly stealthy, but at low speeds, the engine wasn't that loud—and he knew the higher-pitched sound of his bike. He began listening as hard as he was looking.

Unfortunately, the action was slow. Valuable time was gobbled up as he and his brothers searched... time in which his mind went down all kinds of trails, none of which were good.

A text message came in from Wes, almost as if he'd read his mind. *Derek is checking the hospitals.*

Zane's grip tightened on the steering wheel. He didn't know if he had the stones to do that. Derek was a machine, though. He'd do what needed to be done.

Movement suddenly caught the corner of Zane's eye. His head snapped around, but it was a raccoon waddling across the road. Yet another thing he had to worry about if Emily was careening around on a bike.

How had the Lunatic gotten her to do this? And straight out of his bed?

He rubbed a hand over his face. Why had he left her? He'd let down his guard after he got her away from Hunter earlier in the day. He'd thought she was safe if she was in bed with him. That was the way it normally worked. He protected his charges from sleep raiders who came into their sleeping areas. He'd never had to worry about it working the other way around.

He went down a secondary road. He knew his pattern was haphazard, but driving in a grid would make him crazy. Driving at a crawl was putting him close to the edge as it was.

This was taking too long.

Where would she go? Most everything was closed. He had no idea where Hunter lived, but hanging out watching television didn't sound like the two of them—especially not on a night with a full moon.

With a press of a button, he called Wes back. "Check the bars. This Lunatic is at full charge. The two of them will be somewhere with energy or doing something active."

"There are five of us out hunting now," Wes reported back. "I'm calling Devon to wake up Cael. She can go into the dream realm to get him if she has to. There are times to break the rules."

Breaking the rules. Emily wouldn't have done that before.

"Thanks, man."

Zane disconnected and let out a snarl. This was why Lunatics were so hard to battle in the first place—they worked in the waking world. He doubted there was anything a Dream Weaver could do to help from inside the dream realm.

Hunter Mahina had run circles around him from the start. Hell, around all of them.

Running in circles.

Zane stopped breathing. No, they couldn't have gone there. He knew *it* was closed.

He took the next turn anyway and pointed his Camaro toward the outskirts of town. Where did a person take a dirt bike?

Somewhere with dirt, of course.

His heart pounded. He wanted to step harder on the gas, but he was learning to look before he leapt. It took forever to get across town, and when he made it to Solstice Adventure Park, it looked like the trip had been in vain.

The lights were off, except for the security lights, and the main gate was closed and locked tight. He nosed his car up close to it and let his headlights span out as far as they could penetrate.

It was then that he noticed the pedestrian gate. The latch had been flipped, and it stood wide open. It didn't even look as if it had a lock.

He stared hard at that gate. It was plenty wide for a dirt bike.

Off in the distance, he heard a buzz. He shut off his car

and pushed open the driver's-side door, all in one motion.

The hornet-like buzz was clear in the still night air. Dirt bikes. In the darkness. He couldn't see them, but they were here.

"Emily!"

The hornets droned on.

Zane tried to text and run at the same time. He bumped right into the open gate when he passed through, and he had to stop.

Adventure park, he texted to anybody and everybody. *They're here. Help!*

He ran onto the expansive property. He could pick out the sound of his own bike now. It was coming from the general location of the motocross course.

"Gods," he hissed.

He'd never run so fast in his life, but once he made it there, he didn't know what to do. Two dirt bikes were running the motocross track solely by the light of the full moon. A security light stood over the spectator section where he stood. It lit up the bleachers, the turn on the flat portion of the course, and the bike entrance area. The chain-link fence in front of him separated the riders from the spectators, but the rest of the course was lined with trees.

Massive, tall trees that would win in any collision.

The sound of two-stroke engines got louder. They were coming down the slope to where it flattened out and turned. He hopped onto the bleachers and waved his arms, trying to get their attention.

The rider in green wobbled as she turned in jerks rather that one smooth arc, while the blue rider hugged the inside curve. She was going slower, but she made the pass safely and took the lead.

Blue. Emily had borrowed his riding equipment, too. It would provide her some protection, although as he squinted, he saw cross-trainers on her feet. He hoped that helmet was strapped on tight. Knowing Emily, it was.

She wasn't that far gone.

She couldn't be.

"Hey," he yelled at the biker who followed her back up the rutted dirt slope. "Hunter! Get her off the course."

The Lunatic didn't hear him—or she ignored him—as she disappeared into the darkness. That green... He recognized that bike, too. Another rider had ridden it the day he and Pete visited.

Another of her life-coaching clients?

Zane climbed up another step on the bleachers, although he didn't know how that was supposed to help. He tried to follow the sounds. The security light overhead was as much a help as it was a hindrance. How were their eyes adjusting back to the darkness? The moon was bright, but it wasn't fluorescent.

He clasped his hands atop his head. He didn't know what to do. How could he get them stopped? He didn't want to surprise Emily and break her concentration. She needed all her attention on the trail before her. It had ruts that were a challenge to navigate under a full sun.

"Come on, Emily, get out of there."

The two women weren't going anywhere near as fast as he and Pete had gone, but they were both inexperienced riders. The only thing keeping him from hyperventilating was that it didn't sound like they were going faster than second gear... when they remembered to shift at all...

What he did hear, though, were lots of squeals and laughter.

Great. They were laughing while he was having a heart attack.

Could he catch Emily on foot when she slowed for the curve? That kill switch on the handlebars was practically made for this situation. It was the only idea he had.

He heard his name and footsteps pounding his way. Backup had arrived.

"Sweet Aphrodite," Tony said as he skidded to a stop. "What do they think they're doing? This is crazy."

"This," Zane said, "is *Lunacy*."

"Shit. What do we do? What's the plan?"

"You're asking *me* for a plan?"

The riders came full circle again, and dirt flew in the air from Hunter's back tire as she learned how to plant her foot and lean. Throwing up his arms, Tony trotted over to an area where he could breathe.

"Crazy woman," he snapped. His gaze trailed over the biker in green. "Crazy, hot woman."

"We've got to get them off those bikes."

"How?" Wes asked as he arrived on the scene. He was breathing hard.

Zane hopped off the bleachers and moved into position. They really did need a plan. "We need to break the hold this Lunatic has on Emily. Take her out, and Emily will come to her senses."

He hoped.

"Whoa." Wes took a step back. "I'm okay vanquishing night raiders in the dream realm, but I'm not hurting a human."

"She's not human," Tony growled.

"She's as human as we are," Zane said. "She's the child of a goddess. We just need to get her away from Emily."

"How?" Wes asked.

Zane didn't know.

* * *

Emily was having the time of her life, even as the bike beneath her juddered over bumps. They were winding their way up the hill. Trees stood guard, helping define the path. Without a breeze, exhaust hung in the air. She tasted dirt and felt its grit in her teeth, but the energy was electric.

Neither she nor Hunter were very good, but she was proud that she'd gotten the bike moving and was staying upright. Well, most of the time… This probably wasn't how she was supposed to learn, but the motocross course was empty except for the two of them. If it was busy and bright, she probably wouldn't have worked up the nerve to try it at all.

But tonight, she felt bold.

"Whoops!" Hunter squealed when she hit a soft spot and her bike wobbled. She nearly went down, but she wrenched it upright and stopped to catch her breath.

Emily pulled up beside her. "Are you okay?"

Hunter gave her a thumbs-up. "This is fun," she yelled.

"So much!" Emily yelled back. With their engines idling, it was hard to hear.

Hunter leaned closer. "Is your Oneiros going to be mad?"

Emily winced. If Zane woke up while she was gone, he'd freak out. "He'll be worried," she said loudly. "He's become the worrywart. Not me."

"He'll blame me."

"I know. I'm sorry about that, but it's our last shot to do something like this." She looked at the bike she was straddling and felt a little sad. "Apparently, I'm supposed to be the responsible one. The rule follower."

"That's not you anymore."

Emily looked at the darkness around them. They were trespassing, and she'd run out in the middle of the night. She hadn't even done that as a teenager. The more she thought about Zane, the guiltier she felt. "Maybe it should be."

"That's for you to decide, not anybody else."

Yes, and she would. But after tonight. Tonight, she was having one last adventure. "Let's go faster."

"Ooh, someone's getting saucy."

Was that a dare? Emily gunned the accelerator. "Race you."

* * *

Zane rushed out on the track when things got quieter. He still heard the engines somewhere out in the darkness, but they didn't seem to be moving anymore. What happened? Had someone wiped out? Was anybody hurt?

"Oh, shit." He braced himself when engines stopped purring and started growling again.

The riders came flying toward him, down the slope. They took the turn, and plumes of dirt flew. He tried to see color through the dust, but he recognized Emily not from the color of her jersey but the tilt of her head. He stood inside the fence, ready to lunge out to slap the kill button on her handlebars, but they were going faster now. He didn't know if he could catch her.

His thigh muscles bunched, and his weight went to the balls of his feet—but he froze when he saw her veer off toward the jump.

"No!"

He watched in horror as everything slowed down. Emily lined up for the small incline, dirt flew as her tires gripped, and then the bike launched into the air.

Time warped into fast forward as she came down again. Unfortunately, her back wheel didn't clear the mud puddle. It landed in the squishy mess and slipped, throwing her out of balance. She tipped, her tires spun, and centripetal force swung her in a circle. Dirt and mud sprayed as she landed, bike outside the puddle, but her firmly in it.

"Emily!" Zane took off for her.

His brothers exploded into action, and Hunter skidded to a stop.

"Emily?" she called. "Are you all right?"

Emily groaned loud enough for Zane to hear.

"I've got the bike," Wes said as he rushed in to pull it out from under her... and off her... "Is your leg okay?" he asked as he heaved the bike upright.

"Em, are you hurt?" Zane dropped to his knees beside her.

Her voice was muffled inside the helmet. Hands shaking, he lifted her goggles.

"Ew," she said mournfully, "*mud.*"

He was surprised to find her brown eyes sparkling. She grinned at him with a mud splatter on her cheek, and she looked so damn cute, he momentarily forgot how terrified he'd been.

But then Hunter's bike revved.

Tony pounced before Zane could.

"Uh uh." Tony plucked Hunter off her bike, and it fell over. The engine cut out, and the Solstice Adventure Park was doused in silence again. "You're not going anywhere, Lunatic."

"I didn't do anything," she cried. "Let me go, Oneiros."

"I don't think so."

Hunter squeaked and tried to wiggle away, but Tony wrapped his arms around her. "Stop it."

Fiery and indignant, she kicked at his shin. "You stop it."

"Ow," he yelped when she connected.

"You big oaf." She pulled her helmeted head back and was ready to head-butt him—or more likely, ram her head into his chest—when she caught a look at him. "Oh!"

That, apparently, changed things.

"On second thought…" she purred.

Tony scowled down at her, not trusting her sudden change in attitude. She wobbled her head at him. Seeing what she wanted, he cautiously helped her remove her helmet. Her long, dark hair spilled out, and she looked at him with big eyes.

"Hi, I'm Hunter."

Tony stared at her with his mouth agape. The angry tension in his face turned slack as his gaze ran over her face.

"What's your name, handsome?" she asked.

He seemed to have forgotten it.

"Tony," Zane yelled.

"Tony," Hunter repeated. She smiled.

"Damn it." Zane caught Emily's hand. "Can you stand?"

Mud sloshed as she got her legs underneath her, but she slipped when she tried to plant her feet.

"Ah! Sorry," she said when she nearly pulled him in with her.

He dug in his heels and helped her climb out of the mess. From the waist down, she was coated in mud. Sloppy, gooey mud. The sneakers on her feet were goners.

"Does anything hurt?" He brushed a gob of mud from her forehead before it could fall into her eye. "Other than your pride?"

She flicked her hand, trying to get the mud off, but it clung. She grimaced in distaste, and he helped her take the glove off.

She was coming down from her high.

Seeing she was safe and unhurt, his worry left, and his anger returned, full bore. He turned on the dark-haired woman who'd cause all the commotion. "You could have gotten her killed. Get your claws out of her, Lunatic."

"Hey," Emily said. "That's mean."

He didn't care. He took a step toward Hunter and jabbed a finger at her. "This stops now. Do you understand?"

Hunter paled. They had her cornered. Three Dream Weavers versus one Lunatic.

Good. Maybe fear would make her listen.

"She's not one of your playmates anymore," Zane growled.

"Stop it." Emily caught his sleeve and yanked him back. Her eyes weren't sparkling anymore. "This isn't her fault."

"The hell it isn't," Tony said.

Hunter became more agitated. Her gaze snapped from one Oneiros brother to the next until her attention finally landed on Wes. She cleared her throat.

"Wow," she said, her voice sultry. "That half-pipe looks like an awesome ride, doesn't it?"

Zane took a step back as he felt power pulse. "Wes, don't listen to her."

Wes was already turning around to cast his gaze across the park to the half-pipe. It loomed over them on the far side of the complex, sitting further back in the shadows. It was closed, awaiting snow and the winter season, but that didn't seem to matter. His face lit up. "Yeah."

Next thing Zane knew, his brother had snatched up Emily's helmet from where it had fallen on the ground. He swung a leg over the dirt bike and hopped on the kick-start.

The roar of the engine was loud in the night.

"Wes, snap out of it," Tony yelled. His voice jumped

when Hunter wiggled in his arms, rubbing up against him. "Hey, stop that."

"Want to dance with me in the moonlight, big boy?"

Zane held up his hands as the situation suddenly veered out of control. Wes zoomed off on the bike, heading straight for danger, and Tony... Well, Tony had his mind on much different things.

"Tony!" Zane snapped.

Shit. She'd mesmerized both his brothers. With barely a suggestion, she'd flipped everything upside down.

What was he supposed to do? Protect Emily? Save his brothers?

He heard footsteps pounding as someone ran toward them. Five of them had been hunting. "Over here," he called.

But then the Lunatic lifted her face to the full moon. When she lowered her chin, her dark eyes glowed with power.

"No," Zane roared. He leapt between her and whichever of his brothers was trying to come to their rescue.

Off in the distance, a dirt bike whined.

"Go get Wes," Zane yelled over his shoulder. "I've got this."

"Do you, Dream Weaver?" Hunter rubbed sensually against Tony, and his brother grunted.

"Zane?"

It was AJ.

"Go."

AJ hesitated only a second before following orders. He turned on his heel and raced to the half-pipe. *"Wes, get off there."*

AJ, the quiet one, was yelling. That was as bad as it got. The Lunatic was winning.

"Go home, Oneiros. Take Emily with you, and I'll let your brothers go."

She was trying to use her influence on him, but Zane glared at her. She was stunning, a true daughter of a goddess, and she had the upper hand. She took her power from the moon, while he was at full strength in the dream realm. The only power he had here was his anger and his love for those around him.

He pulled from that well of strength. He wasn't leaving this for another day. They were settling this now.

"You've had your fun," he said, "but this is it. You stay away from her from now on."

"She's my friend," Emily said, even as she watched what was happening around her with growing awareness.

"She's not your friend, she's a Lunatic."

"Stop calling her that. It's rude and… and insensitive."

"Em, she's the one making you do these things. It's gone too far."

Mud flew as Emily whirled around. "So I always have to be the sensible one? The fuddy-duddy?"

Fuddy-duddy?

"Rules are sometimes there for a reason." Zane couldn't believe the words coming out of his mouth. Off in the distance, he heard his dirt bike revving, Wes whooping it up, and AJ yelling *stop* at the top of his voice.

Had the entire world turned upside down?

"You can't put the genie back in the bottle, Zane." Emily slopped toward him looking more like a swamp monster than a genie. "I want to be free from all the rules in my head. I want to be able to get wild every once and then."

"I'm onboard with that. Hell, I'll get wild with you. I'm just trying to make sure you don't get hurt—or hurt anybody else." Zane flung out his hand. "Emily, look where you are! Remember how worried you were about me when you found me riding here? Well, I know how to ride, and it was daytime."

She blinked.

He pointed at the half-pipe where, honestly, things were getting dodgy. "Look at what she's done to my brothers with only a few suggestions." Emily looked at the commotion happening over on the half-pipe, and Zane could see the fogginess in her brain starting to clear. "Do you think that was his idea? He came here to help you."

Suddenly, Emily's eyes went wide. "Ohmigosh, Wes! He can't ride that thing on a dirt bike!"

Zane didn't want to look... for his brother's sake—or his bike's—but he did. His heart skipped a beat. "Lunatic," he snarled.

He whirled around to confront Hunter, and his eyes nearly popped out of his head. "*Tony!*"

His brother, the Dream Weaver, and Hunter, the Lunatic, were deep into a full-on make-out session.

Tony's shirt was off. His arms were still around the dark-haired woman, but he was holding her, not restraining her. Her arms were looped around his neck, and they swayed together, their feet shuffling, as their mouths mated.

Emily gasped.

"They're dancing together under the moon." She let out a squeak when Tony's jeans suddenly dropped to his knees. "*Naked.*"

"*Anthony,*" Zane roared, "wake the fuck up!"

Hunter stepped back from Tony and rubbed her lips together. "Too bad we're enemies, *stud.*"

She trailed her fingers over his muscled chest and, impulsively, leaned in to kiss him again. Then she darted off to her bike.

Zane made a move toward her, but she held up her hand.

"You wouldn't have your dream girl if it wasn't for me, Oneiros. You owe me." She grinned at Emily. "Thanks for sticking up for me. I *am* your friend."

Zane stood dumbfounded as Hunter jammed her helmet onto her head and zipped away, escaping into the night. Laughter trailed after her.

"Best full moon ever!" she whooped.

He watched her go. Four Dream Weavers. She'd just handled four Dream Weavers without lifting a finger.

"Tony, pull up your pants."

"*Ow!*" Wes suddenly wailed when the engine of the dirt bike cut out.

"You're lucky it's your ass that hurts," AJ yelled at him. "You could have broken your neck, you idiot."

Zane spun around, but he blew out a ragged breath when he saw AJ yank Wes into a hug and pound him on the back.

"Fuck," Tony muttered. Out of them all, he looked the most shell-shocked. He zipped up his jeans, but he stared in confusion in the direction Hunter had gone.

Zane picked his brother's T-shirt off the ground and shoved it into his chest. "You okay, big man?"

The look in Tony's eyes alternated between terror and fury. "What. The. Fuck?"

Amid the chaos, Emily stood frozen like a kitten in a bull-fighting ring.

"Maybe I did get carried away," she said softly.

Zane sighed. He could see the blush on her cheeks even in the moonlight. "You're not the only one."

She put her hand to her chest and found a glob of mud. She flicked it off in distaste. He caught her hand and pulled her further away from the puddle of gunk.

"It's okay. Everything's all right now."

She looked around as if seeing everything for the first time. The adventure park, the motocross course, the number of his brothers who were running around in the middle of the night... "What was I thinking?"

"You weren't. She egged you on."

"No, she didn't."

Zane raised an eyebrow.

Emily lifted a hand to her temple, and her brow furrowed. "I was going to meet her at Night and Day. I didn't have my car, and I didn't want to take yours." Her face crumpled. "So I stole your bike instead."

"It's fine. I'm not worried about the bike."

"Hunter saw me arrive on it, and she wanted to try riding, too." She looked down at herself. "Oh, Zane. *Mud.*"

He shouldn't laugh—but he did. "Good thing I have a washing machine, too." Walking up to her, he pulled her into his arms and pressed his face into her hair. "Who's the *dolt* now?"

She tried to squirm away. "Zane, you'll get all muddy..." Her fingers dug into his sides when she realized what he'd said. "You were awake."

"I heard you." He looked at her cute, mud-smeared face. This time, he wanted to get it right. "I love you, Emily."

She blinked fast. "I love you too."

He pulled her up close, mud and all, and soon they were dancing, lip-locked, under the full moon.

Her eyes were sparkling again when she pulled back, and she touched her lips. "Um, I think we should go help your brothers."

Zane looked across the park to the winter play areas. AJ was in over his head with both Wes and the bike. "I'll go help those two."

"I've got Tony."

They both looked at his bewildered brother.

"Looks like you got the bigger challenge." Zane shot her a grin before darting off. "Good luck with that."

CHAPTER TWENTY

Emily sat on a cloud, looking down on the city of Solstice. It was a beautiful autumn day, and the leaves on the trees were bursting with color. From her vantage point, she could see swaths of reds, yellows, and oranges. Over on her left, she spotted High Score's building and her neighborhood. If she squinted, she could see the roof of her house.

The cloud lifted as it caught a thermal and drifted to another part of town. There was the park with its patch of wildflowers and people the size of ants walking around. Or scootering...

Her heart skipped a beat, and the cloud moved along. A breeze took it toward the outskirts of town, over the adventure park, and her pulse began to race. Looking down, she saw motocross racers skidding, jumping, and falling. She tensed until the rider climbed back on his bike and hurried to catch up.

Even then, she couldn't relax. It was all so chaotic, loud, and dangerous.

And that was in the sunshine.

What had she been thinking? How could she have thought that riding on that course in the middle of the night was a good thing to try? She couldn't believe she'd even gone onto the straight open roads on one of those things. With no lights, no insurance, and no idea what she was doing.

A wind gust came through. It carried her cloud past the adventure park and out to Comet Tail Lake. Her toes uncurled, and the cloud dropped so she could take a better look. The surface of the water was peaceful, still as glass and soothing.

She heard a plop behind her and glanced over her shoulder. Zane was here, looking like he'd just jumped onboard. Puffs of white cotton candy lifted from under his bare feet. He looked around at the cloud and the white drawstring pants he was wearing. "No mud up here," he said with a laugh.

Oh, the mud. It had gotten everywhere.

Thunder rumbled off in the distance, but he lifted a hand, and birds started to sing. Tufts of the cloud continued to break away as he walked toward her. He sat down beside her and swung his legs over the edge with hers.

"Hey, Comet Tail," he said as he looked over the landscape beneath them. "That's where Wes and I went dirt biking with Pete."

And again, her cloud started to rise. It rotated away, and they floated along until she spotted The Chalet, the restaurant where he'd taken her on their first official date. Hooligan's bar didn't count. The cloud leveled out and hovered.

"Nice," he said, approving of her choice. "We should go back there while the colors are still blooming."

"I'd like that."

They sat quietly for a moment with their legs swinging back and forth. "How are you doing?" he finally asked.

The sky began to darken. He lifted an eyebrow, and butterflies suddenly flittered around. One landed on her finger. Its light weight tickled as it opened and closed its wings.

"No nightmares tonight," he said. "Let's try to work through things another way."

"What do you mean?"

He ruffled his hair. "I know you don't believe me when I tell you certain things. That's why I'm here, in your dream.

We need to talk. I need you to understand some things."

"Like what?"

"Like I really am a Dream Weaver."

"I know. You're an Oneiros. I read about them… you."

"Right." His mouth twisted, and he stared off into the distance. "You studied up on us, but there are some things you don't know. We deliver dreams, but we're also responsible for keeping the balance in the night world. We protect our charges from beings that would harm their sleep… beings like your friend, Hunter."

"Hunter?"

He turned toward her and hooked his leg up on the cloud. "She's a Lunatic, Em, with a capital L. She's a daughter of Selene, the Moon Goddess."

The butterfly took flight again, weaving and bobbing along its way.

"Lunatics take their power from the moon, and they can make people do crazy things—especially when the moon is full, like tonight."

The sky began to darken, and Emily felt the flicker of fear. She didn't want to be up here during a storm. Or at night.

"Do you remember what you did tonight, Em?"

Remember? She could feel the vibration of the dirt bike beneath her. She could feel the dust coating her skin. "How could I have been so impulsive?" she asked.

"It wasn't your fault." He dipped his head to look her in the eye. "She was influencing you."

"But I was the one who hopped on the bike to go meet her." Oh, Emily's stomach hurt. The risk she'd taken was unfathomable. And so unlike her…

"It was her moon, the Hunter's Moon. I think that gave her some extra oomph." Zane's serious expression brightened. "Hey, *oomph*."

Emily shook her head. Now was not the time, although… "That is a good one."

He pushed a tiny cloud away from her head. "I need you to understand why I acted the way I did. Lunatics and Dream

Weavers are natural enemies, and she messed with you."

"She's not my enemy," Emily said automatically. "She's my friend… or I thought she was."

"I know."

Had she been that gullible? Had she truly not seen Hunter for what she was? Emily began to click her fingernails. "I liked who I was when I was with her, Zane. I like feeling free and curious, not so cautious all the time."

"You can still be that way, if you want."

"Was I just a target to her?"

A bat suddenly swooped in, chasing her pretty butterfly. Emily gasped and reached for it, but Zane put his arm out to keep her from falling off the cloud. He pointed at the bat, and it veered away, flying as if it were suddenly drunk.

"Funny thing is, I think she likes you, too. She stopped to make sure you were okay when you wiped out, even though there were three Dream Weavers there. She could have just ridden off."

"But what she did to your brothers…"

"Yeah, that was bonkers… especially the Tony thing." Zane rounded his eyes. "Outside of the dream realm, we don't have the *oomph* she does."

A laugh hiccupped out of Emily, but she cut it off. "Stop it."

"Never." He took her hand. "She'll probably stay away from you now that you're onto her. If she doesn't, though, make sure to be aware of the phases of the moon. You can resist her suggestions."

"You're not telling me to stay away from her?"

"That's up to you. I don't like her, but you do—and she did get us together."

Yes, she had. Why had she done that? Emily's mind churned. Had it been for the thrill of it? Hunter had sensed that Zane was an Oneiros from the start. Had she wanted to see how close to the fire she could get? Or had she truly wanted to help? She was an unconventional life coach, but she'd had good insights on a lot of things.

"You seemed immune to her. How did you do that?"

Emily didn't know how she felt about the whole situation, but she didn't want to be under the influence of mind control again, if that's what it was. If Zane had any tips or tricks, she needed to know them.

"I was angry and focused." He rubbed his hand over his bare chest. "And scared spitless. My heart nearly exploded when you went for that jump."

"Sorry." Emily stared at her feet dangling over the edge.

He was as touchy about what had happened tonight as she was. She could understand why. She'd gotten carried away. Looking back, she could see now how her escapades had grown. "She was at low energy when I met her."

"Her power should be waning after tonight," he said, "but I'm going to keep an eye on you. If I tell you that you're getting out of control…"

"It just means I should step away from the dirt bike." Emily understood now.

"Exactly."

"Okay."

"So, are we good?"

She squeezed his hand. "We're good."

That seemed to satisfy him. He stretched and looked around at the skyline. In increments, it brightened. They sat together, soaking up the calm.

"This is my last dream ride with you, Emily."

"What?" she said in surprise. "You won't be my Dream Weaver anymore?"

"I'll still take care of you in your sleep. I'll guide you into the dream realm, but I won't hitch rides on your dreams anymore."

"But I want to dream about you."

"Then you will, but the dream will be under your control." He pushed the strap of her white nightgown from where it had slipped down her arm back onto her shoulder. "That representation of me will do whatever your brain thinks I should do, but the real me will be off taking care of other sleepers. Other dreamers."

"Are you still going to take rides on their dreams?"

He scowled when she caught him. "I still believe dream rides can do some good, despite what my brothers think."

"Then why not mine?"

"We're together, but you should have your privacy. I don't want to cross that line with you, and I don't want you worrying that I will." He waggled his eyebrows at her. "You might not have noticed, but I've been getting more responsible these days."

"I've noticed, even if I've been getting chaotic at the same time."

"Meet you in the middle?"

She liked that idea.

He leaned in to give her a soft kiss. "Since I'm here, and it's my last dream ride, is there anything you want to do?"

Emily looked around the puffy cloud. She felt the wind brushing her hair against her cheeks and felt the sunlight warming the back of her neck. She felt invincible, like she could do anything, try anything—but in the safety of a dream this time.

There was only one thing that came to mind, because she wasn't about to do it in real life. Not even at the suggestion of a Lunatic. "Sky diving?"

"Why did I know you were going to say that?"

In the blink of an eye, she found herself wearing a helmet and goggles again, plus a parachute on her back. At least this adventure didn't involve mud. She hoped.

"Ready?" he asked.

"What? With no planning or double-checking our packs?"

He obediently turned around so she could check the parachute on his back. He was outfitted just like her, and she tested to make sure their harnesses were cinched up tight.

"Ready," she finally declared.

He took her hand. "One, two, three..."

They jumped together, falling and flying through the air, and laughing all the way down.

EPILOGUE

"Rise and shine, Em," Zane said as he woke her up. The weekend was here, and he'd finished with his charges early. He'd left Emily in bed so he could make them breakfast as she finished out her last dream of the night, but he couldn't wait any longer.

He watched as she rubbed sleep out of her eyes and raked fingers through her tousled hair.

She looked at the tray of food in surprise. "Are you bringing me breakfast in bed?"

"I sure am."

"Why?"

"To celebrate your new job." He set the tray table over her lap as she propped herself up against the headboard. The smile on her face was enough to make him consider doing it for her every day.

"You didn't have to, but thank you."

He kissed her cheek. "It's not every day that High Score gets a new product owner."

The tirade she'd gone on in the fishbowl apparently hadn't been as out of line as she'd thought in her head. She'd spoken some truths that others heard, primarily Kevin, their CEO. The old product manager for her team was transitioning to a different role, and Emily was moving into his place.

She took a sip of her juice as she eyed the breakfast

burrito with hunger. "I hope I do a good job. I've been a project manager for so long."

"You'll do great." He had no doubts.

He passed her a card.

"Aw, you're so sweet."

Sweet, yeah, that was him. He had to tell his brothers that one.

He watched as she ripped open the envelope. She pulled out the card, but she fumbled it when something slid out. She quickly caught the piece of paper before it fell off the bed, and her eyes rounded when she read it.

"Harbingers of Mayhem?"

Zane lunged for the table tray and saved it in the nick of time. He moved it out of the way as she scrambled up to her knees.

She was blinking and reading the printout again to make sure she hadn't made a mistake. "You got us two tickets to see Harbingers of Mayhem?"

"In Perihelion City in three weeks. You'll have to tell your new boss you need the time off."

"Zane!" she squealed.

He caught her when she launched herself at him. Laughing, he pulled her up close as she nearly squeezed the wind out of him.

"I never thought I'd see them play live."

He hugged her back. It was time the two of them started having adventures of their own. "That's why I'm here, Em, to make your dreams come true."

THE DREAM WEAVERS

They are the Oneiroi, Greek daemons of dreams. As dream weavers, their mission is to watch over sleeping humans—for without dreams, chaos can reign. So the Oneiros brothers blend in with the waking world by day and watch over their charges by night, protecting humans from the creatures who would prey upon their sleep. But what happens when the Oneiroi have dreams of their own? And what if they fall in love with those they're duty-bound to protect—or the enemies they've sworn to fight?

DREAM MAN
Book 1

Devon dreams of her fantasy lover. To reach him, she performs a love spell, yet even the simplest of spells can have repercussions. When Cael shows up in flesh and blood, she has to decide if he's the man of her heart... or the demon of her dreams.

DREAM WALKER
Book 2

As a child, Shea Caldwell suffered from sleepwalking. Now, she's moved on to erotic dreams—especially about sexy Derek Oneiros—but she's afraid to invite him into her bed. For you see, Shea is dangerous when she sleeps. But so is Derek, and he may be the only one who can save her.

DREAM RIDER
Book 3

As a Dream Weaver, Zane Oneiros isn't supposed to hitch rides on the dreams of his charges, but he can't help himself when the dreamer is Emily Hutchins. Beautiful Emily is his work friend, but in her dreams, Zane wonders if he can find more. When they share a kiss, everything changes. Cautious Emily becomes more daring, and Zane worries that meddling with her dreams may be the cause. Soon he's battling to get the old Emily back and make their dreams turn real, not the nightmares.

DREAM LOVER
Book 4

Tony Oneiros doesn't like Hunter Mahina. She's a Lunatic, a daughter of the moon goddess, and he's a Greek god of dreams. While he's trying to help people sleep and dream, she's keeping them up at night doing crazy things. And he's not immune to her charms. When they kiss under a full moon, the chemistry is combustible. Tony isn't sure if she used her powers to influence him, but he needs to find out -- and protect his dreamers from her, while he's at it.

EXCERPT FROM DREAM LOVER

Hunter rolled onto her back with a groan when her phone dinged the announcement of a new text message. She was awake, but she wasn't ready to get going. She was a night owl by trade. Anything related to mornings was a struggle for her, and it was the weekend.

Sunlight brightened her bedroom to the point where the curtains were glowing. Grabbing the empty pillow beside her, she flung it over her face—and then had to adjust it so she could breathe. She really needed to look into sun-blocking shades.

"Ugh."

Who was texting her at this hour, anyway?

She wriggled on the bed, trying to find a more comfortable position, but her toes were out from under the covers. She needed her toes covered in order to sleep. Flouncing again, she tried to find the missing sheet, but that just succeeded in waking her up more.

Her growl was muffled by the extra pillow.

Her clients didn't usually reach out on the weekend, although she did have a brunch meeting today. But that was brunch, and this was definitely breakfast time. Was he canceling?

If he was canceling, then she could sleep in. She should check.

More likely, though, it was one of her sisters. They weren't early birds any more than she was, but with everyone based all over the world, it was easy to get confused on time zones.

Giving up, she blindly reached for her phone on the nightstand.

One quick peek, and she was awake. "Emily!"

She missed her friend and former client. She rubbed her eyes and read the message, hoping that Emily wanted to get together or talk or something. They had fun together, but their escapade the other night had put a damper on their relationship.

The "or something" in the text made Hunter sit straight up in bed.

Tony wants your number. Should I give it to him?

Tony. Tony Oneiros. The big, muscled, hunky, bad-tempered Dream Weaver—who also happened to be a great kisser.

"He what?" Hunter squeaked.

Her heartbeat leapt from its resting rate into the danger zone in one second flat. He wanted her number? After what she'd done?

Or after what they'd done?

That, she could understand. It had been a great kiss, a steamy, knee-weakening make-out session. He'd better want her number after that.

But his brothers hadn't fared as well when they'd challenged her, had they? Poor little Dream Weavers stuck with no powers outside the dream realm. That night had been a whirlwind, a glorious jumble of activity and messiness and emotion.

"Ohh," she said in a huff when she caught on, "he's trying to trick me!"

She kicked at the sheet that now seemed to be everywhere, and it tangled around her legs. She had to fight to extricate herself before she could launch herself out of bed and begin pacing around her bedroom. She read the text again.

Nope, she hadn't misread it. Tony Oneiros wanted to get in touch.

Her stomach tightened. He'd been good at the touching part, too. His big hands spanning her waist... His palms sliding down to cover her butt... She shook her head.

"Oh, Hunter, you've gone and done it this time."

She scraped her hand through her hair and flipped it to the side.

Her full moon had been one for the record books. Her sisters couldn't believe that she'd taken on four Dream Weavers by herself and lived to tell the tale. Half of them thought she was a hero, while the other half thought she was nuts—which was saying something.

Maybe Emily could give her some background on what this was all about. Hunter lifted her phone to text... or call... but she couldn't.

"Dang it." She was trying to stay on the right side of Zane Oneiros, Emily's boyfriend. He'd been the one Dream Weaver who hadn't fallen under her influence.

And he was the brother of the sexy, yummy one who had.

She chewed on her lip.

That was the beauty of her moon powers. Her subject had to have some interest in order to respond to her suggestions. She knew that. It was why Zane had been all growly and incensed. He'd been immune to everything she'd said, but his brother, the delectable Tony, hadn't.

Which raised the question, could the text be real?

Her belly squeezed, and she stopped pacing right in front of the glowing curtains. Warmth filled her from the inside out, and her thoughts went all ooey and gooey until she got hold of herself.

"Get real." They'd had a moment—a scorching-hot moment—but that didn't mean she could forget what he was. An Oneiros wouldn't cross that line. An Oneiros and a Menae? Never.

She made herself march to the bathroom to throw some cold water on her face.

It was definitely a trap, but why?

A thought occurred to her, one that made her ooey-gooey center congeal into a rock-hard chunk of ice. She knew the Oneiroi vanquished sleep raiders in the dream realm. They didn't intend to do that to her here, in the waking world, did they?

Cold water dripped off her chin. They wouldn't. The Menae ruled under the moon; everyone knew that. They wouldn't risk upsetting the upper echelon. There were still Greek gods out there who were way more powerful than them, and everyone had gotten used to nighttime being the way it was. They liked having the moon there to guide their way.

No, if the Oneiroi hurt her, they'd risk the extinction of their own kind.

And Tony hadn't acted like he'd wanted to hurt her. Even when he'd plucked her off her bike, he hadn't been rough. Just strong.

So strong.

"Oh, hell." Hunter grabbed a towel and scrubbed the water droplets off her face.

This was all her fault. What good had she thought would come from making friends with the girlfriend of an Oneiros? She'd put this all into motion by giving Emily her business card in the first place. The laced-up project manager had just been so frustrated and unfulfilled when they first met. So ready to break out of her structured little world.

She'd been trying to help. Honestly.

Hunter braced her hands on either side of the sink. She'd tried to do a good deed, and she'd succeeded. Emily and Zane were together now, but in the process, she'd outed herself to the enemy. They knew she was here now, and they didn't like it—even though they knew the rules. They were supposed to stick to the dream realm, but they'd come at her in the waking world under a full moon. She'd had every right to "wipe the floor with them," as her sister Strawberry had put it.

But she'd hurt their pride.

She stared at herself in the mirror. Was that what the request for her number was about? Was the blasted Dream Weaver trying to show how tough and brave he was? To get her going? To yank on her chain?

Her eyes narrowed. Of course he was.

She glared at the phone where it sat on the vanity. And she'd fallen for it. She'd gotten up early on a Sunday morning—no, she'd leapt out of bed.

He'd made her pace.

A grumble passed her lips. Oh, he wanted to play with her

head? She was a master at that game.

Snatching up her phone, she began typing. Just as quickly, she backspaced. She needed to word this correctly. She needed to send Tony Oneiros' cute butt pacing. Lifting her phone, she started again. Yes, she typed. Give it to him.

He wouldn't be expecting that. She'd called his bluff.

See how he'd deal with that.

ABOUT THE AUTHOR

When taking the Myers-Briggs personality test in high school, Kimberly was rated as an INFJ (Introverted-Intuitive-Feeling-Judging). This result sent her into a panic, because there were no career paths recommended for the type. Fortunately, it turned out to be well-suited to a writing career. Since receiving that dismal outlook, Kimberly has become an award-winning author of romance and erotica. When not writing, she enjoys movies, sports, traveling, music, and sunshine.

Learn more about Kimberly's books and sign up for her newsletter at https://kimberlydean.com.

www.ingramcontent.com/pod-product-compliance
Lightning Source LLC
Chambersburg PA
CBHW020822260626
47169CB00003B/781